Courage and Clowns
by
Lee Stewart Gilmore

When Lisa Whitford accidentally becomes foster parent to two young children, her once very orderly life is turned upside down At the same time she meets TV Reporter Michael Bradshaw and falls in love.

Unfortunately Michael is still married and a messy divorce won't help Lisa when she decides she wants to have permanent custody of the children. Her life gets even more complicated when the children's father turns up out of the blue and becomes unpleasant, and to everyone's astonishment he decides to fight for custody of children he barely knows. Finally Michael takes an assignment in Ethiopia and Lisa feels as if her world is falling apart..... and that's only the start.

Lee Stewart Gilmore has asserted her right under the copyright, designs and patents act to be identified as the originator and author of the following works.

*Courage and Clowns
Copyright Lee Stewart Gilmore 2012*

CHAPTER 1

In August the trees brown their leaves in the glade
And then grey October, as colours now fade................

Lisa had never thought of October as being grey. There was a crispness about October and the added anticipation of Christmas being only a few months away. Lisa had no objections to winter either. She didn't see it as drab and bleak. To her, there was nothing better than waking up on a winter's morning when it was cold and the sun still had the audacity to shine even though there was very little warmth in it. No, the end of the year didn't make her gloomy the way it did to others she knew.

Life hadn't turned out exactly as Lisa Whitford had planned. Maybe your destiny was planned out when you were young and poor life had no idea how other people could affect its direction. At thirty, she should have been married with children, a mortgage and a loving husband. Lisa had the mortgage, but divorced two years earlier, she would have to forego the loving husband and the children, for the time being anyway. She wasn't unhappy, just a little dissatisfied and that was why she had joined this voluntary project for children. If she didn't have children of her own, there was no harm in borrowing other peoples on a temporary basis.

She pulled the sun visor down above her head as the grey October sun was slightly blinding and turned her car onto the slip road for Stancroft where she was about to meet a new family who may or may not become part of the project. She mentally went over Janet's directions and found Corson Street without any great difficulty. She wished she had made the time to go home and change, but her shop had been so busy this afternoon, she had only just managed to get closed up and on her way by five. She saw Janet's car and pulled in behind it, stealing a quick glance at herself in the vanity mirror. Her long auburn hair with its soft curls looked a trifle messy after a day of running her hands through it, so finding a clasp in the glove compartment, she pinned it back off her face. The two piece suit was definitely out of place here and to say she felt overdressed would have been an understatement. She stepped out of the car glancing across the street as she locked the door.

Corson Street looked as if it was ready for demolition. There were more houses empty than had occupants and where windows were boarded up, the slats of wood had been spray painted with graffiti. The whole place was an eyesore and it was no wonder, she thought, that the people living here had problems. The main one springing to mind was whether it would have been safe to sleep here at nights. Thankfully she wouldn't have to find out.

The door of number twenty-three opened as Lisa was walking up the path carefully dodging the mud and puddles in her stiletto heeled court shoes. She was glad when she reached the safety of the front door where she was greeted by the cheerful face of a nine-year old.

"I'm Jamie," he volunteered. "Mum says you've to go through." He indicated a door that turned out to be the sitting room. Lisa thanked him and joined Janet King, her project head, and Eleanor Campbell, Jamie's mother. Lisa could sense straight away that this was not going to be an easy interview. Suspicion was written all over Eleanor Campbell's face and she noted the disapproving glance she had been given as she seated herself on the sofa. She accepted the cup of tea being offered and listened as Janet continued to outline the work of the project and its volunteers.

Eleanor Campbell put her cup back on the coffee table rather more noisily than she had intended, but she was allowing herself to get agitated. "I know Jamie has been a problem at school lately and things have been difficult since his father left, but bringing in outsiders isn't my way of doing things. I've managed all right for the past two years and I don't want social workers meddling in my life. Most of them have no idea what it's like struggling to try and make ends meet or about how to bring up three kids on your own."

Lisa could see how uneasy this was making Mrs Campbell, and it wasn't the first time the project had been discounted because many people still imagined there was a stigma attached to being involved with the social work department. Eleanor Campbell may have been fairly low down on the social scale, but she was obviously a proud woman who was unaccustomed to seeking help.

Lisa tried to choose her words carefully. "I'm sure it is difficult Mrs Campbell, but we are not social workers. This is a voluntary project. Our aim is purely to spend some time with Jamie on his own, doing things that he would enjoy and at the same time leaving you with some free time for the younger children. It's really only to give you a break and to give Jamie the opportunity of doing something different." She had hoped she didn't sound like some kind of benefactor.

They chatted for almost an hour during which time, Eleanor Campbell remained suspicious and Lisa felt even more uncomfortable in her suit.

They didn't seem to be getting anywhere. Jamie's headmaster had contacted the project because he felt that Mrs Campbell could do with the help and Jamie would benefit from the attention on a one to one basis. It was his craving for attention from his teacher that was causing his disruptive behaviour in class.

Eleanor Campbell glanced at Lisa. "Jamie can be a handful, and no disrespect to you Miss Whitford, but you look very young. Do you have children of your own?"

"No I don't, which is one reason I joined the project and I am sure Jamie and I could survive an evening on our own." Lisa looked in Jamie's direction for some moral support and was rewarded with an enormous grin. He was an attractive looking child with thick dark curly hair that had a sort of wild appearance. He reminded Lisa of a gypsy with his enormous dark brown eyes. And she had no doubt he could charm when he wanted to.

"Maybe it would do Jamie good to be involved in something, and lord knows the kids don't get many treats." Eleanor Campbell was relenting. Lisa saw her opportunity and quickly took advantage of it.

"We could always try one or two evenings and if Jamie isn't settled or you decide the project doesn't suit, then that would be the end of it."

Lisa saw the mother's face soften.

"Well Jamie," she said, looking at her son's expectant face, "we'll give it a try."

They made arrangements for Friday evening and Janet and Lisa said their goodbyes. As they walked back to their cars, Lisa took a longer look around the square that housed about twenty terraced properties.

"What chance do these people have? Just look at this place." It was grim, damp and depressing.

Janet sympathised. "The council are fighting a losing battle on estates like this. The more they repair, the more vandalism occurs. It's a vicious circle. Call me and let me know how you get on with Jamie."

With these parting words, they drove off in different directions.

Eleanor Campbell watched her visitors from the sitting room window. Lisa Whitford didn't look more than twenty-five and she wasn't what you imagine your average do-gooder to look like. She was well groomed and she had a cultured voice. It had a kind of sharpness to it, not abrupt, but maybe just a little cold. And yet, Lisa Whitford's face was kind. She had soft green eyes and a generous smile and despite her initial hostility towards her visitor, Eleanor felt she could trust the petite figure, right down to her highly polished fingernails. The more she thought about it, the more she thought she could get to like her. Janet King on the other hand wasn't quite as impressive, but she looked the type you could rely on to get things done, and quickly. The older woman looked more like a social worker to Eleanor. She was twice the height and weight of her volunteer and her dark hair was cut very short. Eleanor thought this was probably more for convenience than style. As she watched them drive off in their flash cars, she thought how much her husband would have ogled over someone like Lisa Whitford. In his dreams, he may have looked but he could never have pulled someone like her. That thought amused her no end. When he hadn't been carrying on with someone, he had been drunk. It hadn't been much of a life, but at least when he had been here, she had a wage packet coming in each week. Becky was only two when he left and she had been expecting the third.

She walked away from the window and one look at Jamie's face and she could tell he was already looking forward to his outing.
"She's nice mum, isn't she, Miss Whitford. I liked her."
Eleanor looked at her son and fervently hoped he didn't turn out like his father, a pretty face and he was gone. She laughed to herself. He was

only nine; she would have a good few years before she would find out.

"Jamie, run in and tell Mrs Johnston she can bring the baby back anytime, and you and Becky can go and play until your dinner's ready."

Jamie disappeared out of the door. Mrs Johnston lived further along the street and very kindly watched the kids on occasions. Eleanor caught her reflection in the mirror over the fireplace. She looked all of her forty years and more. Her skin looked drab and her small frame had long been carrying too much weight. She ran her fingers through her fair hair that was badly in need of cutting into something that resembled a style. She found it hard trying to manage on the income support she received. She had little money to spend on herself, but she did have three lovely kids, and for that she was eternally grateful. Glancing at the clock, she began to make preparations for dinner.

It was almost seven when Lisa opened the door on her neat little house where there was always a welcome waiting in the form of Freebie, her shaggy little mongrel, wagging his tail and barking with excitement. She opened the kitchen door and let him out into the back garden. She was kicking off her shoes, when the phone rang.

"Hello Meg, I've only this minute walked through the door."
"I did try the shop, but you must have been closed early, it had only just gone five. You'll never make a million if you carry on like that." Meg's cheery voice relayed.
Lisa explained about her visit to Stancroft and how adorable Jamie was.
"You think they're all adorable. I seriously think there is something wrong with your head. That last little girl was a nightmare."
Lisa laughed remembering the last project child. "Yes, well she wasn't my favourite either, but wait until you meet this one."
"I am full of anticipation, or should that be trepidation. Actually I called to see if you were doing anything. Thought I might come over?"
"Great, any time after eight, I need to walk the dog first, and then get in a bath. See you later." She replaced the handset and went off in search of her little companion.

She walked further than she had intended, and was only getting out of the bath when Meg appeared. She called down for her to put the kettle on while she got dressed. When Lisa came downstairs, Meg was slumped in an armchair, with Freebie at her feet. Her red hair was loosely tied back, but it was already escaping in huge chunks. She was getting married next July and since she had decided on a date, her pale blue eyes always seemed full of excitement.

"Guess where I am going on honeymoon?"

"I don't think you're supposed to tell anyone Meg, can't you even manage to keep that a secret?"

"I won't tell anyone else. We're going to Turkey. Keith booked it today." Meg's smile said it all, she was so happy.

"Well, don't tell him you're broadcasting the fact." Lisa said hoping that she hadn't in fact been telling everyone.

"But I'd be sending you a postcard when I'm there, so what's the harm in telling you before I go?"

Lisa laughed. "Most people don't send postcards from their honeymoon, you idiot."

Meg looked indignant. "Well how am I supposed to know? I've never been married before."

"And you won't be married at all if Keith hears any of this. How did you get on shopping with your mother?"

Lisa had wished she had been free to go with them but she was sure there would be other shopping days.

Meg had been her closest friend since they had been children although she was a few years younger than Lisa.

"I have had the most awful day," Meg said exasperated, "Mother has had me in almost every shop known to man looking at wedding dresses, and they are just not me. I'm going to end up walking down the aisle in a pair of jeans."

"I'm sure you'll find something, and I bet your mother is enjoying every minute of this."

Meg pulled a face. "She's unbearable, I wish Keith and I had eloped. This seems like such a lot of fuss for one day."

Meg certainly wasn't the fussy type, spending most of her life in casual clothes.

Lisa laughed at Meg's expression.

"I don't know how Keith puts up with you; he must have the patience of a saint."

"The man's in love with me, I'll have you know." Meg raised her eyebrows to bring some dignity to the proceedings, but it didn't work.

"You'll have to find a partner for the wedding." Meg teased.

"No I won't, I'll hardly be on my own with all of your family there. Anyway there isn't exactly a queue at the door at the moment, and it's your day, so stop worrying about me."

Lisa had made a point of not getting involved with anyone since her divorce, much to Meg's annoyance. There had been dates but none exciting enough to develop and she wasn't exactly on the lookout.

"You can't live like a nun for the rest of your life; you're only thirty for heaven's sake." Meg continued.

"I have no intentions of remaining celibate, I just haven't met anyone I've been interested enough in. Is there some kind of hurry?" They had argued through this topic before and Lisa was getting tired hearing it.

"There's no hurry, but I think three years is long enough on your own. I really think you'll need a man made out of chocolate, and then if you decide, like you do, that after a few dates you're fed up with him, you can always eat him and start again."

"Very funny. Why is it when someone is getting married they imagine that everyone else wants to do the same? Remember I've been there and I don't want to make the same mistake again, I want to foster or adopt and until I've done that, my love life will have to take second place."

Meg knew she was fighting a losing battle.

"I don't follow the social work department's reasoning in this. I would have thought a couple would have been more attractive than a single person, no disrespect." Meg had wandered through to the kitchen and helped herself to more coffee.

"It is." Lisa tried to explain. "But I've done my assessment on my own and if I suddenly produce a relationship, then he would have to be assessed separately and you know how long that would take. It's simpler this way and now that I've got this far, I can't afford to muck it up."

"But Lisa, adults need adult company. I just don't understand how they can object to you having a boyfriend."

"Meg, I am trying to explain it. There's no harm in me having a boyfriend, as long as he isn't staying at the house if there are kids here, until he's assessed. For all I know he could turn out to be a child molester."

"I think I see what you mean. It wouldn't be much of a relationship if after a few months you were still kissing each other goodnight on the doorstep. I suppose they have to protect the kids."

Lisa looked thoughtful, before she added, "And then when I have a child or two, it will be more difficult to get anyone interested because I have kids. But it's what I've wanted to do and if I don't get married again, which is always a possibility, then I could always adopt."

"Well, as I have been saying for a long time, there is something slightly wrong with your head, but it's up to you."

Meg knew there would be no chance of changing Lisa's mind, once it was made up there was no going back.

Tiring of this line of conversation Lisa steered Meg into more talk of the wedding, which wasn't difficult.

"The band is booked now after all the confusion and that's another thing crossed off the list. And mum and I went to look at outfits for her but we didn't see anything remotely suitable."

"What have you decided to do about your father?"

Meg's parents had been divorced for years and didn't speak to each other at all.

"He's being told nothing until after the event. I know that doesn't seem right but we have no choice. I won't have them both there, drawing daggers at each other and mum's made it plain he's not welcome. He hasn't exactly been a father to any of us. In the end it's been decided for me. I just couldn't bear anything to spoil the day after mum has worked so hard to get it right."

"I think you're wise. More coffee?" Lisa rose from the chair and made her way into the kitchen. Meg followed fighting with bits of her hair as she waited for the kettle to boil.

"I must visit a hairdresser this weekend and see what she can come up with for this." She yanked at what was left of the ponytail. "Why couldn't I have been dark or blonde? I don't even know where the red hair came from. I only wish it hadn't chosen me."

"Your hair is a beautiful colour and it's so thick. How can you complain about it?"

"Because it's also the cause of these million and one freckles and I imagine it's going to take a trowel full of make-up to cover. God must have been having a bad day when I passed by."

"Meg that's awful, freckles are a sign of beauty."

"Give over Lisa. I know I am no oil painting. I could do with a little less colour on my head and face. I don't think that's too much to ask."

"Everybody would like to change some part of their appearance but if we could we'd all be six foot and blonde." They wandered back into the sitting room with coffee and toast.

From there, the conversation moved on to Lisa's shop, which had been opened less than a year, and although business was good, it still wasn't as busy as Lisa would have liked. She had chosen the old village where the shops were more specialised instead of the modern town centre with its high street names.

"I could do with investing in more advertising but it's so expensive and I could also do with someone to work one day to let me get to the warehouse instead of me having to do that in the evening."

They chatted the next few hours away. The girls were so close they were more like sisters. As well as growing up together, they had both worked for the same advertising company before Lisa opened the shop.

"I really ought to be making a move; I have an early start tomorrow." Meg slowly untangled her long legs and stretched. "We're doing our presentation for that new electronics company, and if all goes well, it would be a big contract to win. Don't you ever miss the advertising world Lisa?"

"Not one bit. All that rushing about and not even being able to relax when you got home thinking of all the things you had to accomplish the next day. I didn't want advertising to be the only thing in my life. Maybe I'm not as ambitious as you, or somewhere along the line, I lost the urge to be competitive." As Lisa struggled to her feet, Meg was already at the door. It was cooler this evening than it had been for the past few nights and she shivered a little.

"Mother asked when you were coming over for dinner. Shall I tell her Sunday?"

"Wouldn't miss it for the world. It's the only day I get a decent meal and when you're not talking there's even the chance of an intelligent conversation. I'll see you on Saturday though if you want some ideas for a going away outfit."

Meg grimaced and shouted over her shoulder as she made her way to the car. "Can't wait. See you on Saturday."

Lisa waited until Meg's car had pulled away before closing the door. She then let Freebie out into the garden before deciding that tonight was going to be a reasonably early night for her.

The rest of the week passed fairly quickly, and business was better than it had been on the two previous weeks. The exceptionally hot weather through September had stopped shoppers buying decent clothes. Everyone was wearing shorts and tee-shirts and when you mainly stocked designer suits and out of the ordinary items, making a vast profit was extremely difficult. But the weather had changed.

She had telephoned Jamie last night and was pleased to hear the eagerness in his voice when she said she had tickets for the cinema. At six o'clock she was on her way to Stancroft, and she had to admit, she was looking forward to her evening.

"Hello Miss Whitford, come in, Jamie's almost ready." Eleanor Campbell looked much more relaxed than she had been at their last meeting.

"Please call me Lisa, it'll be a lot easier. Hello Jamie. All set then?"

"Yes miss, can we go now?"

"Yes Jamie we can. What time would you like Jamie back home?" Lisa didn't want any unforeseeable problems on their first outing, so it was as well to check with his mother.

"He's normally in bed by nine thirty, if that's all right, he's not very bright in the mornings."

"Yes that's fine. We'll see you later. Right Jamie, let's go."

He ran out of the house and down the path to the car.

"We don't have a car Miss. When I'm older I'm going to learn to drive and I'll have a car the same as this one. Is driving hard?" His little face was inquisitive and Lisa watched as he ran his hand over the upholstery as if it was the deepest, most expensive velvet he had ever seen.

"It's quite difficult at first, but when you get used to it, it's easy. How was school this week?"

"Okay, I only got into trouble once, but it wasn't my fault, not really. You see," he continued in his matter of fact way, "this boy bumped into me and when I pushed him back, the teacher shouted at me."

"If someone bumps into you Jamie, it's called an accident."

"It wasn't an accident, he bumped me on purpose." He replied indignantly.

"Well next time, why don't you tell the teacher, before you push him back and see what happens."

Jamie gave her suggestion some thought before he answered. "But once I've told the teacher, she won't let me push him back."

Lisa tried very hard not to laugh. She could see by Jamie's serious expression that he hadn't followed her train of thought. They had arrived back in Kilmains and as they parked in the open-air car park at the shopping centre, Jamie was taking in everything he saw.

His eyes almost popped out of his head when he stepped on to the escalator and saw that he could look down into the ice rink that was all open and only a rail separated the skaters from where, during the day, would be shoppers.

"Look at that Miss; you can watch the people skate."

"Have you ever tried ice skating Jamie?"

Lisa suspected she knew his answer before he said it.

"No never. Can you skate Miss?"

"Yes I can, maybe some night we could go together and I could teach you."

"Would you really Miss?"

"Look Miss, someone's fallen over." His face had been scanning the ice for one such moment.

"You fall over quite a bit when you're learning, but it is fun. And you needn't call me, Miss, we're supposed to be friends so why don't you call me Lisa?"

Jamie looked pleased at this suggestion and calling her by her first name would seem very grown up, like she was.

Before finding their seats, they queued for popcorn and drinks. Jamie had never been to a huge cinema like this before and he was amazed to find out there were nine different films showing. During his movie, he didn't move a muscle. His face was glued to the screen, where the all-action hero beat up all the baddies in an assortment of cinematic ways. The screen was full of every special effect you could imagine and Jamie was enthralled. She could tell this was going to be the best movie he had ever seen, and she wasn't mistaken. He relived every minute of it on the journey home. He was an inquisitive child, which Lisa liked and easy to talk to. The fact that she didn't know how all of the special effects were done didn't seem to bother him. She had enjoyed this evening. Jamie was a bright little boy and despite the reports Lisa had read, he was well mannered and eager to learn. He was just the sort of child Lisa would have wished for herself.

CHAPTER 2

Over the next few weeks Lisa saw Jamie much more than was usual on the project. Most of the other volunteers only saw their kids once a week, or in some cases, only once a fortnight. Jamie had settled at school and the change in him was quite noticeable. All the child had needed was some attention and individual attention at that, and Lisa had plenty to give. He fell in love with Freebie and the dog was devoted to him. Many a Sunday afternoon would find the three of them exploring the Country Park. Freebie wasn't the only one devoted to Jamie. Lisa herself was becoming more attached to him, and there was no doubt, she loved him dearly.

Eleanor Campbell had relaxed a lot more and she and Lisa always had a chat and a cup of tea when she brought Jamie home. Yes, Lisa was enjoying life with Jamie and his endless questions. Their trip to the zoo had been classic.
"If chimpanzees are like us, why didn't they learn to talk? I mean if they are like us they should be clever enough." He waited expectantly for Lisa's reply.

"I don't think their vocal cords are the same as ours." It was the best answer Lisa could come up with.

"Why are their arms so long?"

"Because they use them to swing through the trees."

"Why do they eat bananas?"

"Well you like bananas Jamie, why shouldn't they." The questions went on and on.

"Why are camels so ugly Lisa?"

"I'm sure they don't think they're ugly. They probably think they look interesting."

"Why does their hump lie over to one side and not stand up like it does in a picture?"

She really didn't know the answer to that one and her head was buzzing by the time they went to have something to eat. Eleanor Campbell always sent Jamie on his outings as well dressed as was possible. His trainers had seen better days, but they were scrubbed as clean as they could be. His clothes may not have been new but they were always clean and freshly ironed and his skin looked as if it had been scrubbed until it shone. He may be from a deprived area, but there was no embarrassment in taking him anywhere.

He had never been to a public library either. His teacher had a little bookshelf in the classroom, and they could borrow books from that, but he had never seen anything like a proper library. He looked up books on all the animals he had seen at the zoo, and then he had to be shown where they all came from in a large world atlas. They had left armed with books for him and by his second visit, he knew where all the children's sections were and could choose his own books. Lisa encouraged him to read and each week his books were returned in exactly the same condition as when he had taken them out. But out of everything they did, she knew Freebie was still his favourite.

Jamie had by now met most of Lisa's friends, and he had been to the shop. Wherever he was taken he was the centre of attention and he loved it. Never once had Lisa had to raise her voice or scold him. He was so well behaved it seemed too good to be true. She was sure she looked forward to their outings almost as much as he did.

Janet had congratulated her on her success at one of the project meetings.

"I haven't really done anything. He's great company and quite a little character and he certainly hasn't thrown any tantrums or shown signs of misbehaving. He's just a little boy who needed some attention."

Janet shuffled the expense reports she had been collecting in and pushed her glasses back up on her nose. She wriggled her nose to keep them in position. "Has he ever mentioned his father?"

"No never, but I'm sure if he wanted to he would have done it already. He's not shy and he obviously doesn't consider his father part of his life anymore. Why did you ask? Do you think it's important?"

"No, possibly not. I think I was just curious, that's all."

Lisa poured another two cups of coffee and handed one to Janet. The project meetings were more of a get together, when the volunteers could meet and bounce ideas off each other. It was also a time to catch up on everyone's news. Lisa had been one of the first to join the project, and since that first day, she and Janet had become good friends. The room was beginning to clear and Lisa shouted her goodbyes across the room. She sipped her coffee and chatted to Janet as she cleared her desk of papers and put them carefully into her battered briefcase. Janet waited until the others had gone and then she handed Lisa a report she had received from Jamie's school. Lisa flicked her eyes over the paper.

"It says here, although he's more settled he's lazy and slow to pick things up. That's not true, he's desperate to learn. We're in the library every week and he takes home at least four books and he can almost recite them word for word by the time we take them back, now does that sound to you as if he's slow?" Lisa pulled the clasp from her hair and ran her fingers through the long curls. She was tired tonight and having to read drivel written by some imbecile who didn't even know the child they were writing about, was irritating. She replaced the clasp at the nape of her neck.

Janet tried to sympathise. "No, from what you say he sounds bright, but I wonder why the school see such a different side to him?"

"I've no idea," said Lisa indignantly, "maybe they don't pay enough attention. He's anything but slow. It's possible he doesn't have a good teacher."

Janet had to laugh at the way Lisa always defended her children managing somehow to focus on their good points.

"Well, I will be answering the report and I will make your views known, if somewhat more diplomatically. Now let's get these cups cleared up and get home, it's been a long day." They said their goodnight in the car park and Janet promised to phone if she had any further word from the school.

Lisa drove the hour's journey home listening to a local radio station's phone in. The topics were amusing and lifted her spirits although she was glad when she finally reached the house and parked the car. It had been a long day and she was tired.

Jamie had been to Lisa's house on many occasions, which was not normally project policy due to the fact that some of the kids came from dubious backgrounds. A seemingly innocent remark made by a child to an unsavoury relative could lead to burglary or vandalism. Not that their group had come across anything like that, but it was always better to be safe. In Jamie's case this was certainly not thought to be a problem, his family were unfortunate, not criminal.

They had tried their day at ice-skating and after only fifteen minutes he had sailed off on his own, with a natural ability that had surprised Lisa. He was even attempting turns by watching other people and after a few falls, he had the hang of it. He skated back to Lisa slightly out of breath.

"This is great Lisa. Could you teach me how to jump, like that girl over there?"

Lisa looked over to see a figure skater rehearsing a routine. "No I certainly couldn't. I said I could skate Jamie, not do acrobatics."

Jamie laughed and skated off into the middle of the rink.

When she had taken him horse riding it had been the same. Not only did he want to know all about the horses, but who fed them, what were their names, how old were they and did they enjoy all the people riding them. By the time they were leaving, Lisa herself knew more about her local stables that she had done before. Life with Jamie was going along quite nicely, she thought.

The shop still wasn't making as much as she would have liked, but even that didn't seem to bother her any more. She was sure it would be successful given a little more time. It was certainly an easier way of making a living than advertising. She had been busy too, organising her stock for Christmas and New Year. People were dressing up a bit more at the festive time and she was looking for good sales prior to the holiday. It would have been nice to have some help, but she was almost positive that after New Year she would be able to hire someone for one, if not two days a week.

It was late one Friday evening when she closed the shop and headed for home. She had been on her feet all day and was looking forward to soaking in a bath, then putting her feet up and watching some television. She had taken Freebie into the shop with her that day because she wasn't sure she would manage home at lunchtime. She stopped off at the park and let him have a run before finally getting home. It was seven thirty when she put her key in the door. The answering machine light was flashing and the phone was ringing as she let herself in. She knew something was wrong the minute she heard Janet's voice. "Thank heavens I've got you at last, I've been phoning for at least an hour."

"I was late finishing tonight. What is it?" she asked hesitantly. She switched on the lamp over the table in the hall and sank into the chair beside it. She could sense the anxiety in Janet's voice. She kicked off her shoes and rubbed her aching feet.

"There's been an explosion in Stancroft, at the soft drinks factory behind Corson Street. It was broadcast on the six o'clock news and as I couldn't find out much on the emergency number, I came over here. The social work department are manning an emergency centre, that's where I am calling from. Its chaos here, they're saying there are at least ten dead and many injured. Lisa, I haven't seen any sign of the Campbells."

Without hesitating Lisa screamed down the phone. "I'm on my way; I'll be there as quickly as I can." She fumbled for her shoes and put her tired feet back into them. She picked up her bag and her car keys; Jamie's little face vividly flashing through her mind. Please God she prayed let him be okay. Five minutes later her car was speeding along the expressway. She couldn't bear the thought of losing Jamie, never seeing him again. Never hearing that infectious little laugh. She fought back the tears, overtaking everyone who looked as if they might hold her up.

As she turned into the estate the noise was deafening. She could hear people screaming. People in pain, people shouting orders and the incredible roaring as flames swept skyward. Such high flames it looked as if the heavens were on fire. She abandoned her car after realising she wasn't going to get any closer and continued on foot along the street and into the square. Corson Street was like a disaster area, like something you only saw on television, not something you were in the middle of. There was the sound of generators turning over, loud sounds, maybe it was all the fire appliances, she really didn't know. But it was deafening and churning constantly in a kind of rhythm. They were abandoned all over the place, wherever they could find a space and the sound of the water gushing in torrents in all directions and the noise, frightening noise. She spotted an ambulance with one of its attendants preparing to bring out a stretcher. She made her way across to it.

"Where's the emergency centre?" She became another of the screamers, trying to make herself heard above the din.

"The school, over there."

He hadn't even looked up but continued with his task and merely nodded in the direction that she should take.

She waded through the water, her court shoes saturated. She remembered her first visit here; she hadn't been appropriately dressed then either. She hadn't even thought of getting changed before she left the house. What had she been thinking of, in hindsight it would have been very wise. Her clothes were already smudged with the thick, black smoke billowing around her, falling and clinging whenever it found something solid. She couldn't stand the noise; her eardrums were bursting as she covered her nose and mouth to prevent the stench from the fires finding its way through to her. She was beginning to choke and she ran the last few yards to the school. She ran close to the television cameras and when she glanced over briefly, she recognised the blonde reporter at the front. She had seen him many times before on her own television screen.

The school was even more chaotic than the square, with people running backwards and forwards along the corridors. The noise however was much more bearable. She had no idea where to go when a voice startled her.

"Can I help you?"

Lisa turned to face a young WPC. "Yes thank you Officer. I'm looking for someone and I don't know where to start."

"Try the main hall. Everyone who comes in is being registered there. It's at the end of the corridor, to the left."

Lisa thanked her, wondering how she had managed to look so immaculate when Lisa, who had only been there a matter of minutes, looked filthy and bedraggled. She entered the main hall and was pleased to see Janet almost at once. The feeling of nausea in the pit of her stomach was easing off but she wasn't sure it would stay like that. She had never been near a disaster in her life. There were people lying on camp beds, bleeding and waiting for help. People coughing as though their lungs would give up. She finally reached Janet.

"Have you found Jamie?" she asked hopefully.

"There's no trace of Mrs Campbell or the children, but they are still bringing people in. Give me a hand with these blankets." Janet handed Lisa a pile of folded blankets and pointed across to where they were needed. Lisa was glad of something to do and was glad Janet was there with her. She distributed her blankets and helped with hot drinks and generally tried to make people as comfortable as possible until the medical staff could get to them.

Staff from social services were manning the registration desks and at the same time they were frantically trying to phone relatives of the many people sitting around, unhurt physically but emotionally drained. In one corner, some minor first aid was being carried out and the worst cases referred to the waiting ambulance attendants.

In the next hour she assisted where she could, sometimes only with comfort. When she finally accepted some tea for herself, she suddenly realised how tired and hungry she felt. She eased her aching feet out of her shoes and wriggled her toes to relieve the pressure. She had been on her feet since before six that morning and they were beginning to object and none too quietly.

"There are a few more people being brought in," the girl at the desk remarked as she lifted Lisa's empty cup. "As it's so crowded in here, they've taken them to the dining room and I thought you might like to take a look."

Lisa forced her feet back into her shoes and limped along the corridor. It had been a long time since she had prayed in earnest, but found herself doing so now. She saw the little girl first.

She must have been about six years old, the same mop of dark curls, the same dark complexion and the same dark eyes. She had to be a Campbell. Then, standing behind her, she saw Jamie. He ran to meet her, throwing his arms around her neck, almost choking her, at the same time as the lump in her throat was trying to do the same.

"I've been looking everywhere for you." She said gently wiping tears from his eyes, but leaving her own to slide slowly down her cheeks.

"I can't find my mum, or the baby. Have you seen them?" His deep eyes searched her face hopefully. His little lips trembled and he stifled more tears.

"Not yet Jamie, but we'll find them darling. Is that your sister over there?"

"That's Becky, she's been very frightened. We were playing in Mrs Johnston's garden, while mum was making our dinner and then there was this big bang and everything caught fire and I didn't know what to do."

"It's all right Jamie, let's get Becky."

The little girl was gazing around blankly. Lisa bent down beside her.

"My name's Lisa, I'm Jamie's friend, there's no need to be frightened."

The child was more shocked than anything else and although she didn't speak, she allowed herself to be taken by the hand and guided back to the registration desk.

"My name's Lisa Whitford. I work with Janet King." Lisa explained to the girl manning the desk. "Would it be alright to take these children through to the main hall?"

She gave the girl their names and after some notes had been taken she advised Lisa to check in with the first aid counter first. Neither of the children had been hurt and after a nurse permitted, Lisa went in search of Mrs Johnston. She found her sitting having a cup of tea, but still visibly shaken from her ordeal.

"Mrs Johnston, I'm Lisa Whitford. I'm a friend of Mrs Campbell, perhaps she's mentioned me to you." Lisa felt so sorry for the elderly lady, sitting amidst all of this.

Mrs Johnston looked up into the young girl's face.

"Hello there, Jamie's mentioned you a lot. Where are the children being taken? You know, I haven't seen Eleanor anywhere, have you?"

"No, not yet, but we'll find her. I'm taking the children with me for the moment. Do you have anyone coming to see you?"

"Oh yes, my son's coming to collect me. They say we can't stay in our houses tonight, in case there's another explosion. I've just to wait here until he comes." She kissed the children and told them both to be good and she would see them soon.

Lisa and the children then trooped back along to the main hall in search of Janet. They found her still running around. Lisa marvelled at how she still had so much energy.

"Well I suppose the first thing is to find them a place to stay tonight, until we establish….." she didn't finish her sentence. "A bed for tonight and then tomorrow things will sort themselves out." Janet's matter of fact way of dealing with the crisis amazed Lisa.

Lisa interrupted her train of thought. "I thought they could stay with me tonight. I can take tomorrow off and we'll wait at the house until we find out what's happening." She hadn't hesitated about making her offer. Becky had been clinging to her since they had left the dining room and it was obvious what the child needed was something to eat and then bed.

It didn't take long for Janet to clear everything with the duty officials and soon Lisa had them both in the car, heading back to Kilmains. They stopped at Macdonalds just before closing time and picked up burgers and drinks.

Once at the house however the children picked at their meals and Lisa decided that maybe a quick bath and bed would be a better idea.

"Where will my mum be Lisa? She'll be worried when she can't find us. Will someone tell her where we are?" Jamie was becoming tearful again and this time it started Becky off as well.
Lisa stroked his mop of curls. "I told everyone at the school where we were going and remember I told Mrs Johnston too. So when your mum gets there she won't be worried. Now let's get you into bed."
She tucked them both up in the same room. She didn't want either feeling alone or frightened if they woke during the night. They were both cuddled up with an assortment of soft toys and exhausted, within minutes they were fast asleep. As she walked back downstairs, for once Lisa thought her house felt like a home. Freebie had decided to stay with Jamie and was curled up at the bottom of his bed, quite contented. She made a quick telephone call to Meg and while she waited she made some coffee and left it simmering on the stove.

It was almost midnight when Meg arrived with at least a dozen reasons why it had taken her so long. Lisa poured the coffee and handed a mug to Meg.
"Have you had a look at yourself Lisa? For someone who is always immaculate, it's nice to see you look filthy and untidy, and I might add, human, like the rest of us. Your feet are black."

"Yes I know, I am in dire need of a bath and a change of clothes. But I haven't had any time yet. What have you managed to rustle up?" It was the reason Meg had come over.
"There's everything in here but the kitchen sink." She lifted the heavy holdall on to the table. "My sister-in-law has thought of everything, including night clothes, but I see I'm a bit too late with those."
Meg had a niece and nephew of similar ages, so Lisa had scrounged some clothes for the morning.
"It's very kind of her at such short notice." Lisa emptied almost the entire bag. There were trainers, jackets, tee shirts, underwear, jeans, and baseball caps. She had even sent slippers.
"I hadn't even considered jackets, she really has thought of everything. I'll call her tomorrow and thank her. More coffee Meg?" Lisa had reached over and switched on the kettle without waiting for Meg's reply. The coffee from the expresso machine had tasted a little stewed, which was hardly surprising since it had been simmering on the stove for almost an hour now.
"Can I see the kids; I promise I won't wake them?" Meg wasn't used to her friend doing things on the spur of the moment. Everything Lisa did was usually carefully thought out. This was so unlike her. They climbed the stairs as

quietly as they could although nothing would have wakened Jamie and Becky after the day they had lived through. They gazed in at the two sleeping children; their dark curls forming almost perfect circles around their heads.

"She's Jamie's double. I don't think I've ever seen two children so alike before." Meg had mentioned on their way back downstairs. "I thought you said their mother was fair haired?"

"She is, so I expect they must take their colouring from their father. I thought I would have heard from someone by now. I can't imagine why they haven't found their mother. But I suppose if there had been any news, we would have heard."

"If it wasn't that this was such a tragedy, I could see you with a couple of kids. You liked showing them to me, you had a kind of proud expression on your face."

"Meg, much as I would love kids, I don't think I would like to get them this way. What if they don't find Mrs Campbell or what if…" Lisa couldn't prevent the tears from filling her eyes.

"Oh Lisa, of course they'll find her, by tomorrow this will all seem like a bad dream."

She put her arms around her friend. Lisa was always unruffled, so seeing her like this had shown Meg another side of someone she thought she had known for all these years. In any of Meg's crisis, she had always come to Lisa. Now for the first time she had to give support, not ask for it.

The phone ringing disturbed them. The voice was official, but sympathetic. They had found the bodies of Mrs Campbell and the baby. They hadn't survived the blast. The official went on to explain that someone from the Child Care Team would be in touch the following day to speak to the children. Lisa then quickly phoned Janet who was devastated and promised to come over as soon as she could in the next few days. As she returned to the sitting room and to Meg, the full extent of what had happened earlier, and the news she had only received, finally sank in. The tears wouldn't stop. What would happen to Jamie and Becky? She cried for Eleanor Campbell and her baby and for the two little children asleep upstairs unaware that their lives were about to change forever.

CHAPTER 3

Michael Bradshaw had been watching her since she had abandoned her car. Flash car for someone who lived around here he thought as he followed her with his gaze into the square.
"Can you get a shot of the girl over there, by the ambulance?"

The cameraman swung round. She was a looker all right, trust Michael; he never missed a pretty face. But it wasn't her looks that were of interest to Michael, although he had to admit she did have something.

She was too well dressed to belong in an area like this, and he doubted she would have relatives who lived here either. So who was she? And what was she doing?

"Bring the camera, let's check this out." Michael thought he might just have found a story.

They watched and filmed her helping with drinks, blankets and consoling the desolated. Her clothes were by now smudged with smoke but she carried on regardless. She was definitely looking for someone. Michael watched as she

scanned all the new arrivals and the disappointment was evident, when, once again, she hadn't found what she was looking for. After a conversation with one of the other girls she rushed out and headed along the corridor. By the time they reached the dining hall she was already hugging a little boy. The relief on her face was obvious, and she was crying. Michael was glad that out of the devastation someone had been reunited, and he was glad it had been her. Satisfied with what he had seen so far, he beckoned his colleague.
"Let's go back outside."
As he stood in front of the camera, he brushed back his blonde hair and wondered why he was still thinking of her.

Michael Bradshaw was an attractive looking man with intense blue eyes and his tall muscular figure could well disguise his need to lose a few pounds. His broad smile had won the hearts of many that watched him from the comfort of their armchairs. He was a likeable character with an infectious laugh and a playful sense of humour. His attention to detail and dedication had gained him the respect of his work colleagues and the adoration bestowed on him by female fans, kept him high in the station's ratings. It was difficult to dislike a man, admired by so many.

The studio editing room was untidy and warm, or maybe he was now beginning to feel the tiredness of the long day.
"Can we separate the sequence with the girl looking for the kids? I won't need that for tonight's broadcast." He lay back in his seat and stretched. He would be glad to get home tonight. He intending finding out some background before he would have any use for those shots. He couldn't suppress the smile when her face lit up the screen in front of him. He knew only her name, it was Lisa and she worked on some kind of project. He was the investigative reporter, what more did he need. Tomorrow he was sure he would have the answers.
"Anyone eating?" He called across to the technicians working with him.
Before long the station editing room was deserted. The next broadcast didn't go out until midnight, leaving enough time to eat and then complete the editing. Her face wouldn't leave him. Not during dinner and not even when he went on air. Michael saw attractive women every day, TV studios were full of them, so what was so compelling about her?

He drove into the square at ten the following morning and was confronted with a very different scene from the one he had left the night before. Gone was the movement of thick black smoke, the remains of which still clung defiantly to the ruined buildings. Gone were the fire fighters, the ambulance crews and more noticeably, gone was the noise. They hadn't started the clear up operation yet and the silence was deathly. And gone too were a whole row of houses, leaving twelve, where there had been eighteen.

"Film the square and the piles of debris. I need to check something at the school." Michael instructed. He left his cameraman to record the aftermath of a disaster that they both knew would affect few people outside the relatives of the families concerned.

"Yes I do remember her, but I'm sorry, I don't know who she is. There were so many people working here last night."

Michael thanked the girl behind the desk. She looked as if she had been there all night without a break. He asked the few remaining aid workers on duty, but no one could remember her. As he was about to give up, an elderly lady approached him

"The girl, the one you're asking about, she left with the Campbell children." Mrs Johnston had returned to the school to find out what she could about her neighbours.

"Are you sure it's the same girl?"

"Of course I'm sure. She told me who she was, her name was Lisa. Now what was her last name? My memories not what it used to be? It was Whitford, I think. Yes it was, Lisa Whitford."

"Do you know where I can find her?" Michael could have hugged the old woman.

"I think she's some kind of social worker." Mrs Johnston had naturally assumed that because Lisa was helping with Jamie.

"Thank you you've been a great help."

Mrs Johnston watched the young man leave. She had the feeling she knew him from somewhere, but she couldn't remember exactly from where. She thought of the two Campbell children. What would happen to them now?

Michael's next visit was to the Social Work department, whose offices were in Hayton, four miles away. He was directed from one office to another and finally when he found someone who could help him, she wouldn't.

"Mr Bradshaw, these children have just lost their mother and I really don't think interviewing them would be wise and as for Lisa Whitford, she's a volunteer and I simply couldn't give you an address." She was pleasant but adamant.

Michael knew he would get nothing more.

"I am sorry, I didn't know about their mother, you see, I only saw them briefly last night with

Miss Whitford. Thank you for your time, I'm sorry to have troubled you."

Michael walked back to his car. He had got most of it wrong so far. He wasn't thinking straight or logically. Lisa Whitford was some voluntary social worker of sorts and she had obviously been connected to the children whose mother had just died. But he didn't exactly know what the connection was. He had no intentions of giving up. There was some kind of story here and he intended finding Lisa Whitford. Apart from the story, she was slowly becoming an obsession. It wasn't a case of wanting to find her; he needed to find her.

Lisa was awake early on the Saturday morning mainly because she had hardly slept. She had no idea what today would bring nor had she any notion of how to handle the kids today. She called Cathy who owned the florist shop next door to her clothes shop and asked her to put up a notice apologising for the shop not being opened. She had feigned a migraine and Cathy was sympathetic. She could tell her the full story another time.

She then started to prepare breakfast. It wasn't long before she heard her little visitors moving about upstairs. She called up from the bottom of the stairs, "I've left out some clothes for you both and as soon as you're dressed, come down and have some breakfast." For some reason she felt she had to make the day as normal as possible. What was she thinking? These children had just lost their mother. Nothing would ever be normal again. She brushed a tear from her cheek as she heard the footsteps behind her.

"Good morning." she said as brightly as she could and saw straight away what her first mistake had been. She hadn't taken into account the fact that Becky was only six and although her clothes looked fine, her face was unwashed and her hair looked as if it would take a week to brush out the tangles. Never mind, this morning anything was acceptable. They only had to find a way to get through it. With both the children seated at the table she lifted over the plates of food.

"Have we to eat all of this Lisa?" Jamie asked, staring at his plate. "I've never seen so much food at breakfast."

This was obviously her second mistake she had cooked bacon, sausage and egg. Her home was short on child friendly food items.

"What did you have at home Jamie?"

"Cereal and a drink. But I bet I can eat all of this." He replied, stabbing a sausage with his fork.

Courage and Clowns

She was glad to see that both were attempting their breakfast, but then they hadn't had much to eat the night before.
"Eat what you can. I am sure Freebie will eat whatever is left." Lisa started filling the sink to clear up the pans. She hadn't made anything for herself because she wasn't sure she would have been able to swallow. What made children so resilient she wondered? Whatever it was, she had none of it.

Jamie chatted away during breakfast whilst Becky remained very quiet. Everything was abnormal and strange to the little girl and nothing Lisa tried would entice her to say much. She had never met Becky on any of the occasions she had taken Jamie out so she was a complete stranger to the little girl. After breakfast and for most of the morning they played with the dog in the back garden and once or twice she actually saw a smile on Becky's face.

The social worker arrived at lunchtime.
"I'm Judith Webster. I'm sorry you were left to cope with all this on your own last night. I'm from the Child Care Unit and I've been assigned to the children."
"Can I get you some tea or coffee?" inquired Lisa, showing Judith into the sitting room.
"Whichever you're making will be fine thank you. Have you spoken to the children yet?"

"No, I had no idea what to say and I thought it might be better left until you got here." Lisa left her for a few minutes while she made the coffee. She returned with the drinks and as they both got settled, Judith tried to fill Lisa in with the details they had come up with on the family and where they thought this would lead. After about twenty minutes, Judith thought it was time to speak to Jamie and Becky. Lisa called them in from the garden.

"This is Judith; she would like to talk to you both about all the things that happened last night." Lisa sat with both of them on the sofa and waited reluctantly to hear Judith explain.

Very quietly and very gently Judith talked about how the blast had happened and how lucky they had been to have been visiting their neighbour at the time because her house hadn't been damaged. She went on to describe how their own house had been nearer the explosion and why their mother hadn't come looking for them. Jamie fought back the tears, but Becky couldn't. They couldn't understand that they weren't going to see their mother again.

"What's going to happen to us?" Jamie struggled to ask, looking from Judith to Lisa for some kind of reason for this.

"We'll have to try and find your father Jamie, and meantime, we'll arrange somewhere for you to live." Judith's voice was emotional and Lisa was grateful that she had been the one who had been sent today.

"We can stay here with Lisa, can't we Lisa, please?"

"I'm sorry Jamie that's not…" Judith was interrupted by Lisa

"Why can't they stay here? At least for the next few days, until we've all had time to come to terms with this. I would like to keep them here. Is that possible?" Lisa had surprised herself by her suggestion but she did want them to stay. Where else were they to go?

"Well, I don't think anyone had actually thought of that as an option, but maybe over the weekend it would be better if we left them here. Jamie at least knows you, and Becky will probably settle because Jamie's with her. It would certainly give our office more time to set something up for them, if you're sure you can manage Lisa?"

"Oh yes, we'll be fine." Lisa smiled at both the little faces. She decided she liked the tall, casually dressed figure of Judith Webster. The naturally waved hair shaped a face with little trace of make-up and the expensive glasses didn't hide the gentle hazel eyes. One telephone call back to the office and the arrangements were made. Lisa's background checks had all been done previously and her fostering assessment completed so there was no reason she couldn't keep the children for the next few days. Lisa had already decided she would like to keep them until their father was traced, but this wasn't the time to mention it. She would take one thing at a time.

Before Judith left, they had agreed that Lisa should take the children shopping in the afternoon. They were desperately in need of clothes, shoes and odds and ends. The social work department would foot the bill for whatever they needed. The children would be away from school probably for the next week and Judith was going to arrange a child minder for Monday, so that Lisa could get to work. They agreed to meet again on Monday evening.

Lisa did feel guilty that she was looking forward to her weekend, but she wasn't sure what she was supposed to be feeling.
"Let's take the dog for a walk then we can go shopping," she suggested. There was an excitement in her voice she couldn't disguise.

The shopping centre in Kilmains was ultra modern, unlike the village where Lisa had her shop. She preferred the old village, but you couldn't argue, the new shopping malls, all undercover had every shop you could wish for, even if it had no atmosphere. The shopping trip was all the fun she had expected.

Courage and Clowns

"Can I really have this?" Becky touched the fabric of the beautiful pink dress.

"Yes, if they have it in your size." Lisa saw no harm in one or two totally unnecessary purchases, if it cheered them up. Maybe she could take them out for dinner tonight or tomorrow and give Becky a chance to wear her dress. She was delighted to find that her size was in stock and her face was beaming. The dress had soft lace petticoats and Becky had never seen anything so lovely. Then there were trousers, shoes, nightwear, underwear, and sweaters and so it went on. It had taken them all of three hours but Lisa was satisfied that they had everything they needed, and of course one or two things that they didn't need.

"Thanks Lisa for all these clothes, you must be really rich to buy all of these." Jamie was struggling to carry all of his own bags, but he had insisted.

"I've enjoyed shopping with you and I'm glad you like your new clothes." Lisa had replied, trying to keep a hold of Becky's hand in the busy shopping area. Jamie couldn't understand how Lisa had enjoyed shopping when she hadn't bought anything for herself, but then adults were a bit strange.

There was one thing she had forgotten to buy and that was a few toys to keep them occupied, but first they had arranged to meet Meg at one of the many cafes. When they finally got there, she was already seated in the corner, the remains of her first cup of coffee in front of her.

"Look Meg," cried Jamie excitedly, throwing himself into the seat beside her and grinning from ear to ear. "Look at all this stuff Lisa bought for us."

"You look as if you've bought the entire shopping mall." Meg glanced at the array of shopping bags. "I am surprised that you managed to carry all of those."

"These bags are all mine." Jamie proceeded to pull out his new trainers for Meg to admire.

She was suitably impressed. "Very smart, you're really going to look something in those. And what did you get Becky?"

"I got a pink dress." The little girl said quietly, still clinging to Lisa's hand.

They ordered more coffee and milk shakes, and of course you had to have cakes as well. Lisa very quickly explained what had happened during Judith's visit and the fact that the children would be staying for the next few days.

"They both look as if they've settled." Meg commented as she watched them run across to the sweet shop. "And something tells me there's more to this?" She eyed her friend with a kind of amused suspicion.

"Well, the Social Work department still have to trace their father and that could take a few weeks, and I'm going to ask if they can stay with me until then. What do you think?" Lisa waited for the reaction.

"Don't you have to be qualified or something? I mean, surely they are more likely to leave them with someone who fosters already." Meg didn't want to see Lisa get attached to these kids and then lose them.

"I am qualified, what do you think the past year and the assessment were all about?" Lisa knew this was the attitude she was going to be up against, not just from Meg but from the social workers.

"Calm down, I was only trying to look at it from another point of view. If that's what you really want then I wish you luck. But don't forget they do have a father to go back to whenever he's found."

"I haven't forgotten but we don't know how long that will take. I'll have to convince everyone they would be better off with me, and I can do that." Lisa was determined and very stubborn when she was like this so Meg decided it would be better to try and move to another subject as soon as she could.

"What will you do about work?" She needed to ask this one last question.

Lisa was ready with her answer. "They'll be back at school next week so all I have to do is arrange someone to collect them after school and stay until I get home."
"I see you have this all worked out. Who is this someone?"
"I don't know that yet, but I'll find someone. It can't be that hard finding a childminder." Lisa was not going to be put off by something so trivial and Meg could sense it.

They continued chatting until the children returned armed with their purchases. They had enough sweets to decay all of their teeth in one go, but as today was a different sort of day for all of them, it didn't matter. Meg finished the last dregs of her coffee. "I need to run now. I have to meet a dressmaker at half past four and mother will have a nervous breakdown if I don't turn up."
"Why couldn't you find a dress that fitted in the shop? Were you too big?" Becky was puzzled. Meg was tall but they made tall dresses she thought.
"Thank you very much Becky." Meg's mock anger made them all laugh.
"I know I am rather large, but this is a special dress, a wedding dress because I'm getting married soon." Meg thought this would be the end of Becky's contribution to the conversation

and she was surprised when she continued talking.

"I'm getting married when I grow up, and I'm going to have a house like Lisa's, all pretty with a garden to sit in." Becky had spoken more than she had since she arrived.

"I think you'll have a while to wait." Lisa took the small hand in hers as they left the café and made their way back to the car park. They said goodbye to Meg and loaded the car.

"I like Meg," said Jamie with conviction. "She's very jolly, isn't she?"

As Lisa drove out of the car park she thought this a very apt description of her friend.

Michael Bradshaw returned home at around two o'clock on the Saturday afternoon. The tall, dark figure of his wife was coming downstairs as he laid his keys on the table in the hall.

"Going out again?"

He hadn't really needed to ask the question. The green eyes flared at him.

"Perhaps if you were here a little more often, I wouldn't need to be out." She straightened the pencil skirt on her linen suit, a new purchase that same morning. She picked up a clasp from the table and tied her long sleek hair in a twist at the back of her head. Satisfied with her appearance, she made her way to the front door. The heels on her new, pale green Cartier shoes clipped on the Italian marble floor.

"Don't hurry home." He murmured to the back of the door as it slammed behind him. He picked up the telephone directory and wandered into the kitchen. She had been attracted by his fame; he had been attracted by her looks. The attraction on both sides had long since gone. Over the past few years they had come to loathe each other, and although they had no life together, she wouldn't agree to a divorce. She was having affairs, but as long as she was discreet, he couldn't care less. To leave her would have meant having his personal life all over the papers, and the station was very much against any kind of scandal. In saving his career he had given up any chance of a personal life.

Yes, Kerry Bradshaw was a nasty piece of work, and it was probably safer having her where he could keep an eye on her. He flicked the pages of the directory and dialled the first number.

"Hello, is that Mr Whitford? I'm sorry to disturb you but I'm trying to trace a Miss Lisa Whitford … I'm sorry I must have the wrong number.

He had around twenty more to try. It took him the best part of the next hour. By call number twelve, he was no further forward. No one appeared to be related to her either, this seemed a waste of time maybe he should leave it for now. He had given the social work department his card but maybe they wouldn't pass it on, or worse still, maybe she wouldn't phone even if she got his message.

He dialled the next number on the list. The answering machine voice was very precise and articulate. "Hello, this is Lisa…"
Success! He replaced the receiver. He sat back in his chair and loosened his silk tie. Now he had more than a phone number, he had an address. He ripped the page out of his notepad and picking up his jacket and keys, he headed for the car. Kilmains was only seven miles from Glasgow; he would be there in no time.

As Lisa pulled into the car park at the house, she could hardly help noticing the sleek Mercedes sports car parked further along. The kids were already out of the car, as she started unloading the many bags.
"Right, let's get this lot inside…" She hadn't finished her sentence when a voice interrupted.
"Miss Whitford, my name's Michael Bradshaw."
As she turned around she found herself looking into the bluest eyes she had ever seen.

"I know who you are Mr Bradshaw, but I am wondering how you know who I am? Jamie take some of these bags please."

Before Jamie had a chance, Michael had lifted the few remaining bags and closed the boot.

"Didn't you get my message? I wanted to talk to you about last night?"

"What message Mr Bradshaw?"

"It doesn't matter, I'm here now. Can I speak to you for a few minutes?"

They had reached the front door. Lisa thought for no more than a second. Spending a few minutes with such good-looking company certainly couldn't do her any harm.

"Please come in Mr Bradshaw but I don't know if I'll be of any help." She couldn't imagine why he wanted to talk to her.

As she opened the door the dog appeared to investigate the owner of the voice he hadn't recognised. He decided he wasn't as interesting as he had sounded and instead the little dog ran off into the garden with Jamie and Becky. Lisa dumped all the bags on the dining room floor and filled the kettle.

"Would you like some coffee Mr Bradshaw?" She was hoping he would stay long enough to have some.

"Please, white, no sugar." He looked around the blue kitchen. The paint was blue; the cups the tea towels, the kettle everything was blue even down to the handles of the spoons.

"I wouldn't need to be an investigative reporter to tell you're partial to blue."

He had made her laugh, and that pleased him. She had a beautiful smile and her whole face lit up when she laughed. He was badly smitten, and he knew it.

They lifted their coffee through to the sitting room. The room was definitely feminine. Again the soft blue, but this time contrasted with pink. Almost everything was delicately and tastefully edged with lace. The expensive, pink and blue porcelain figures were strategically placed to look like finishing touches rather than ornamentation.

"What can I tell you about last night?" She brought the conversation back to the reason he had come.

"I watched you last night and you weren't exactly dressed like a rescue worker. Then I saw you when you found the children and I presumed they weren't yours and, reporter that I am, I thought I sensed a story."

He didn't want a story now. Sitting there so close, he wanted her.

"I'm sorry to disappoint you, there's no story here. The children are staying for the weekend that's all, and I would prefer if you didn't make a story out of that." She felt no need to tell him any more.

"Will you have dinner with me tonight?" His thoughts were spoken before he realised he had said them. He had to see her again. The fact that she had said there would be no interview meant that soon she would be showing him the door, and he had to prevent that from happening.

"I don't think so Mr Bradshaw. If that's supposed to entice me into giving you an interview, then it's failed miserably." She had been taken aback by the suddenness of his proposal but she presumed that was how reporters worked. "In any case, I have two children to look after." She knew how the media worked. She had spent two years trying to get good copy for some of her accounts at the agency. Journalists were never backward in coming forward.

"It's not like that. I would like to take you out to dinner and I know a little country pub where the children would be very welcome. They even have a play area at the back. Please say yes and I promise, no interview and no story."

Lisa was tempted. What harm could a little dinner do, and it would be good to have a night out, especially in such celebrated company. "Well, yes it would be nice, thank you." She wasn't sure why she had agreed except perhaps for no other reason than she wanted to. He was delighted.

"I'll get home and get changed and I'll pick you up at seven, and thank you for saying yes."

With that, he was gone.

Lisa spent the next few hours getting the children ready for their night out. Becky was almost dizzy from twirling around in her dress and Jamie too seemed quite excited at a night out for dinner, dressed up in his new clothes. They were ready a little early and Lisa felt nervous and excited. She had to admit she was looking forward to her night out and looking forward to seeing Michael Bradshaw again.

Promptly at seven, he returned, dressed in beige trousers and a casual shirt. His body was well tanned and his chosen colours seemed to emphasise it. Lisa was glad she hadn't overdressed, her plain skirt and blouse were smart but not over the top. They were only having dinner in a pub; a dress would have seemed a little much.

Michael had noticed the remarkable difference in the children. The little boy wore dress trousers in pale blue with a blue and yellow striped shirt and the little girl was stunning in her pink floral dress. That one would be a heartbreaker one day he thought and what a change from last night. Gone were the sorrowful faces and here tonight they looked like two normal happy children. He was amazed at their resilience.

As they drove to the pub he couldn't help feeling that he liked the idea of being a family. That's what it felt like. Lisa and the kids, they felt like a family. He had never known that feeling before.

The pub was quaint and the kids were thrilled when they were handed their own special menus. Once they had ordered Jamie and Becky were desperate to go outside and play until their meal was ready.

"So tell me, why were you so anxious to take us out tonight for dinner?" Lisa wasn't convinced that his reporting still wouldn't come first.

"I did want a story at first. But when I saw you with the children today at the house, you all looked so natural as if you belonged together. I suddenly didn't want to do anything to spoil that for you." She knew he was being honest.

"Officially I only have them for the weekend, after that I really don't know. Their father has to be traced and I don't think anyone knows yet where he is." Lisa was watching Jamie and Becky through the window and her face gave it all away.

"I get the feeling you'd rather he wasn't found for some time anyway? Am I right?" Michael was watching her closely and it was obvious that she cared for these children and what would become of them.

Before she knew it, she was telling him about her divorce and how much she had wanted children. She explained about working on the project and how she hoped to foster or adopt one day. The more he heard the more he wanted to know. But for now their meal had arrived. The food was delicious and even after eating their way through their main course, Jamie and Becky still had room for apple pie and ice cream.

"Can we go back to the play area Lisa?" Jamie was enjoying his night out and didn't want to waste a minute of it.

Michael was enthralled with the kids.

"If you like after we have coffee, we can go for a walk along the river bank. There's a little bridge and if you look over, the water's so clear you can see the fish swimming. How does that sound?" Michael had suggested.

"So what you mean is we can play until you've had coffee? Thanks. Come on Becky."

Jamie's powers of deduction always worked in his favour.

They both ran off leaving Michael and Lisa to have their coffee alone.

"I don't think that's exactly what I said." Michael smiled at Lisa. "They're lovely kids. How could any father leave them? If you ask me, he doesn't deserve to get them back. Do you know why he left?"

"No, the kids don't talk about him at all. I'm not even sure how long he's been away. And you were right when you said I hoped he wasn't found for some time. That's a terrible thing to say, I don't really mean it. Children are always better with their natural parents. Their mother was a lovely woman she didn't really get a fair chance being left with three kids to raise and then being taken the way she was, it's so sad."

"You're going to make a wonderful mother Lisa I can tell. Whether it's these kids or someone else's you'll be devoted to them."

"I hope you're right. I'd hate to take on a child and then discover I couldn't love them. It would be awful."

Lisa had gone quiet thinking how terrible that would be.

Michael sensed her change in mood. "They say that maternal love is the purest form of love and you already show that when you look at Jamie. You'll never have difficulty loving a child. In fact I think you'll love them to the detriment of everything else."

"What a strange thing to say. I don't think you know me well enough to make that kind of assumption." Lisa knew however, he was probably right.

Michael felt he had said more than enough. "Let's go find them and have our walk."
He gently held her arm as he helped her to her feet and she could feel the surge of pleasure running through her body. It was a long time since she had trembled at someone's touch. Michael had walked along this river path many times before but always alone. He did lots of things alone. He searched for her hand as they walked along and when he found it, it felt like the most natural thing in the world for Lisa to clasp his hand in return. His grip tightened as he smiled and squeezed her hand even tighter. This felt good.
"What kind of fish are in the river?" Becky was already way ahead of them on the path. "Will there be lots of goldfishes?"
"No I shouldn't think so Becky, more likely to be trout." Michael called after her.
She didn't know what trout was but she wanted to see anyway.

Lisa watched her companion intently as they walked along. He wasn't at all what she had imagined. He wasn't the over confident face on the screen any more. He was really rather nice. People had been smiling at him in the pub, obviously recognising him and as he smiled and said a few words to one or two of them, Lisa had the feeling that underneath the outwardly cheerful appearance, he was in fact unhappy. She wondered why that might be. They reached the bridge.

"Oh look Lisa, lots of trouts," Becky screamed. "Can I have a closer look?"

"Lots of trout Becky and if you get any closer you'll be in the water." Lisa held the little girl as she leaned over to get a better look.

"Jamie don't you want to see?" Lisa noticed that he was showing little interest in the fish.

"People are going to catch them and eat them, that's disgusting." His little eyes were filling with tears.

Michael bent down quickly and put his arm around the little boy, his blonde hair a stark contrast to Jamie's dark curls.

"People aren't allowed to fish here Jamie, so these little ones won't ever get eaten."

Lisa was surprised at the gentleness in his voice. She took Jamie's hand. "Let's turn back now I think you're probably tired and it's been a long day."

The child was silent throughout the journey home. As he sat staring out of the car window Lisa wondered what was going through his mind. Becky on the other hand had fallen asleep. Her long dark eyelashes resting on her flushed cheeks. It wasn't long before the car pulled up at the house and without hesitation

Michael gently lifted Becky and carried her along the path.

"I'll take her upstairs and then while you're getting them into bed, I'll make some coffee." Michael seemed to be making himself at home and Lisa saw no reason to object. Once they were tucked up in bed Becky woke for a brief few minutes.

"Will mummy be back from heaven tomorrow to take us home?"

Lisa hadn't been expecting a question like that and was taken unawares. "No Becky, mummy has to stay in heaven. God will look after her now."

"God isn't nice if he won't let mummy come home."

She sobbed into her pillow for a few minutes and then almost as quickly as she had awakened she was fast asleep again.

Lisa hadn't realised that she was asleep again and was explaining that God only took good people who got sick and couldn't stay here any more. But Becky couldn't hear any of this.

Lisa tucked the quilt around the sleeping body.

"Lisa?" Jamie's voice called softly from the other bed. "God won't ever take my dad then will he, if he only takes good people that is?"

What an odd thing for him to say thought Lisa but she felt that more conversation on the subject

of death, God and heaven could probably wait until morning.
"It's late Jamie, go to sleep." She placed a kiss on top of the dark head.
She wasn't sure what to make of Jamie's comment but stored it away to mention to Judith on Monday evening.

Michael had the coffee all ready and he smiled at her as she walked in. She liked his smile. She had to be honest, she liked him. What a pity the evening was coming to an end. He had even let Freebie out into the garden and as the little dog returned he only looked briefly in Lisa's direction and made his way upstairs to begin his night vigil, guarding his friends, the children. She knew he too within a few minutes would be sound asleep. Michael played with his coffee cup twirling it between the strong hands.
"Lisa, I have to see you again, but before you say anything there's something I have to tell you. I'm married but let me explain."
She knew something had to burst the bubble. Everything had been too perfect but she certainly hadn't expected to hear this. She had presumed he was probably divorced.
"Lisa I've been married in name only for years and until now I've been able to live with that. I haven't looked for anyone else and I suppose that in a lot of respects it's been convenient.

Then all of a sudden I meet you and I know we've only known each other for a day, but there's something very special about this. If there's the slimmest chance of anything here then I'll sort out the rest of my life. Will you at least think about what I've said?"
She listened closely and although he sounded genuine enough she did wonder if he had ever told anyone else the same story. She wanted to believe him but she wasn't a fool.
"Michael, I've had a wonderful evening but maybe it's better if we just leave things the way they are. I really have enjoyed myself but I have no intentions of confusing my life by having an affair with you. I don't need any skeletons in my cupboard and if the social work department found one, they would drop me so quickly. I've worked really hard to get where I am and nothing's going to spoil it. I'm sorry Michael, I can't afford to mess things up now." She was sorry indeed. She hadn't met anyone like him before and she would have liked to see him again, but it wasn't worth the risk.
"No Lisa, I can't let things go, not like that."
Before she knew what was happening she was in his arms. His kiss was hard and passionate and as he felt her body respond, he kissed her again, this time much more gently. She had been taken by surprise but she was even more surprised to

discover that she was, in return, kissing him with the same eagerness.

"I'll call you tomorrow. Think about what I've said? Goodnight Lisa."

He was gone.

As she rested against the closed door her body was shaking. A body aching for the man who had just left.

CHAPTER 4

Lisa's thoughts were jumbled when she woke up on Sunday morning. In two days her world had turned upside down. She had spent a very restless night and was tired and confused. She had spent the last two years not interested in a relationship, so why was Michael so different?

If there was the slightest chance that she would be allowed to keep Jamie and Becky until their father turned up then that was what she wanted to do more than anything. What if he didn't want them? What then? Maybe Michael would wait, but what if he didn't want to wait. She didn't even know how long that might be. Why had he turned up to complicate her life? Why now?

The telephone rang bringing her out of her own thoughts. She searched for her slippers and made her way downstairs. She lifted the receiver.

"Hello," a crisp voice said. "I'm Mrs Davidson, the social work department asked me to call you. I believe you're looking for someone to look after

two children tomorrow?" The voice although crisp was also soft and lilting.
"Oh yes," Lisa had forgotten all about Judith saying she would find a child minder. "I need someone from about eight thirty until just after five, if that suits you?" Lisa suspected her caller was older, maybe late fifties or early sixties.
"That would be fine. What ages are the children?"
"Jamie's nine and Becky's six. Did the social work department tell you anything about their background?" Lisa thought it would be wise for her caller to understand what the children had been through.
"Yes they did and I'm only too glad to be able to help. I'll see you tomorrow at eight. I'm looking forward to meeting the children."
Lisa liked the sound of the voice at the other end of the telephone line.
"Thank you Mrs Davidson, I'll see you tomorrow."
She replaced the receiver and switched on the kettle to make some tea. This could be the only quiet ten minutes she would get all day because before long the children would be awake.

The telephone rang again. Lisa wasn't much of a morning person and it was unusual for anyone to ring this early and she'd already had one call. She lifted the receiver again.

"Good morning, how are you?" Michael's voice was husky and sensual.

She was conscious of the tremble running through her body. How could anyone sound like he did first thing on a Sunday morning?

"I'm fine," she replied. "But I'm not accustomed to people calling me this early." She hoped the tremble hadn't reached her voice. It was reaching everywhere else.

"Did you sleep well? I have to admit I didn't and that's your fault." He accused. "I didn't want to leave you last night."

"I didn't sleep well at all," she admitted.

Michael continued, "I'm going to be in the studio all day today, but I was hoping we could get together later for a chat, say about nine?"

"Michael, this isn't going to work," she heard herself saying. "I've thought about it and maybe it's better not to see each other." She had wanted to say anything but that.

"Lisa please, just an hour tonight and we'll talk, what harm can that do?"

She knew only too well that seeing him again was only going to make this more difficult, but she agreed.

"Make it about nine thirty, the kids should be asleep by then, and Michael I'm not promising anything."

She wasn't at all sure this was wise.

"I know but we need to talk. What are you all doing today?"

"I'm not sure yet," she replied. "Possibly visiting a friend, but the kids aren't up yet, so we'll have to see."

"Have a pleasant day and I'll see you later. Take care." And the line was dead.

She replaced the receiver and, singing to herself, she made some tea. She had only sat down with the cup when she heard some movement from upstairs followed by the sound of little footsteps on the stairs. Becky's voice was still sleepy.

"Can I put on new clothes today, please?"

Lisa ruffled the mass of tangled curls. "Yes of course you can. Shall we go and choose something?"

Becky beamed with delight and raced back upstairs. Lisa took one last gulp of her tea and followed. Between them they arranged an outfit for the day by which time Jamie was awake. They both appeared much happier this morning thought Lisa as she left them to get dressed and she had promised that if they were quick they could help with breakfast. At the thought of food Jamie was dressed and downstairs before Becky.

The kitchen became a disaster area as they both mixed up batter for pancakes, stirring instead of whisking, which Lisa had thought would cause less mess. She was wrong. In the end however, the pancakes were delicious and topped with lemon juice and sugar, breakfast was a success.

"What would you like to do today?" she asked them both. "I was thinking we might visit Meg." Both were in agreement. They had liked Meg and were looking forward to seeing her again. It wasn't long before they were organised.

"Can Freebie come too?" Becky had asked and as she was holding his lead in her hand, there wasn't much chance of saying no. So Freebie came too.

Meg was delighted to see them. Visitors were one of her favourite pastimes. It was a great excuse for sitting down and not doing anything, like housework for example.

"Why don't you stay and have something to eat? Mother wasn't expecting you today with all that's happened. She's coming here and Keith's coming over and as it's dry we were going to barbecue. The kids would love it."

Becky's little voice piped up in the background. "We went to the pub last night for dinner, then Michael took us a walk to see the fishes and there was this bridge and when you looked over you could see the fishes swimming about. It was great Meg." Becky had rambled through her story so quickly Lisa had no opportunity to stop it. She hadn't wanted to mention Michael but she had forgotten that the children might talk about him.

"Hold on, hold on." Meg had lost track of the conversation, which wasn't surprising under the circumstances. "Which pub and who's Michael?"

Jamie joined the conversation in his matter of fact tone. "Michael is Lisa's friend and he's really nice."

Meg threw a glance at Lisa. It wasn't the first time that Lisa had been on a date and never mentioned it until well after the fact. And now there was a 'Michael'.

"Where did Michael spring from?" she asked, fully realising that Lisa hadn't wanted to be asked at all.

"Michael Bradshaw, but I only met him yesterday, so I haven't exactly had the chance to tell you." Lisa knew there was no point now in trying to gloss over the night out.

"Michael Bradshaw from television, that Michael Bradshaw?" Meg asked.

"Yes." Meg's face was a picture.

"You had dinner with Michael Bradshaw and you weren't going to tell me? I saw you at four o'clock yesterday and you didn't mention him." Meg was open-mouthed as she waited for Lisa to explain.

Thankfully Lisa was saved by the arrival of Keith and after saying hello, he had two excited children and a dog rushing out to help him set up the barbecue.

"Well, are you going to tell me or not?" Meg asked after everyone was out of earshot.

Lisa explained how he had arrived, and then about dinner and finally the circumstances immediately prior to his departure. Meg's astonished expression made Lisa smile and add, "It's not as exciting as it sounds. He's married and although he did say he would sort his life out, I can't afford to be mixed up in anything, especially a divorce."

"He's adorable, you must be tempted?"

"Of course I'm tempted but can you imagine if the press got a hold of this they would have a field day. 'Temporary child carer has affair with TV presenter.' The social work department would love that. I think that I would suddenly become totally unsuitable as a prospective parent to any child."

The thought of it made them both laugh.

"Has he said if he'll contact you again?" Meg asked

"He's coming over later tonight." When Lisa saw the suspicion on Meg's face, along with a know-it-all grin, she added, "To talk, that's all, so don't give me that look."

Meg raised her eyebrows and still grinning mischievously, she whispered, "If I had Michael Bradshaw to myself late at night, I wouldn't want to be talking to him and if you take my advice, I'd forget the social work department for one night and enjoy yourself. Who's going to know? I certainly won't tell anyone, in fact I shall go to great lengths to deny it when the press ask me for an interview."

"You're an idiot Meg, don't encourage me."

The conversation was halted at this stage by the arrival of Meg's mother and the barbecue chef's, Jamie and Becky, looking for food. The next hour was spent preparing the meal and from the shrieks outside, Lisa could only presume the kids were having a great time. Keith was very patient and it looked as if he was enjoying himself too. Meg and Lisa wandered out into the garden where Meg's mother had been sitting with her glass of wine.

"Help me Keith, this won't turn over?" Becky screamed as her burger landed on the patio.

"No problem, we've plenty more." Keith unwrapped another burger and left Becky to stand guard while it cooked. He came over and sat down. He was a very slim man with fair hair and very pale grey eyes. His five foot ten figure was perched on a garden chair with his long legs stretched out in front of him

"They're lovely kids Lisa. How's the perfect little mother coping?"

"I doubt I'm anywhere near perfect but we seem to be managing. At least they're still living and I've had them for two days so I can't be doing too badly. I've been trying to keep them busy so that they don't have time to think about what's happened. But I have to admit, I'm enjoying it."

"I think you've done wonderfully well, considering," said Meg's mother Marjory. She was also tall like Meg but heavier. They had the same fair skin although Marjory's hair was darker than Meg's was. There was no doubting they were mother and daughter. She had always treated Lisa like another daughter and she marvelled at how she was coping with her new situation. The conversation naturally turned to talk of the wedding, which was Keith's excuse to bail out and go back to cooking. After what seemed an eternity, they eventually had enough burgers cooked and Meg and Lisa had produced some salad and some vegetables and at last everyone was ready to eat.

"What are these tree things?" asked Becky with her usual subtlety.

"It's broccoli," Lisa explained. "Would you like to try some?"

She screwed her face up at Lisa. "No, it still looks like trees. I don't think I'll bother."

Jamie was again rather quiet, but Becky more than made up for it.

"Keith, Meg's having a wedding dress made. She told me." Becky continued through a mouthful of burger.

"Yes I did know Becky because it's me she's going to marry." Keith had managed to sound fairly serious.

Becky was very pleased because she liked Keith and Meg and it was nice that they were getting married to each other.

"What will you be wearing? Do you get a wedding suit or something?" She continued with her questions.

"Yes, but it won't be quite as fancy as Meg's."

"Men never get fancy clothes to wear. They always look the same."

At this point Keith had to laugh. Becky was a character. "I'm beginning to feel sorry for whoever marries you."

Becky wasn't the least put out. "Lisa says I've got to wait a long time before I get married."

"Yes I expect you will have to wait a while." Keith was enjoying his dialogue.

   They had stayed rather longer than Lisa had intended and eventually the time came to leave. Lisa kissed Marjory on the cheek and promised to visit soon.

"Thanks for having us."

"Give me a call later." Meg winked at Lisa as they walked out to the car.

"It may be quite late, perhaps tomorrow would be better?" Lisa suggested.

"No, tonight." Meg wasn't prepared to wait to hear the second instalment of the Michael Bradshaw saga.

On the way home they stopped off at the park and let Freebie have a run around. Jamie and Becky chased him until they were all exhausted and ready to go home. The two children settled in front of the television until it was time for their baths. As Becky played with the bubbles, she asked Lisa if she was going to marry someone too.

"Not at the moment Becky. Did you have someone in mind?" Lisa replied as she covered Becky in soap.

"I liked Michael so you could marry him and then Jamie and I could stay here and be your children. That would be a good idea, wouldn't it?" The child continued innocently.

"Well I don't really know Michael well enough, so I don't think I'll be marrying him." She joked as she placed bubbles on Becky's nose. "Becky, don't you want to live with your father?"

"I don't think so. Jamie doesn't because he said he doesn't like him and he says I don't either, but I don't remember."

Lisa knew she would have to get to the bottom of this and again she stored it away for Judith.

At last the children were safely tucked up in bed and Lisa had just under an hour before Michael arrived. Time enough to have the peaceful cup of tea she had been trying to have all day. She tried to sort things out in her head. She knew there was no way she would be happy seeing Michael while he still had a wife living under the same roof. On that account she was decided. So where did she go from here? Nothing in her life could be planned until Mr Campbell was found. She realised that she didn't even know his first name. She also had no idea how long the social workers would try to find him or what would happen if they didn't. Lisa had lots to ask Judith tomorrow evening. She was amazed at how much her life had changed in the last few days. She thought of Michael. It had been so long since she had been in a relationship and she had forgotten how good it felt to be held by someone. Here she was at thirty, undecided about everything and no one to help her with her decisions.

Michael arrived on time and after she had made him a drink, they wandered through to the sitting room.

"I've thought about this all day long." He didn't see any point in holding back. "I've made some major decisions about my life and whether or not you decide you want to be with me, I shall be leaving my wife. I spent an evening with you last night and I didn't think it possible to feel like that about anyone anymore. I know we've only met, but I know how I feel about you. I'm thirty-nine years old and I have nothing in my life except my work and a few close friends. And no matter how close your friends are they are no substitute for a relationship. Suddenly what I have isn't enough."

"Michael, before you say any more, can I explain. Having the children here these past few days has made me realise that what I need from life is what I am getting from them. I don't need to complicate things. I can't wait any longer for this, I have to do it now and I can't let anything or anyone prevent me from doing this. There is no room for a relationship."

"Lisa, with me you could have your own kids or adopt as many as you want. I'm not trying to prevent you from doing anything. I just want us to be together."

They talked for hours and seemed to be going round in circles.

"Michael, until yesterday I didn't even know you, and now you're turning my world upside down. We don't even know each other." She was so confused she didn't know what to think.

He crossed the room to where she was sitting. His arms were around her, powerful arms and his kisses were wild and forceful. She wanted him. Her whole body cried out for him, but not like this. None of this was right.

"I want you so much," he murmured.

She pulled away from him, embarrassed at how she felt.

"Michael, I can't, not yet."

"I know my darling." He stroked her hair, sending shivers running through her. "I'm sorry, I just don't want to wait."

Lisa was still hesitant. "I need to sort things out. This is all happening too fast for me." She lay back and rested her head on his shoulder. His cologne was making her quite heady but it was still subtle. She liked it. She enjoyed the feeling of simply having him there. Michael Bradshaw was going to be very hard to resist, but she had to make sure everything else was in its rightful place and she had to be sure they really belonged together. She was even beginning to convince herself that they did. From that moment her mind was made up. She was going to find a way to have the children and Michael.

His kisses were now gentle and lingering, but just as arousing. She could feel his hand on her back against her bare skin and his touch made her body respond uncontrollably. If he stayed any longer she wouldn't be able to resist him. She didn't want to resist him. She wanted him more than ever.

"Lisa, I know you want me, as much as I want you," he whispered.

Her resistance crumbled as her arms were around his neck pulling him down towards her. Their lips met and once more they were locked in a passionate embrace, his tongue probing her mouth, then moving down her neck to stop at her shoulder. With his every touch her body jerked. She gasped with excitement. No one could have resisted feelings like these. He lifted her gently and carried her upstairs. Lisa felt the coolness of the quilt against her skin as he slowly undressed her, using his lips and tongue to initiate each new uncovering of her skin. His experienced hands stroked her gently until her body screamed for him to take her. As he pushed inside her, she gasped in delight. His breathing was heavy, and as they moved together their loving was fierce and desperate. She climaxed in spasms of sheer ecstasy and when he continued relentlessly she found her self again beyond the point of no return. She gave in as he brought her again and again to the limit of pleasurable endurance, before using all his strength he pushed inside her to bring them both together to the ultimate region of passion.

Complete and satisfied they lay side by side. Whether lust or love, this was how it should be.

"Whatever happens darling, we're going to be together." He murmured. He stroked her hair gently as he spoke. "Lisa, I love you…no, don't say anything…I know I do. I have thought of nothing else since the first moment that I saw you. Whatever way we do this, we'll end up together, believe me."

"I'd like to believe you. There's nothing I would like better. I didn't intend tonight to happen, but I'm not sorry that it did. I just can't see you again here at the house."

"Does that mean, you intend seeing me again, I thought maybe you were just using me and then you'd throw me out." He was laughing, balancing his head on his hand; his elbow perched on the pillow. Lisa pushed his arm away bringing his head into contact with the pillow. She kissed him gently.

"I'm not in the habit of using men and casting them aside, in fact, I can't believe you're here at all. I can't bear the thought of not seeing you for months."

"Nobody said anything about not seeing each other. I certainly have no intentions of leaving you for months. We just have to be careful. We don't want your name mixed up in my divorce or the social workers finding out about me. But I don't see how they can object to what you do as long as the children aren't involved. Surely you'll be able to have some evenings out?"

"Of course I can". She replied, foreseeing all the problems this was going to throw at them.

"Then leave the rest to me. Don't worry, everything's going to work out."

Lisa wasn't sure that she could keep up the pretence, but for Michael she was certainly prepared to try.

"I'm not sure where I'll be staying, but I'll leave you a number where you can contact me and you can give me the shop number and then I won't have to phone the house." He scribbled a number on the pad beside the phone in the bedroom.

"It's my programme controller's home number. I've spoken to him because I had to warn him that my wife would probably make a meal of all that's going to happen and I didn't want him to find out through the press. His name is Josh Ridley and he knows about you. All you do is leave a message with Josh and I'll contact you."

He smiled like a Cheshire cat, he had obviously thought of everything.

"Michael, it's almost two o'clock, I really do have to throw you out now." She spoke gently, not wanting to break the magic. Her head was still trying to take it all in.

"I know, I suppose I'd better go before I fall asleep."

"I really do wish you could stay." She had reached for him, but he was already on his feet.

"At least I'll have something to come back for. Remember, whatever you read or hear from now on, you have to ignore. My wife isn't going to take this lying down and she'll drag up anything she can. I love you and even if this takes months, I'm only at the other end of the phone. I'll find ways of seeing each other and if you need anything, ring Josh."

"I'm going to miss you." She admitted soulfully.

"Not half as much as I'll miss you. Take care sweetheart, and stay there, I'll see myself out." His last kiss was hard and brutal on her lips.

"That's so you don't forget me." He again brought his lips down on hers with force.

"I don't think there's any chance of that Michael." She heard the stair creak gently as he made his way downstairs and the click as the front door closed. Lisa wasn't a deceitful person and the next few months were going to be difficult. She didn't like the idea of creeping about and seeing someone in secret but they had no other choice. She had no way of knowing how long it would be before she saw him again, but exhausted she soon fell into a deep sleep, with Michael in and out of her dreams.

Monday morning came all too soon. Lisa had the children up and dressed ready for Mrs Davidson's arrival. She had slept well, but not long enough and she was slightly tired. Her life really had gone haywire. Normally on a Sunday evening she would have soaked in a nice long bath, watched some TV and been in bed by midnight. Not that she regretted for one minute her evening with Michael, but it would have been nice to have had a lie in and a quiet morning afterwards. Unfortunately that wasn't this Monday morning as she tried to clear away the breakfast dishes and at the same time try to keep the children fairly calm. The doorbell rang a few minutes after eight. Mrs Davidson looked like anyone's grandmother. She was not very tall, slightly stout with masses of white hair in thousands of tiny curls sitting on her shoulders. The little gold-rimmed glasses sat in the middle of the cheery weather-beaten face.

Lisa made some tea and they chatted for about fifteen minutes. The children were introduced and promised to behave before disappearing into the garden with Freebie.

From her accent Lisa had thought that Mrs Davidson came from the highlands, but she was in fact from Skye.

"My son and his family moved down here, so I came with them." The elderly lady explained.

"I'm enjoying it. I like all the shops and having plenty of places to go and the theatre here is excellent. And of course registering with the social work department as a childminder means I can do some useful work when I want to without really being tied to a job. It all works very well."

Lisa got up from the table and gathered together her things for work. She had no qualms about leaving Mrs Davidson in charge. She suspected she would be much more capable than Lisa herself was.

"You have my shop phone number, in case of emergencies, and I should be home about five thirty. And the children can help you find anything you need." Lisa called goodbye to Jamie and Becky.

"We'll be fine don't worry." Mrs Davidson was already putting the cups into the sink and appeared to be quite at home.

In the space of four days Lisa had a completely new life. One that she could quite happily settle into. She remembered she had promised to phone Meg the evening before but as the evening had turned out slightly differently to what she had planned, she had forgotten all about it. She would maybe get a chance to ring her during the day if only briefly to apologise.

She was also trying to push thoughts of Michael out of her head but that was proving more difficult. She parked her car behind the shop. This was such a different Monday morning. She was smiling to herself as she opened up for business.

Monday was a quiet day, so she busied herself doing a general tidy up and rearranged clothes on the rails. She had some new stock to go out so she was busy pricing her garments when the door opened at lunchtime. It was Cathy from the florist's shop.

"Who's the secret admirer?" she asked of Lisa as she placed a beautiful basket arrangement on the counter.

"Are these for me?" asked Lisa surprised. She picked up the card. They were from Michael, although the card wasn't signed, it read; 'The dreams of today, are the realities of tomorrow.'

They were beautiful Chrysanthemums, one of Lisa's favourite flowers. She was glad Cathy didn't have time to wait and ask a lot of questions. But she knew she would be anxious to find out whom they were from at some point in the next few days. She and Cathy often had a quick coffee on quiet days. Lisa normally went home at lunchtime to see to her little dog but there was no need to do that today. On some occasions she took him into the shop with her.

The shop was busier in the afternoon, but she was still glad when five o'clock came and it was

time to go home. As she opened the front door the children and the dog greeted her. They were all trying to get her attention at the same time.
"Hold on. Let me get in first. Have you had a good day?" she asked. She called a greeting to Mrs Davidson as she took off her shoes.
"Slippers Freebie, that's a good boy?" The little dog sped up the stairs, returning with one slipper in his mouth. "Next one?" she said, taking the first slipper from him. Off he went again and returned with the second slipper. "Good Boy." Lisa patted his head. "You are clever." The little dog wagged his tail. Jamie and Becky were thrilled with Freebie's trick.
"He is clever isn't he?" Becky was cuddling him to death and the dog wasn't complaining.

Lisa followed the smell of food into the kitchen. Whatever was cooking smelt delicious and was totally unexpected.
"I've rustled up some shepherd's pie for dinner, I hope you don't mind, everything's all laid out ready?" Mrs Davidson was saying as she put some plates in to warm. "Now you sit down and I'll get you a cup of tea." She was already filling the kettle.
"Mrs Davidson you needn't have gone to all that trouble, it's very kind of you." Lisa looked around the kitchen. The table was all laid and dinner was finishing off in the oven. It was too

good to be true. Lisa asked how their day had been.

"My grandchildren are all grown up now and I do miss children around my feet. I've really enjoyed my day and Jamie and Becky are no trouble. And the dog is adorable." With that she reached for her hat and coat.

"How much do I owe you for today?" Lisa asked. She had no idea what to pay Mrs Davidson and Judith hadn't mentioned anything about the money side of it.

"Oh don't worry, the social work are taking care of today. It's been really nice meeting you my dear. Goodbye children."

Lisa walked her to the door after offering her a lift home. Mrs Davidson had declined the offer as she said she liked to walk and she didn't have very far to go. They said goodbye.

The dinner was delicious and having it cooked had saved Lisa a lot of time this evening.

"We helped Mrs Davidson with the washing up at lunchtime and we didn't break anything." Jamie announced stuffing more dinner into his mouth.

"Jamie, don't talk with your mouth full. You seemed to have a good day and you liked Mrs Davidson?"

"We did. She's really nice and good fun for someone so old," added Becky.

Tact was never going to be Becky's strongpoint.
"Come on then. You can help me clear up before Judith arrives." Lisa was pleased to see that Jamie was more cheerful this evening.

Judith arrived slightly late but it had suited Lisa as she tried to get changed with minutes to spare. They were all seated when Judith announced that they had found a place for the children at the end of the week. She was hoping that Lisa would be able to keep them until then. Judith had no hesitation in asking Lisa because she could see a marked difference in these kids already. After what they had been through, it would have been normal for them to be withdrawn. Instead here were two very settled and remarkably happy children. Whatever formula Lisa Whitford had, was working.

Becky was sitting with the dog on her lap, he was sound asleep. Jamie was stretched out on the floor at Lisa's feet. The whole sight was remarkable.

"Are you enjoying staying with Lisa?" Judith asked.

"Oh yes, we went to the pub for dinner, then we had a barbecue and we saw fishes in the river, not goldfishes, they were trout." Becky's garbled account of the weekend made Judith laugh. They didn't seem like the same children she had seen on Saturday. Nor did they appear to be the same children she had read about in a report at the office.

Lisa needed a few minutes to speak to Judith without the children listening so she suggested they take Freebie and play upstairs. The three of them clattered upstairs. Once it was quiet Lisa broached the subject of keeping the children longer than the week.
"I would like, if possible to keep them until their father is traced. Is that possible?" She waited with anticipation for Judith to reply,
"I would love to say yes because the children are so settled here I have no hesitation in saying it would be the best thing. But I do think it would have to go in front of the Children's Panel. We could apply for a temporary order, if you're sure that's what you want?"
"Yes it's what I want. Do you have any news of Mr Campbell?"
"There's no news yet, we've absolutely no idea where he's gone. There's no family on either side, so he had no one to tell and if he did tell anyone, we'll never know. I have also no idea how long it will be before we know anything. Are you prepared to have the two of them until whenever it is?"
Lisa had no hesitation.
"Yes, I don't care how long it takes. But I have some concerns about one or two things that

they've said about their father." Lisa recounted the details to Judith.
"I have no idea what that means, but of course we'll make some enquiries. Now you're going to need Mrs Davidson, shall I find out is she's available long term until we know exactly what's happening?"
"Yes if you could, the kids liked her and she said she had a good day with them. She would be ideal."

Lisa called the children and explained what was happening. They were both delighted that they could stay with Lisa. Lisa left them watching television as she and Judith walked to the door.
"Someone's been lucky? These are beautiful."
Lisa was caught off guard. She had forgotten Michael's flowers. They were sitting on a table in the hall where she had put them down when she first came in.
"Yes, they were from a friend."
Judith noticed that Lisa hadn't volunteered that a boyfriend had sent them, but something this size didn't just come from a friend. Janet King hadn't mentioned a boyfriend either when they had spoken earlier on the phone. Having to take other people into consideration in a situation like this often made things much more complicated, and they had to be careful where the children

were concerned. She would have another word with Janet in the morning.

"I'll call in to the shop tomorrow if that's okay with you and let you know if the application's going ahead?" Judith had suggested.

"If you make it lunchtime, I can close for an hour and we can have coffee." Lisa offered, still annoyed that she had been stupid enough to leave Michael's floral tribute out on display.

Judith Webster almost danced out to her car. It wasn't often that a temporary placement showed such possibilities.

Lisa had only switched off her bedside light when the phone rang.

"I'm sorry, did I wake you?"

"No I've only this minute come to bed." She wouldn't have cared if he had wakened her at three in the morning.

"How did things go tonight?" Michael's voice was distinctly mellower than the night before, as if he had to whisper because she was in bed.

Lisa related the events of the evening.

"So, I'm a definite third in line for your affections. This really isn't good enough." He mused.

"You should make that fourth, you've forgotten the dog and he's definitely before you because he was here first."

His laugh could have been heard without the aid of the phone. He continued in a more serious tone.

"I'm moving out of the house at the weekend, by which time the fat will really have hit the fire. It's probably best if we don't see each other for the first few weeks, just in case. Will you survive without seeing me?"

"I'll have to try, won't I? And excuse me, I managed for thirty years without you, I'm sure I can survive for a few weeks."

He laughed again and apologised for not being able to see her sooner.

"I forgot to thank you for the flowers. They really are beautiful."

"Now tell me you would rather have had roses or carnations?" his voice teased.

"I do actually like carnations now that you mention it."

"I did think you were going to be a hard woman to please and I was right. What am I going to do with you?"

"Are you looking for suggestions?" she asked. "I could give you a few."

"I may take you up on that. Goodnight sweetheart, sleep well and I'll talk to you soon."

The line had gone dead. Lisa switched off the light with Michael still in her thoughts. Michael would always be in her thoughts from now on. That was one thought worth holding on to.

CHAPTER 5

Mrs Davidson arrived promptly at eight the following morning much to Lisa's relief. She seemed perfectly happy that the children were staying at least for the rest of this week and was delighted that she had been asked to look after them. Lisa left for the shop once again thinking that she must phone Meg when she got there.

She had only been there for a matter of minutes when her first customer arrived and before she knew it time was getting on. She hoped the rest of the day would continue like this, it really was time this shop was making more money. Cathy appeared with a large bouquet, more intrigued than she had been on Monday but again with no time to stop and question Lisa. This time it was carnations, lots of carnations and the card read simply 'I thought you'd have gone for roses'. She took the bouquet through into the back room and was about to put the kettle on for coffee when she heard someone come into the shop. More customers, this was turning into a good morning. She left them browsing as the door opened again, this time it was Meg.

"You're hopeless Lisa. You were going to call me on Sunday night, what happened?" Meg said, exasperated with her friend.

"I'm sorry, I ran out of time. Can you stay and have coffee and if you can, would you like to make it. Everything's ready in the back." Lisa said as she accepted another sale for wrapping.

Meg took herself into the back shop and made the coffee. The bouquet didn't go unnoticed. She returned with the two mugs and handed one to Lisa as the customers left. She threw a questioning glance at Lisa.

"I couldn't phone on Sunday, it was too late." Lisa replied taking a long gulp of her coffee.

"What do you mean too late? Was it midnight late, or early hours of the morning late?"

"If the children hadn't been in the house it would have been Monday morning late."

Lisa glanced over her coffee cup to watch Meg's reaction.

"You did sleep with him, I can tell, oh Lisa, I can't believe it. What's he like?"

This wasn't like Lisa. So he had to be special, really special.

Lisa's face coloured as she said, "He's fabulous Meg. I didn't want him to go at all."

Meg couldn't hide her surprise. "I'm glad to hear that you are capable of the feelings we lesser mortals have. Did he send you the flowers?"

Lisa laughed. "That's the second one. Yesterday it was a basket of chrysanthemums."

Meg was impressed. Not only was Lisa smitten, it appeared that he was too. That thought pleased her no end.

"So what happens now?" Meg was watching her time as she was supposed to be at the printers, not visiting her friend for coffee. But she wasn't leaving until she had heard the full story.

Lisa continued. "He's moving out of his house this weekend and we won't be able to see each other for the next few weeks and then, well, I'm not sure what's happening. He does phone though every day."

"I still can't believe I'm hearing this and what about the kids. What's happening there?"

Lisa quickly explained about Judith's visit and the kid's staying for a while longer and about the children's panel.

Meg had finished her coffee and was ready to leave. "If you'll be in tonight I could come over?"

"Yes, that's great I haven't arranged to go anywhere. See you later."

Meg picked up her bag and her pile of folders for the printers and left feeling happy that life had taken a turn for the better where Lisa was concerned. She thought it quite amusing that within a week Lisa had picked up two kids and a man, without even trying to get either. She was looking forward to tonight to be able to have a longer chat. Michael Bradshaw, how lucky can you get!

Lisa finished her coffee and washed up the cups. Standing over the little sink, she suddenly realised that maybe she was falling in love with Michael. She pushed the thought out of her head just as quickly as she had been thinking it. She hardly knew him, but she was wondering how she was going to survive the next few weeks without seeing him.

The phone rang bringing her out of her daydream. It was Michael.
"Thank you for my carnations, they're beautiful." She hoped no one would come in for a few minutes.
"I aim to please. Now tell me that they were the wrong colour," he teased.
"No they're perfect but could you please not send any more the florist who has the shop next door to mine is getting suspicious and I don't want to start telling her lies about whom they're from."
"Okay, no more flowers, for at least a week. Are you sure you wouldn't have preferred roses? My

budget could stretch you know." He asked jovially.

"No I'm not a great fan of anything with thorns. They're lovely but every time you go near them they stab you for no reason." Lisa replied.

"Reminds me of my soon to be ex-wife. She's kind of deadly. As you can imagine she's not taking this very well. My home life is a living nightmare and will only get worse as the week goes on, so I may move out sooner. I'm spending more time at the studio because it's quieter." He said more seriously.

"Are you sure this is what you want to do Michael?" She couldn't believe she was giving him a chance to change his mind.

"Never been more sure of anything in my life. I'm really missing you and to think this time last week I didn't even know you. I can't wait to see you again. Please tell me you haven't had second thoughts?" he asked.

"No but I want you to be sure, that's all," she said hesitantly.

"You have nothing to worry about. I'll call you later. It may be around midnight because I intend staying here until I really have to go home."

She said goodbye and hung up. Could she be falling in love so quickly? She would never have believed it was possible, but she certainly felt more for him in this short time that she had for anyone before. She was longing to see him again.

The shop was relatively quieter in the afternoon so she caught up with some paperwork. At five she locked up and drove home. It was a lovely thought driving home to a house with people in it.

She wondered what the kids had been doing all day. She wondered about Freebie too. She hoped her little dog wasn't feeling abandoned by her but instead was enjoying all this extra attention. For so long there had been only the two of them and now his little life was full of other people. She wondered whether to a dog, this was an advantage or a disadvantage. It was a pity she couldn't ask him.

Her journey took about twenty minutes and on arriving home she discovered that dinner was again all prepared, and Freebie was delighted that his mistress was back. The little dog jumped around her ankles.

"Hello there," she said cuddling him. She was missing having him in the shop with her.

A couple of minutes later he was back at Becky's side, so maybe he wasn't suffering after all. She was glad he had taken so well to the little girl, as it was a distraction for her at the moment. She thanked Mrs Davidson for again preparing dinner.

"There's really no need to do all of this but I do appreciate it." She said taking the cup of tea that she was being offered.

"I like to keep busy and the kids usually watch a bit of television between four and five so it gives me something to do. You must be tired when you get home. There's nothing worse than a long day and then having to cook a meal as well. So don't you say another word? I'm off home now, so have a nice evening and I'll see you tomorrow. Goodnight my dear." The elderly lady said putting on her hat and coat and off she went.

Dinner was again delicious and both the children cleared their plates. There was apple pie for dessert and as Lisa hadn't had cooking apples in for some time, Mrs Davidson must have bought them. She must remember to offer her money for anything she was picking up. She really was more than a child minder. Lisa had also noticed freshly vacuumed carpets. She hadn't expected a cleaner as well. The woman was a treasure.

After dinner they all helped wash up and before long the kitchen was back to its pristine condition. Lisa made some coffee as the kids lounged in front of the television. She took off her shoes and wriggled her feet. This was all so very much what she had hoped but it had occurred to her it could be a honeymoon period and everything could suddenly change. The children were certainly easier than she had expected and she was going to make the most of it.

At seven thirty she suggested they have their baths before Meg arrived and then they could stay up and see her for a little while. Jamie moved first and Lisa went up to run his bath. She left him soaking and went back downstairs. He was quite capable of washing himself and it wasn't long before he re-appeared in his pyjamas.

"Is it possible to wash too much?" he asked. He was thinking that having to bath every night was a little unnecessary.

"No Jamie, it's not. Most people shower or take a bath every day. Why do you ask? Are you afraid you'll wash away?"

He just laughed at Lisa and plonked himself back down on the floor in front of the television. With Becky washed and changed, Lisa left them to have a shower herself and was only changed when Meg arrived. She poured a glass of wine for them both and they settled down in the sitting room. Becky was rambling on in her usual fashion about Mrs Davidson and how she liked her and Meg was listening intently and asking questions when she had the opportunity. Becky didn't really pause for breath once she had

started. After an hour Lisa said it was time for bed and both of them moved without prompting. After she had said goodnight she made some coffee and took it through to Meg, who was sprawled out on the sofa in her usual manner. She always made herself at home.
"Should I be arranging another two places at the wedding?" Meg mentioned seeing how much the kids had become part of the household.
"Meg, I'd love them to be there, but there's no guarantee I'll still have them. And it's months away. But it would be nice. We'll have to wait and see."
"I have a feeling you'll still have them and don't ask me why I think that. I just do. I'll be prepared, in fact there may be three extra places needed." She said thinking about Michael.
"I hadn't thought that far ahead, but yes hopefully Michael might be there." Lisa liked the idea of planning things with him in mind.
"Have you decided what you're doing about your dress?" said Lisa changing the subject.
"I think I may go with the dressmaker. She had loads of different patterns and at least she'll make something that suits me, and we can always change it as we go along. And it would cost half the price of the dresses I've looked at. I really grudge an obscene amount of money on a dress I'll only wear for a day and then store it

away in a trunk." Meg grimaced at the thought of this dress.

"You'll look fabulous and I think the dressmaker is the better option. What about the bridesmaids?" Lisa knew Meg's two nieces and as they were both blonde and pretty it wasn't going to be difficult to find something that suited them.

"I'm going to let them choose something. My sister-in –law can worry about that. But I don't think they'll be hard to please, unlike me." Meg pulled another face. "We haven't decided on a colour yet, so there's plenty of time."

The time passed by as they chatted. They watched Michael on the news at ten and Lisa stared at the face on the screen. A face that she now knew so well. His eyes weren't nearly so blue on the television but his smile was the same. She couldn't believe how lucky she was.

They were still chatting when the phone rang. Lisa glanced at her watch; it was fifteen minutes past midnight. She lifted the phone in the hall.

"Hello there, are you on your own?" The sultry voice enquired.

"No, Meg's here. We were watching you on the news earlier." She loved the sound of his voice.

"I think I'll just come over and wish you goodnight." He said with a hint of suggestion in his voice.

"No you won't. You stay where you are. We have to keep to what we agreed." She would rather have said yes, come over, but that wouldn't have been very clever.

"Couldn't handle it then. Is that what you're telling me?" he mocked. She could hear him sighing.

"Michael, you're a clown. Go home and go to bed."

"I'd rather be in your bed. Why don't you invite me over?"

"Michael don't do this." She knew he wasn't serious, but at the same time if she had said yes, he would have been there.

"Okay, I give up. I'll speak to you tomorrow. Goodnight darling and sleep well."

"Goodnight Michael." She didn't want to say goodbye but she put the phone down.

She returned to the sitting room where Meg had replenished the coffee.

"How's the man of the moment?" she asked as Lisa picked up her cup and settled down again into her chair.

"He's fine. Meg I wish you could meet him, I know you'll like him."

"Like him?" joked Meg. "I'm besotted with the man and I don't even know him. Do you know how many times I've watched the news purely because he's reading it? Most times I don't even hear what he says. If he announced the four-minute warning, I'd miss it. I'd be so busy drooling over him I'd miss the end of the world." They both laughed.

Meg waited another while before getting up to go. "I'll give you a call, but if anything exciting happens you could maybe remember to ring and tell me, before I read it in the newspapers or for that matter hear it on the news at ten."

"I promise." Lisa felt guilty enough about not phoning Meg on Sunday. They said goodnight.

Lisa went to find Freebie to let him out for a few minutes. He scrambled down the stairs as if his life depended on it. Lisa stood out at the back door while her little terrier nosed about. He wasn't a real terrier but his origins were definitely there. He had a shaggy coat the colour of a golden Labrador. He had a little beard, so he looked like a little old man. He had the cutest little inquisitive face. He came back in and waited for his treat. Lisa gave him his chew stick and started switching off lights. She really had to get an early night at some point.

She made her way upstairs with Freebie at her heels and to her surprise he jumped onto the corner of her bed. He had obviously decided that Becky didn't need protecting tonight. Lisa was quite glad to have him back. As she turned off the lamp she heard him sighing with contentment. Freebie wasn't feeling neglected, he was only trying to look after everyone at the same time. Within minutes they were both sleeping.

Wednesday morning came all too soon. Lisa would have liked to take the day off but the business wasn't quite ready for a five-day week. Over the next few months she was hoping that she could close one day midweek or even maybe Monday to give her two days off. She struggled out of bed and washed and dressed. Neither of the kids was awake, so she left them sleeping and made some coffee. She wondered what Michael was doing now. The clock said seven thirty and she could now hear Jamie and Becky talking. She went back upstairs and helped Becky get dressed. They chatted away during their cereal, saying that Mrs Davidson was taking them shopping with her today. Lisa remembered she would need to leave out some money.

As usual Mrs Davidson was there at eight and Lisa asked about the shopping trip.
"It wasn't for anything in particular, just a few odds and ends. Is there anything I can get you?" She asked Lisa.
"They could both do with another change of clothes. Sports trousers and sweatshirts, if that wouldn't be too much trouble?" Lisa hated to ask but the first shopping trip had only covered

enough clothes for a few days and they really could do with some more.

"No trouble at all. I'll enjoy that." Nothing seemed to phase Mrs Davidson; she took everything in her stride. Lisa left some money and went off to work.

The day was busier than Lisa had expected and she was pleased considering she had wanted to take the day off. Maybe she wouldn't be able to close midweek after all. Judith called in at three having been unable to time it for lunch. She had managed to get a hearing for Friday morning, which was short notice, but Lisa was thankful that at least she only had a few days to wait. She couldn't wait to get home and tell Jamie and Becky. Judith couldn't stay long and they said goodbye after making arrangements for Friday.

Shortly before five a parcel arrived by courier. It was a small box wrapped in floral paper with a ribbon and a bow. She opened the box to find the cutest little rag-doll clown with a porcelain head. There was no card. She placed the clown back in his box and left it with her handbag in the back shop. Well she had clearly said no more flowers, but she wasn't expecting a present every day although it did make her feel special. Michael definitely made her feel special. She closed at five and was pleased with her takings for the day. Maybe business was picking up at last. Her whole life seemed to be picking up. At home she placed the little clown on her bedside table.

Thursday passed and finally it was Friday morning. The children were up early and dressed smartly in some of their new clothes. Mrs Davidson would be coming over about ten o'clock to let Lisa get off to work. They set off for the hearing with plenty of time to spare.

Judith met them as they arrived at the offices. There was a conference room on the third floor and that was where the hearing would take place. She was beginning to feel nervous. What if they said no? Jamie and Becky didn't seem to be the least bit bothered about attending and Lisa hoped they would cope with any questions they might be asked.

The panel consisted of four people, three women and one man. They were all introduced and Lisa and the children took their seats opposite.

By the time Judith had spoken to the panel, Lisa hardly recognised the description of herself. She was thankful that Judith was there to put their case forward, and she certainly did that. The children answered their questions politely and looked at Lisa each time to make sure they were saying the right things.

She was so proud of them. The decision took thirty minutes, and they were granted a temporary order for three months. Lisa could hardly believe it. She wanted to jump up and kiss everyone, but she refrained from doing so. The children were delighted too.
"I don't know how to thank you." She was at a loss for what to say to Judith.
"It's me who should be thanking you. I think you're doing a wonderful job. Now I suppose you're in a hurry to get to work. Can I help by taking the children home?
"Thanks that would be great. Mrs Davidson should be there by ten. Do you think she'll be available long term?" Lisa hadn't really thought what she would do for three months if she lost her child minder.
"I'll certainly ask her, but if she can't we do have other people on our books. We'll also have to register them for school as soon as possible, but we can talk about that later." Judith set off with Jamie and Becky suggesting they might go for a coke first before they went home. Lisa made her way to the shop.

Friday seemed like a longer day than normal. There were plenty of customers but Lisa really wanted five o'clock to come so that she could get home to celebrate. There was now so much to be done. As Judith said they would need to be registered at one of the local schools. They would need uniforms and more everyday clothing for winter. She would have them for Christmas. A Christmas day spent with children in the house. She couldn't think of anything she had ever wanted more than that. She was getting quite excited at the prospect of the next three months.

Michael telephoned at four to find out how she had got on. He was delighted and he could hear the excitement in her voice as she planned shopping trips and talked about re-decorating bedrooms. He promised to phone later in the evening. He wished he could be a part of all the excitement.

Lisa couldn't wait to get home when the time came. Mrs Davidson hadn't only prepared dinner; she had again been doing some housework.

"Mrs Davidson, you're only supposed to be here for the children. You shouldn't be doing all of this." Lisa more than appreciated everything her helper was doing

"I'm enjoying myself. There isn't much to do in my own house with there only being me and I'm only too pleased to help where I can." Mrs Davidson busied herself as usual in the kitchen.

"Did Judith tell you that we got a temporary order for three months. Isn't it wonderful?"

"Yes I'm delighted for you all, and she did ask me if I could stay on and I told her I'd love to, so it looks like it's all going to work out fine. I can come over in the morning and get the children off to school and come back in time for them coming in. How would that suit?" Mrs Davidson was more than happy with the arrangements. She liked Lisa a lot and the children were charming. It was hard to believe they had been through so much. She loved them both already and she was looking forward to being occupied for the next few months.

After Mrs Davidson had gone home, they had dinner and washed up in time to watch a film that Jamie had shown an interest in seeing. During dinner, Lisa had asked them both if they would like to have their own bedrooms. They were both thrilled. Jamie would stay in the larger bedroom they both shared at the moment and Becky could have the smaller front room. Becky's questions were endless. What colour would it be? What would the curtains be like? She continued right up until bedtime.

"Come on Freebie, time for bed." She called and the little dog followed her upstairs.

An hour later when Lisa looked in, Freebie was sound asleep at the bottom of the bed. The little dog's squashed face buried deep into the quilt. Michael called at ten.

"Can I come over? I really need to see you." His voice was anxious.

"Michael I thought we had agreed that you shouldn't be here. You said we would need to be careful." She replied. This really wasn't a good idea.

"I'll park away from the house and walk so no one will see the car and I'll make sure that no one sees me. Lisa for an hour, that's all?"

"I don't like this Michael but I do want to see you. This once only."

"I'll be there in twenty minutes." He rang off.

His news wasn't very cheerful. He had already moved out of his house and his wife was being more difficult than even he could have imagined.

"She's accused me of having an affair." He stated

Lisa was amused at the disbelief on his face. "Michael, what do you call this then?"

"What I mean is, she's been having affairs for years and I just ignored them, I wasn't interested anyway and as long as she was discreet, I didn't care. She seems to be under the impression that's the only reason I could ever consider leaving her. Nothing to do with the fact that she's intolerable, money grabbing and unfaithful. Can you believe it?" He swallowed his glass of wine in almost one go.

Lisa couldn't help smiling.

"What's so funny about that?" He asked, none too happy with her reaction.

"Michael, you're amazing, for once she's right. You are having an affair, whether you like it or not."

"It gets worse. She's determined to find out who it is. I'm sorry Lisa I hadn't expected this. I knew she would play the wronged wife but I am worried she'll come up with something."

Lisa could see that he was disturbed.

"Well I don't think the brightest thing was to come straight here. I thought you were intelligent." She smiled at him. "Apart from you being here twice there's nothing to connect you and me so how will she find out anything unless she follows you and has your phone tapped. After tonight we don't see each other until this dies down and there'll be nothing for her to use against you."

She refilled his glass.

"This was the last chance I knew I would have to see you. It's much too soon for her to have made any enquiries. Come here and at least let me know this is worth all the hassle."

She fell into his arms. His mouth sought hers with an urgency that surprised and aroused her.

"How long are you staying?" She asked.

"How long will you let me?" He replied.

Within minutes he had her undressed and ready for him. His lovemaking bore the same urgency she had felt when he kissed her. He didn't waste any time in bringing her to an elated state of bliss and at the same instant the power of his love flooded into her.

There was no going back now she knew that. She never wanted to love anyone else. They lay together, satisfied and contented.

"I think there may be something in the papers on Monday so be prepared and if anyone contacts you, deny it. I really don't think anyone will suspect you but no harm in being ready for them."

She looked into his eyes, the long eyelashes shading the brilliant colour.

"I love you." She whispered as she felt the fire of his lips touching hers. When she had a moment to breathe she asked where he was staying.

"I'm in a hotel until I find a place but that's going to take a few weeks. It won't take Kerry long to find out where I am either way."

They got up and as Michael dressed, Lisa pulled on her housecoat. Once again she hadn't intended sleeping with him but for some reason when he was there nothing else seemed to matter. They made coffee and sat on the sitting room floor with their backs resting against the sofa.

"Just think of the fun we can have when this is all over and we can stay together."

His eyes were full of mischief as he played with her hair, which was hanging loosely over her shoulders.

"I may need to take a course of vitamin pills in preparation." She glanced at him out of the corner of her eye.

"A compliment, I like that. It means I'm doing something right in all this mess." He kissed the tip of her nose.

It was almost two o'clock again that he got up to go.

"I'll keep in touch and remember what I said, phone Josh."

"I've remembered, don't worry I'll be fine."

He put his arms around her and kissed her, moving one hand to probe under her robe.

"Get out of there or you'll be here all night." She pushed his hand away.

"You seem to be making a habit of throwing me out." His tone was accusing but he smiled.

"Yes, so please go." She gave him a gentle push towards the door.

"I'll remember this. You're a heartless woman."

"Yes, and you've no idea how heartless I can be, now go."

She opened the door and guided him towards it. She gave him her sweetest smile.

"You're a rogue but okay I'll go." He laughed and moved into the doorway.
"I love you." He mouthed as she closed the door.

The papers didn't wait until Monday. One of the tabloids had run the story on the front page. His wife was out to get sympathy. According to the paper she had no idea why he had left her.

Lisa put the paper away. She didn't want the children recognising Michael in the photograph. At least she only had a paper delivered on a Saturday morning because it had the week's TV magazine with it. The rest of the week they wouldn't see a paper.

She was glad to leave the children with Mrs Davidson and seek the sanctuary of the shop. Saturday was busy enough to leave her little time to think.

When Meg arrived at lunchtime she was pleased to be able to take a short break.
"I take it you've seen the morning papers?"
Lisa broached the subject knowing full well that Meg would have read them.
"Yes I have it was quite a shock. Is this because of you Lisa?"
"No Meg, it's not. The marriage was over long before he met me. The whole thing's just bad timing, that's all."
Bad timing was an understatement thought Meg.

"Listen, I'm sure you've thought this all through but surely it's a bit of a risk. Are you sure you want this?" Meg hadn't forgotten her part in encouraging Lisa to go ahead with this, and she wasn't sure she wouldn't be regretting it before long.

"I love him Meg, I really do."

Meg looked at her friend thoughtfully. Lisa hadn't looked at another man since her divorce. Of course there had been dates but she never wanted any of them to get serious, in fact she had taken great pains to make sure they realised it from the start. This time though, she could see Lisa was hurting. She did love him.

"What are you going to do?"

"You must think I'm crazy getting involved with him. We have to lie low until this all dies down." Lisa stared into the empty coffee cup she was holding.

Meg had to ask her next question even though she knew it might not be received well.

"You are sure he feels the same way Lisa?"

"Yes positive. He's left a phone number in case I need him for anything. He's genuine Meg, I know he is."

Lunch over, Meg left promising to come over on Sunday at some point.

The rest of the day passed quickly and Lisa was glad to be getting home. Her feet felt as if

they belonged to someone else. She wished they belonged to someone else. Mrs Davidson was a Godsend. Lisa had no idea how she would have managed without her. She insisted that she stay and have dinner with her and the kids. An idea that met with some resistance but eventually Lisa won and Mrs Davidson stayed well into the evening. Lisa enjoyed her company and at nine o'clock they drove her home.
"It was very kind of you Lisa, I've had a lovely evening." Mrs Davidson opened the car door.
"I'm the one who should be thanking you, you've done so much. I'm not sure I would have coped otherwise. Why don't we make this a regular Saturday evening? I would enjoy that."
The old lady was surprised by Lisa's offer.
"Are you sure. Won't you want to go out on a Saturday evening?"
"You'll probably have noticed I don't do a lot of that at the moment so I don't think that will cause us any great problems. It's settled then no arguments."

Lisa missed her own parents and Mrs Davidson was becoming more like a mother to them all.
They said goodnight and returned home to discuss their shopping trip tomorrow. It had been a long day for the kids and they fell into bed at ten with no objections. Lisa watched television

until midnight and having decided that Michael wasn't phoning she went to bed.

Sunday morning was spent shopping. They were kitted out with more day clothes, school uniforms, school shoes, school bags and an assortment of things to put in them. Lisa was glad the authorities were footing the bill for this lot because she had spent an absolute fortune. It was hard to imagine that two such little people could cost so much to keep. They had bought some toys and fabric and wallpaper for Becky's room. Jamie couldn't decide what he wanted and he was quite content to wait until next week for his wallpaper. He hadn't found it very exciting picking new quilt covers and the like. He was much more interested in his new computer game. Becky had a new ragdoll. Her name was Molly she had announced. They had lunch in the town centre before going home to start the paper stripping.

Becky had chosen a paper similar to the one in Lisa's room except that instead of blue the little flowers were pink and lilac with mint green stems. The contrasting material was mint green and would be trimmed in pink. There was a new bedside lamp in the same colours. They spent the whole afternoon stripping the old paper and by teatime they were exhausted. The children had worked so hard.

"Let's call it a day." Lisa suggested
"I didn't realise decorating was such hard work." Jamie threw his little aching limbs into a chair. "And we'll have all of this to do next week in my room. Maybe I should just leave it the way it is?" Lisa hit him over the head with a roll of wallpaper and he giggled and ducked out of reach.
"You're not like a mum Lisa. You're good fun. If they don't find my dad can we stay here for ever?"
Lisa was caught unawares by this unexpected question.
"We'll need to wait and see Jamie." She had to be careful not to make any rash promises.
His little face became serious and Lisa found his very dark eyes hard to read.
"Can they make us go with him?"
"Jamie, why don't you want to live with your father? You must tell me if there's something wrong?" She probed but without success.
"I just want to stay here."
She realised she was getting nowhere again, so like before the conversation stopped there. She wondered if Judith had come up with anything. She had also forgotten to ask their father's name.
   She kept the children up long enough to see Meg. Becky was eager to show off her room and dragged Meg upstairs as soon as she arrived.

Left alone with Jamie, Lisa tried again. She knew there was more going on behind those dark eyes than he was admitting. He certainly changed at the mention of his father's name but gave no further reasons for his dislike or his fear of him. Finally she gave up and they went upstairs where Meg and Becky were discussing the intricate details of the plan for redecoration.

"I think that's enough for one night. It's time for bed." Lisa had no problem getting them into bed. Apart from being exhausted, Jamie wasn't very talkative and Becky wanted the next few days to pass quickly so that she could move into her new room.

An hour later in the quiet Lisa and Meg once again found themselves discussing the wedding.

"Wouldn't it be great if Michael partners you? I think I quite like the thought of a celebrity at my wedding."

"You've got a celebrity…me. That should be enough for you." Lisa pointed out. "Surely we'll have some sort of life by then."

The telephone rang ending their conversation. It was Michael.

"How are you? I suppose you saw the papers yesterday?" He asked

"I could hardly miss it. How are you?"

"Well to say I'm not flavour of the month with my producer would be putting it mildly but at

least he knows my side of the story so it's a case of riding out the storm. What have you and the kids been up to?" Michael sounded tired. His voice lacked its normal fervour.
Lisa rambled through their weekend.
"Have you missed me, even a little?" His voice had become quieter but she could almost hear him smile.
"No, not at all we've been much too busy." She joked. She was missing him more than she wanted to say.
"I'm extremely hurt by your remark and I'll remember it for when I see you next." He sounded anything but hurt.
"Okay, I admit I miss you Michael, satisfied?"
"Much better. I'll be able to sleep now. I may not be able to phone over the next few days but remember..."
She interrupted. "Yes if I need anything, phone Josh."
"You make it sound as if I'm going on at you but I don't want you to think I'm ignoring you."
"I wouldn't let you so stop worrying Michael. I'll be busy with the kids and Meg's here at the moment, so I don't think I'll be lonely." She was finding his attention very welcome.
"I didn't realise you had company. I'll let you go. Goodnight sweetheart, I'll talk to you soon."
She returned to Meg.

"There's no need to ask who was on the phone, you're positively glowing." Meg accused; pleased that Lisa cared enough for Michael to let her feelings show. This was so out of character for Lisa. Not at all like her normal efficient, confident self. Meg hoped this would all work out.

"I don't know how I'll manage not seeing him for months. Why has everything happened at the same time?"

Meg lifted the cups and headed into the kitchen, calling over her shoulder, "Where there's a will, there's a way."

Lisa couldn't help thinking of another proverb 'out of sight, out of mind' and hoped that Meg's was the right one.

Meg left shortly afterwards, reminding Lisa that from now on they both needed all the beauty sleep they could get. Lisa said goodnight promising to call if there were any new developments.

Judith called on Monday and announced that the children were being accepted at the local school and that Lisa should take them in the morning. That evening Lisa arranged with Mrs Davidson to pick them up afterwards and from then on Mrs Davidson would come over at eight in the morning and see them off to school. The school was only a few minutes walk from the house but Lisa would be pushed for time in the morning and the arrangements seemed to suit. As she sat on Monday evening she realised she didn't want them going away to a man she didn't know even if by law he was their father. She looked in on them both. Becky's dark curls formed a ring around her head. She was a beauty right enough. Her chubby little hands lay on top of the quilt and resting against her legs on top of the bed was Freebie. At some point during the night he always found his way back to Lisa's room.

Tuesday morning arrived.
"Jamie, where's your tie?"
"I don't know, maybe I didn't get one?"
"Yes you did and it was there last night. Now go and find it." Lisa was going round in circles. Some kind of system had to be found for school mornings. This was chaos. Breakfast wasn't ready, neither of them was dressed and Becky couldn't find her shoes. At least Mrs Davidson would be picking them up and that would go according to plan. After what seemed an eternity everyone was ready. Although the school was only a few minutes walk they were going in the car this morning and Freebie was going to the shop, so he was there too. After a quick word with the head teacher, she was finally on her way to work. It was just as well that she was self-

employed because she couldn't imagine any employer putting up with her comings and goings over the past week.

Her shop was a sanctuary not only for her but also for many of her regular customers. She listened to their problems and sometimes shared a cup of tea with them. Since opening, she had made many new friends.

Rena Thomson was one of them. In her sixties, white haired and always smiling she always made time for a chat.

"Hello Rena, how are you today?"

"Can't complain Lisa. Well I could but where would that get me." She laughed. "I'm looking for one of those sweaters you had last week. The one's with the high neck."

"I only have two left. One in lemon and one in burgundy." Lisa walked across the shop and lifted the sweaters down from the shelf.

Rena studied both items.

"Lemon makes me look a bit sickly. I think I'll go for the burgundy."

Lisa wrapped the purchase while Rena carried on with her conversation.

"Did you do anything exciting at the weekend Lisa? I expect when you're young and single there's plenty to do."

Lisa quickly explained about the children and about them staying with her at the moment.

"Well that should keep you busy. You'll have no time to call your own." Rena picked up her bag and off she went.

Then came Mrs Grieve. Grieff would have been a better name. There wasn't a day went by that she didn't have something to complain about. If it wasn't the buses it was the politicians or the lack of something decent on TV. The list was endless. Today was no exception.

"Did you see the paper today? More carryings on from that TV reporter Michael what's-his-name. He's certainly not what he appears on the television, all smiles and charm, and his poor wife. It's a tragedy, that's what it is." She rambled on and on. "He's found someone else, that's what they're saying and the wife just gets left behind. That's what comes of being a celebrity. You can pick and choose. Well must go, see you soon."

After all that she hadn't even bought anything. Lisa hadn't seen a paper, so she had no idea what she was on about. She locked up for a few minutes and ran across to the newsagent.

There were two full pages of accusations from Kerry, his wife and no comments at all from Michael. They were an attractive couple she thought glancing at one of the photographs. She finished reading the article. Michael was being made out to be a very unpleasant character. Lisa studied the finely chiselled features of Kerry Bradshaw and she disliked her. Kerry Bradshaw looked evil. She put the paper away and thought no more about it for the rest of the day.

The children had enjoyed their first day at school. Both appeared to have made friends already which was promising. Mrs Davidson had taken them to the park and they were ravenous by the time Lisa got home. They were tucking into their spaghetti as if they hadn't eaten for days.

The weeks passed by without any major developments. They continued with their decorating and the kids liked their school. They were both settling into their new life with Lisa and she couldn't remember a time when they hadn't been there.

Lisa and Judith had kept in touch each week and the only thing they had uncovered was a report from a few years back when Mrs Campbell had been treated at hospital for cuts and bruises. The police had been involved but no charges had been brought so the file was closed. It did seem possible that Jamie could be harbouring resentment because his father had left him. It could be nothing more sinister than that. It might be that they would never know.

The children were very much a part of Lisa's life now and the thought of having to hand them over at some point didn't bear thinking about. Jamie was much more his old self again, inquisitive and funny and very much at home, and it was easy to see he was devoted to Becky and very protective of her. He hadn't outgrown a cuddle and he spent many hours curled up on the sofa with Lisa while Becky played with her doll or the dog.

Michael hadn't been in touch very often and the papers were beginning to lose the story so Lisa was hopeful that her future was getting a bit closer. It wasn't right that he was going through this on his own. She wanted to be there for him but circumstances prevented it. She felt very much an outsider in his life. As the days passed it seemed he was getting no closer, and although never far from her thoughts, his smile was getting harder to imagine and his touch like an eternity away.

CHAPTER 6

Kerry Bradshaw looked around the offices of Chadwick and Company, Private Investigators, and she wasn't overly impressed. The walls were in need of a coat of paint and some cleaning would do no harm, but she had been reliably informed that Eddie Chadwick was good at what he did and she needed someone good. In fact, he was going to have to be bloody incredible.

"You know who I am Mr Chadwick?"

"Yes I do Mrs Bradshaw, I read the papers." He took in all before him from the designer suit, which he suspected had cost more than a few months of his earnings, to the cold calculated expression on the otherwise impeccable face. She was stunning. How could any man leave her? He didn't doubt for one minute that she was a cunning piece of work, but she was about to employ his services, so what he thought really didn't matter.

"Now Mrs Bradshaw, what exactly can I do for you?"

"I want you to follow my husband. I want to know where he goes and who he sees."

"Is he having an affair Mrs Bradshaw or is that what you're hoping I'm going to prove for you?" Eddie didn't beat about the bush.

"Of course he's having an affair that's why I'm hiring you. Are you capable of doing what I'm asking?" Kerry didn't like the man and she wasn't hiding it.

She was a real charmer he thought. He smiled showing perfect teeth in too wide a mouth that had a tendency to make him look as if he was about to laugh.

"I'm glad you're amused Mr Chadwick. I doubt you'll be quite so cheerful if I withdraw my offer." She was getting colder by the minute.

He would have to watch this one. He couldn't afford to turn down work like this. She had offered plenty for proof of the affair.

"I'm sorry Mrs Bradshaw. Of course I want this job. Now can we get some details?"

The interview had lasted exactly one hour and it was the longest hour he had ever spent. He had a list of the places Michael Bradshaw frequented along with a list of his friends and one or two other bits of information, enough to make a start.

She stood up and ran her hands over her hips, straightening her skirt. A gesture that Eddie couldn't help noticing or perhaps one that she had made sure he noticed. God, but she was lovely and what a figure. Those legs must go on forever he thought. She was out of Eddie's league but he could at least dream. Eddie was good at dreaming. He opened the door and held it for her. He didn't close it straight away. He watched as she walked along the long corridor towards the elevator. Her walk could be described as nothing short of suggestive. What a woman!

He returned to his desk more to calm down than anything else. First things first, he lit a cigarette and as he took a long drag he flicked his eyes over the notes he had taken. He knew a lighting technician at the television studios; it might be worth a quick call. He was off to a good start having arranged to meet his contact for a coffee. The meeting brought nothing however. Michael Bradshaw was a workaholic. He spent most of his time at the studios and even went out on outside broadcasts when no one else was available. In all, his contact couldn't say anything against him. He was popular and he certainly had never heard any rumours about him. No, Michael seemed genuine and everyone liked him.

The rest of the day was spent checking restaurants and pubs that Kerry Bradshaw had suggested. It was the same story. Everyone liked him and he was generally in mixed company more often than not he was with cameramen and technicians from the studio. No one seemed aware of any particular escort. There was nothing left but to follow him. If he was having an affair he would slip up, they all did, and Eddie would be there to catch him. Of course this could all be a total waste of time if he wasn't having an affair at all. Eddie had already decided that her ladyship wouldn't be at all pleased at spending a lot of money to find out her husband was whiter than white.

Eddie Chadwick was forty-two years old and he looked fifty-two, too many years of heavy drinking had taken their toll, and lost him his wife and his job on the police force. He wasn't bitter he deserved everything life had thrown at him and he knew it. Now three years on and no drink, he was picking himself up again and he wasn't sure why. His appearance lacked the tidiness normally taught by years of discipline but he supposed somewhere along the line he had stopped making an effort. He ran his fingers through his now thinning dark hair and rubbed his tired eyes. Eyes that had once been vivacious and alive were now dark and lifeless.

He drove over to the hotel in the centre of town where Mrs Bradshaw had said Michael was staying. The reception clerk had been very

informative. Mr Bradshaw was in and would he like to have him paged. He thanked the lad and said no that he would go find him. He by-passed the bar and entered the coffee shop. The waitress was young probably a student. She looked over at him.
"Coffee's fine, thank you." He called over to save her walking to the table for his order.
He sipped his coffee and lit a cigarette. From his vantage point he had a clear view of the foyer area. If Michael Bradshaw were about, he wouldn't miss him.

He waited for two hours drinking coffee until at last he spotted Michael coming out of the restaurant. He watched as he got into the lift. The indicator told Eddie the lift had gone to the basement car park. Eddie had a note of Michael's Mercedes on his list and as he hadn't parked in the hotel car park he made his way out to the front of the building. You didn't use indoor or multi-storey car parks when you had someone under surveillance because if you ended up on different floors you'd lose them. His car was parked on the street opposite the car park entrance. A few minutes later Michael's car appeared. Eddie followed him all the way back to the studio. After what seemed like hours, it was three to be exact, Michael came out of the studio and headed right back to the hotel. Eddie decided that tonight wasn't going to be the night and turned his car in the direction of home.

The next few days were the same. They travelled to the studio or back to the hotel. Then back to the studio or maybe across the city for a news item but always back to either the studio or the hotel. Unless Michael Bradshaw was having an affair with someone in the hotel or the studio, then Eddie was beginning to think he wasn't having one at all. The guy was boring. His third day over he called his employer.
"Nothing to report as yet. All he does is work and sleep."
"Well, that has to change. Just keep following him, that's what you're being paid for." The voice was so cold.
"Certainly Mrs Bradshaw but I did say I would call every few days with an update."
"Try and have something to report next time." She hung up.
Eddie had to wonder how someone who looked so terrific could have absolutely no personality an even less charm.
 At this moment his sympathies were with Michael.
"You should have left her years ago my son." He muttered to himself as he drove home. He stopped off at Frank's coffee stall.
"Working on anything at the moment Eddie?"

"Yes I'm working for this woman. The kind you'd love to take somewhere and show her off but I just can't think of anywhere I would actually want to take her."

"Never known you to be stuck with any female Eddie." Frank replied.

"Well, I'm stuck with this one and I'm going to have to work for every penny. Goodnight Frank."

He balanced his paper cup on the dashboard and drank his coffee on the way home.

Kerry slammed the telephone receiver back into position. This Chadwick character was costing plenty. He had better come up with something. Michael had accepted their sham of a marriage for some time now. It suited him to have a wife, even if he didn't sleep with her. And she enjoyed being on the arm of such a popular celebrity. She had no intentions of giving that up, not at least until she found someone with more money and more prestige. Apart from that, no one dumped her. He had to have found someone else or why this sudden rush for a divorce? Well, it wasn't going to happen just because it suited him.

She was standing in front of the full-length mirror in the bedroom. She allowed her silk dressing gown to fall open. She admired the flawless skin and her equally flawless body. At thirty-five she had the same figure she had at eighteen. She had never had any trouble attracting men. They usually couldn't wait to get their hands on her and she still felt angry that Michael could resist her. He hadn't looked at her since he'd found out about one of her little affairs. It hadn't been the first but it was the first he'd known of. Michael was good in bed so why should someone else have him when she couldn't. Her current beau worked at the showroom where Michael had bought her Mercedes last birthday. He was kind of rough but he suited her purpose. She dialled his number. He wouldn't refuse.

The new bedrooms were a great success. Becky was over the moon.
"Oh Lisa this is lovely." She said placing Molly, her rag-doll on the bed. Lisa was pleased she had decided to do the rooms. She had never seen Becky's face so radiant. It had taken longer than she had expected to finish the decorating but at last they were ready.
"I'm glad you like it Becky. Let's go downstairs and get a drink." She quickly made tea and poured some juice.
Becky was eager to go to bed and as soon as her juice was finished she changed into her

nightdress. Lisa had a little surprise for her. She had made Molly a nightdress from some remnants of fabric.

"Lisa you're so clever. Look Molly a nightdress." Becky threw her arms around Lisa's neck.

"I hope we stay here with you Lisa, I don't want to leave."

"Let's not worry about that at the moment, now off to bed."

Lisa popped her head into Jamie's room. It was dramatic to say the least. He had chosen a sort of zigzag pattern that Lisa thought was loud and overpowering but with a contrast at least it was bearable. The most important thing though, it was his choice and he loved it.

Judith had phoned earlier in the day to say that they still had no word of their father. James Campbell was his name. She had offered the information that they were searching in the Birmingham area, but as yet nothing had come up.

Lisa went back downstairs to sit with Jamie who hadn't finished his drink.

"Jamie what kind of work did your father do?" She asked.

Jamie thought for a few moments. "He drove big trucks." He decided.

Lisa wasn't sure how big a big truck would be to Jamie, so she was none the wiser.

"My dad was always shouting. Will he still be like that?"

"Would you like to tell me about your dad Jamie?"

"He wasn't very nice to my mum. We used to hear her crying all the time when we were in bed and he came home. Sometimes he was very drunk and you could hear lots of things being knocked over and that was when mum used to cry." The child was fingering his juice glass on the table. He hadn't looked up for the last few minutes.

"Did you ever see any of these things being knocked over?" Lisa continued cautiously. Now that she had Jamie talking she wanted to find out all she could about James Campbell.

"No, we were too scared to go down Becky and me. Becky was only little then and she used to cry too. Then we were too frightened to sleep in case he came upstairs."

Mrs Campbell had obviously lied when she said Jamie missed his father. The child was terrified of him.

She thought out what she was going to say next very carefully.

"Jamie, listen to me. At the moment the Regional Council are responsible for you. They are people like Judith and they decide where it would be best for you to live. Do you understand that?"

"Yes, and they picked you to look after us."

"In the meantime Jamie but once they find your dad he has the right to ask for you back, because he is your dad. If you're frightened of him and you don't want to go with him, then you have to tell us and we can try and do something about it. Do you understand me?"

"So if we tell all the things dad did and these people think they're bad things too, they won't let dad hit us again. Mum said if we told anyone it would make things worse."

"Jamie, I'll never let anyone hurt you again, I promise you, come here."

She held out her arms.

He held on to her, as if he would never let go and she was determined that he wouldn't have to. She didn't care how long it took or what she had to do. No one was going to take them from her now.

"I'll take care of you Jamie, always. I won't let anyone take you away from me."

She took him upstairs and helped him get into bed.

As she bent to kiss the crumpled curls she realised he had already fallen asleep. She knew very well that she wasn't in a position to make the sort of promises she had voiced but somehow she was going to keep them. The phone rang. It was Michael.

"I thought you had taken the shop number so that you didn't have to call the house?" She asked.

"I know darling, but that depends where I'm calling from and tonight I'm at Josh's so I know it's safe to have a conversation with you. How are you?"

Her heart was racing. It was so good to hear his voice again. "I'm fine. We've been keeping busy." She told him about the new bedrooms and about her conversation with Jamie.

"Any bastard who beats up his wife and kids doesn't deserve to live never mind have them back. Surely that will give you a stronger case. The social workers couldn't possibly consider giving those two kids back to some animal."

"I suppose first of all, Jamie has to repeat all of what he knows and they have to believe it and I don't know whether we have to have any proof. But I won't give them up. I don't care what anyone says."

"I'd like to meet the person who might try and separate the three of you. I don't give them much chance of succeeding. I'm sure you're pretty determined when you set your mind to it." They spoke for over an hour. He related his conversations with his lawyer about Kerry.

"Someone suggested she might hire a detective, but I think that's a bit dramatic even for Kerry."

"Be careful Michael, maybe she has?"

"Well all I can say is the poor guy must be bored stiff. All I'm doing is working. I'm not really taking the idea seriously. Now the reason I called. Can you get someone to look after the kids tomorrow evening and come over to Josh's?"

Lisa hesitated. "Do you think that's wise?"

"Josh's wife Linda is having some of her friends over so you should get into the house without being too conspicuous, and if we leave at different times it should work. Now can you get someone for the kids?"

"Yes I'm sure I could ask Mrs Davidson. She has dinner with us on a Saturday evening and I don't think she would mind staying on. I don't suppose there's someone I could arrive with?"

"That might be better. Colin's coming over to do some work with Josh so you could stop off at his house and come with him. He lives on the south side. I'll give you his address and I'll phone and arrange it with him. Don't worry Lisa, these are my friends. No one is going to find out. You be at Colin's at eight unless you hear anything to the contrary."

She scribbled down the address Michael had given her.

"I'll see you tomorrow." He continued. "And if you get a chance tomorrow contact the social

work and make them aware what this character Campbell is like before he turns up. And promise me you'll be careful. I don't want him anywhere near you or the kids."
She promised him and said goodnight.

The following day Judith had received Lisa's news without much surprise. She had known things weren't quite right but now at least she had something to work with. And Mrs Davidson was delighted to stay and watch the children.
"You have a lovely time. You don't get out often enough and don't worry what time you get home."

Lisa found Colin's house without any trouble. She left her car there and travelled the rest of the way with him. He chatted amiably on the journey over. He had worked with Michael for a few years and he also had little love for Kerry.
"She'll try and squeeze every penny she can out of him." He had said as they pulled into the driveway of the old sandstone villa. The house was beautiful and Josh met her at the door and led her straight through to his study at the back of the house where Michael was waiting.
"God it's good to see you." He stood up and rushed to the door to meet her, his powerful arms almost crushing her slender body. She felt safe and secure with Michael.
"How are the kids. Driving you crazy yet?"

Courage and Clowns

"Michael I can't give these children up. That means though, once I've said I'm not involved with anyone then that's how it would have to stay until things are definite. You understand that don't you?"

"If that's what you want it's fine by me. I'd like to help if I can but if you want me to stay in the background then I can do that too. I'll wait if it takes the next five years. Lisa I just want to be with you."

"I wasn't expecting it to take that long but it would be less complicated if I did this on my own." She explained.

"We'll work something out. We've managed to see each other tonight and there will be other nights too."

"I love you Michael." She allowed his kiss to burn deep into her. It was hard to resist the feelings rushing through her body.

"What you and I really need is a few days away. Somewhere safe and on our own."

"Michael be practical. We've only managed one night so far." She said lying back against his arm.

"I am the most practical person you'll ever know and I'll come up with something."

They talked for some time before Josh interrupted them.

"Can I interest either of you in some supper?"

Michael lifted himself out of the leather armchair. "Yes, I think it's time I introduced Lisa to everyone." He took her by the hand and led her through to the dining room.

They were a nice crowd and made her feel very welcome. She enjoyed the rest of her evening. If she couldn't spend time with Michael alone, then this was a very pleasant alternative. The evening started breaking up around midnight.

Colin made more of his part than was intended. "Come along dearest, I think it's time we were going." He reached across for Lisa's hand.

"Don't overdo it Colin, I don't think the house is bugged." Josh had replied, getting up to see them off.

"I'll call you tomorrow sweetheart." Michael placed a kiss on her forehead.

Colin was good company. She liked him and he had an infectious sense of humour.

"I haven't seen Michael this happy in years and he tells me you've fostered two kids. You must have a big heart?"

"They're lovely kids. Their mother died in the explosion in Stancroft, that's where I met Michael."

They chatted until Colin was home, and Lisa had transferred into her own car.

"Thanks for tonight Colin, it was very kind of you."

"I'd do anything for Michael and I know he would do it for me if things were reversed. Goodnight Lisa, it's been lovely meeting you and I hope I see you again."

The roads were quiet and she was home in no time. She had a quick cup of tea with Mrs Davidson before she called her a taxi. It had been a wonderful evening and she wasn't particularly tired. She popped her head into each of the bedrooms to check the children were still asleep and then she switched on the late film. Not being able to concentrate she lifted the telephone and dialled Meg's number.

"Hi Lisa, what's happening?" She heard Meg's cheery voice.

"How did you know it was me?"

"No one else would even think of calling me at almost one in the morning," Meg replied.

"I'm sorry were you in bed? I had forgotten how late it was."

"No I'm not in bed. Anything new to report?"

Lisa told Meg about her evening and how much she had enjoyed it.

"So he's not just a pretty face then? I'm impressed he obviously does want to see you and he'll go to any lengths to do it. I'm jealous. Keith's getting very lax in his old age; it's time he was getting a bit more romantic. Maybe you could drop a few hints?"

"Keith's devoted to you, how can you say that. You're dreadful."
They chatted for at least another twenty minutes before Meg decided it was time for her bed. As Lisa replaced the telephone she noticed a message on the pad. Judith was callingping in to see her on Monday.

Sunday passed quietly and Lisa caught up with some washing and ironing. The kids were quite content to amuse themselves. They were perfectly settled and happy and Freebie had most definitely accepted them both as part of the household.

Judith arrived on Monday at lunchtime and Lisa closed up and made some coffee.
"I've discussed the current situation and we all agreed that we should speak to Jamie at the house where he's more comfortable and I was hoping you could make it some evening this week. We don't want to leave it too long now that he seems to be prepared to talk. Meantime should James Campbell turn up he won't be able to do anything until this had been investigated. How does that sound?"
Lisa refilled the coffee cups. "It sounds great and I only hope Jamie is as talkative as he was last time."
"Now that he's spoken about it once it shouldn't be as difficult getting him to repeat it." Judith

Courage and Clowns

seemed satisfied that everything would work out. They arranged a night for later in the week and then she left to catch up with her other appointments.

In the afternoon another little parcel arrived. Inside was a similar little clown to the one on the bedside table. The card read 'All clowns need company'. He was a clown, but a very romantic one.

She opened the top drawer of the counter unit and gazed inside. The little photograph she had cut out of one of the papers smiled back at her. She stared at the blonde hair and the blue eyes. He did have a beautiful smile. She put the photograph back into the drawer. It wouldn't do for anyone to walk in and find her drooling over the scandal of the month. She wanted everyone to know about Michael but not yet, that time would come.

When Judith and her senior officer called in at the end of the week, Jamie hadn't disappointed them. He related countless tales of drunken abuse and nights when they had visited the hospital. Both he and his mother had been treated at the casualty department as a result of his father's outbursts. Incidents, that Judith knew the hospital would have on record.

"I told mum I wouldn't tell anyone Lisa. Will everything be okay now?" Jamie was understandably upset and Lisa put her arm around his shoulder.

"You did really well Jamie, I am so proud of you. No one is going to hurt you again and you did the right thing by telling Judith."

She told him to go upstairs with Becky and play so that she could talk to their visitors for a little while. The two kids did as they were asked and a few minutes later you could hear them both laughing as if nothing had happened.

"What's going to happen now?" Lisa asked tentatively.

"We'll have to write a report and check the hospital records but it's looking as if there's a strong case for James Campbell not getting custody. But that's not really for me to decide."

"You don't mean that there's still a chance he could take Jamie and Becky? No, that can't be possible. You heard what Jamie said. You believed him didn't you?"

Judith tried to calm Lisa.

"I'm only saying, the decision isn't mine to make. The social work department will decide after all the evidence is checked, but I can't see James Campbell getting custody if we can prove all of this."

Lisa wasn't satisfied she wanted someone to tell her he had no chance at all. She wouldn't let him take them.

She said goodnight to them and called the children downstairs. She made some supper and they sat in front of the television until it was time for bed.

The next month passed and nothing changed. Life continued but in the background there was always the constant threat that James Campbell could turn up and disrupt their lives. The children had become the centre of Lisa's life and she loved them both. She wasn't going to let anything come between them. She received lots of phone calls from Michael but she had only seen him once since the night at Josh's and that hadn't even been for very long. Knowing that he was always there in the background had kept her going.

The papers still persisted in running articles about him but these were getting fewer and further apart. She longed to be with him and looked forward to the day when all this would be far behind them. It seemed like a long time since her life had been uncomplicated. Christmas was only a few weeks away and at the moment it was the brightest light on the horizon.

It was early on a Saturday morning when Judith phoned.

"Lisa, James Campbell's turned up." The voice at the other end of the phone was quieter than normal.

To Lisa, it was like a bolt hitting her. She sat down clutching the phone. Somewhere in her mind she had convinced herself he wouldn't be back, and now he was.

"So what happens now Judith, will the children be taken away?" She couldn't bear the thought of that.

"No, for the time being the children stay with you. He can't just waltz in and claim them especially with all the investigation going on. I'm meeting with him on Monday morning and I'll let you know what happens." Judith rang off. The day was completely ruined and with a heavy heart she went upstairs to waken the children.

Eddie read his newspaper again, for the third time that day. It was Saturday evening and following Michael Bradshaw was extremely boring. If he was having an affair, which Eddie seriously doubted, then he was holding out well. Thankfully, Michael's car was coming out of the hotel car park. At last, something to do even if it was only another journey back to the studios.

The car though didn't head north to the studio, but took the slip road for the motorway, heading south. This was promising. He followed the car until it pulled into the driveway of a sandstone villa. He checked the addresses he had been given by Kerry Bradshaw. The house belonged to a married couple called Ridley. The man worked with Michael so there was probably nothing here but it might be worth a wait.

He watched the others arrive, mostly female in two's and three's, but no one on their own. The last to arrive were a couple. She was a pretty little thing with beautiful auburn curls and a lovely smile. She had the kind of face that stayed with you after she'd gone. They started leaving again about midnight. The couple first and then the rest in dribs and drabs and lastly Michael, still on his own. He had taken one or two photographs as they had arrived and it was possible that his employer might spot someone who could be worth watching. He left Michael at the hotel and went home to develop his prints.

There was her face again. She had a kind of haunting effect he thought as he flicked through the photographs. It wouldn't do to show Kerry Bradshaw any sub standard work so he carefully checked that each face was clearly visible in the shots. He would phone his illustrious employer in the morning.

It was late when he woke on the Sunday. He checked his cupboard for a clean cup and finding none attempted some washing up. This surveillance carry-on certainly disrupted his housework. He smiled to himself. He wasn't the tidiest of characters but this was even bad for him. He may not be housewife of the year but he would have to at least make an effort. The kettle boiled and with a cup of coffee he felt a bit more human. He cleared a week's mail from the table and sat down. This case may be making him money but it wasn't taxing his brain. He felt drained and lethargic. Michael Bradshaw may look as if he had it all but as far as Eddie could see, he had nothing, he didn't even have a life.

After his coffee he lifted the telephone and after some cautious deliberation, he telephoned Kerry Bradhsaw. What anyone really needed on a Sunday morning was someone as cold as her. So he was very surprised when she invited him over to the house.

He showered and put on a suit. He wasn't dressing for her but he wanted to look respectable and courteous. Though why he was bothering he didn't know. As he crawled along the street looking for the house he was unaware that Kerry had an ulterior motive for the invitation.

She led him through to a drawing room of antique furniture and paintings. Some of which he had to presume would be original. Very nice he thought either she or Michael had very good taste.

"Now tell me you have something interesting to show me?" Her voice was warmer maybe she mellowed on a Sunday.

He produced his photographs and told her where they had been taken.

"I thought you might recognise someone?" He said lounging back and enjoying the very expensive settee.

"Who's this?" She held up Lisa's photograph.

"She arrived with this one here." He handed her a picture of Colin. "And they left together too, looked very much an item."

So, Colin had a new girlfriend too she thought. What on earth was someone so pretty doing with someone as insipid as Colin? There was no accounting for taste. She handed the photographs back to him.

"Nothing else?"

"Nothing, that's the only place he's been, apart from work."

This wasn't progressing very well. She had to make him try harder for his money.

"Can I offer you a drink Mr Chadwick?" Her silk suit clung to her in all the right places.

Her pleasant manner was slightly unnerving. She had a terrific body and he found himself aroused by her. But he still didn't like her. He accepted the drink and he knew that she purposely allowed her fingers to caress his hand as she handed him the glass. He had to be reading these signs wrongly. She wasn't making a play for him? She couldn't be.

Kerry knew exactly what she was doing. His loyalties had to be completely hers and she knew only one way of doing that. She sat opposite him, crossing the long tanned legs. She had his attention and the rest was child's play. Eddie might have been down on his luck in recent years but he wasn't stupid nor did he think for one minute that she was interested in him. If she wanted to hand herself to him on a plate, he certainly wasn't going to refuse, and he didn't.

She made it perfectly clear there would be more of the same, if he showed some results. He had every intention of claiming more, results or not. Two could play at her game. She wasn't doing him any favours but she was high-class crumpet. Anyway he had enjoyed her and she'd been more than satisfied. He hadn't made a mistake on that score.

Kerry slammed the door as he left. Damn him! It wasn't often a man left her feeling that the next time couldn't come quickly enough.

Judith watched James Campbell carefully. He was uneasy sitting in her office and she was uncomfortable having him there. He wasn't as tall as she had imagined he would be. He had the same thick dark curls and the same dark eyes as the children but there the resemblance ended. His features were sharper, giving him a kind of weasel like appearance and he was very thin.

She explained the situation regarding the children and the fact that they were with a foster carer. She had also to tread carefully around the matter of the investigation. She wasn't really sure why he had turned up at all. He hadn't once asked how the children were doing but he wasn't happy at all. He could see no reason why he couldn't just take them. They were his kids after all. He was becoming more agitated as the minutes passed.

"Mr Campbell there's no need to shout, I'm not deaf."

She was losing her patience with him and he was becoming extremely rude. He wasn't even listening to what she was saying.

"I don't know what you people think you're doing. But no bloody social workers are going to mess me about and tell me what to do with my own family."

"Mr Campbell please sit down." She tried to calm him down but he was having none of it.

"You're all interfering busybodies that know nothing." And with that he stormed out of the office.

Judith knew that wasn't the last she would see of him. She re-read the reports that were lying alongside a clutter of paperwork on her desk. The police had on three occasions contacted the social work department when Mrs Campbell and Jamie had been treated with cuts and bruises. Janet Campbell maintained they were the result of falls and household accidents, so the case had been dropped. It hadn't slipped her notice that there had been no further accidents in the years he had been away.

Her supervisor agreed with her.
"Call him and ask him in again?" She said. "Let's get this resolved and see if we can get another order to keep these kids in care. He's done it before and he'll do it again."

Judith called Lisa and told her about the meeting. She assured her that he had no idea where the kids were and he wouldn't be told. She also felt it necessary to tell her that he was a very unpleasant character and one that she wouldn't trust. She left it until later in the afternoon before she called him back and arranged another appointment, one that she really wasn't looking forward to. In a perfect world there would have been nothing more satisfying than re-uniting a father and his children. This wasn't a perfect world however and James Campbell wasn't what you would call a father. He wasn't someone a child could trust or depend on.

The day finally came and she was surprised when he didn't come alone. Judith introduced Carol Morton, her supervisor.

"I'm Mark Gibson, Mr Campbell's lawyer," said the well-dressed and articulate figure. He was distinguished with dark hair greying at the temples.

"Please sit down Mr Gibson. Mr Campbell didn't advise us that you were coming." Judith offered them both coffee. James Campbell declined.

Mark Gibson continued. "My client believes he is being denied access to his children. Is that correct?"

"No, he is being denied custody at the moment due to the allegations of physical abuse against his late wife and one of the children. Access is completely different and I don't think Mr Campbell remained long enough on his last visit to discuss this." Carol Morton wasn't the least bit off balance. She had been the Child Care Officer for five years, and not many people got the better of her. At almost fourteen stone and being six feet in height, there weren't many who even tried. "Now as far as access goes, this is how it works. Our office, bearing in mind that the children's wishes would be taken into account would supervise any visits. We cannot force them to see you at the moment."

"Mrs Morton I fully understand what you are saying." Mark Gibson saw a very worthy opponent. He glanced from the imposing figure of Carol Morton with her mousy hair tied back in an unflattering ponytail, to the more casual fair-haired appearance of her colleague.

"I would like to advise that I shall be applying for custody on Mr Campbell's behalf, and access rights for the time being. I shall also await some evidence to back up the allegations of abuse."

"I'm sure Mr Gibson when you have contacted our legal department, our evidence will be made available to you. I'll arrange a supervised visit for Mr Campbell, provided the children are not distressed at the prospect and I'll contact you with a date and time." Carol made some notes on her pad.

"Thank you Mrs Morton, I look forward to hearing from you. Good day ladies."

Both Mark Gibson and James Campbell left the office.

After they had gone Judith was prompted to say, "Where do you think James Campbell has the money to hire a lawyer like Mark Gibson? He doesn't look as if he comes cheap."

"Yes that was a surprise, wasn't it? Who knows? We have no idea where he's been or whether he's been working. But I agree he doesn't look as if he has two brass farthings to rub together. If this goes to court do you think Jamie's capable of standing up and saying what happened in front of his father?" Carol was doubtful.

"I think we'd have to rely on Lisa for that one. I think we need to see her and let her know what's happened and what the implications are. She's going to be devastated."

"Do you have any idea how long she would be prepared to have the children? I know the order is for three months but this is going to take longer than that."

Judith had no hesitation in voicing her opinions on the subject. "Lisa's devoted to them both. I don't think she'll give them up without a fight. I'll arrange a meeting with her."

Their conversation over, Judith returned to her desk and the mountain of paper work still waiting for her attention.

Lisa had tried very hard over the weekend to keep the children cheerful, but the news had certainly had a profound effect on them

"He'll take us away I know he will." There was no comforting Jamie and he became very withdrawn. Becky just constantly sobbed whenever she saw Jamie was getting upset and although she didn't remember her father, she understood from Jamie that he was a man to fear. Even Freebie couldn't cheer her up. The little dog was at a loss to know what was wrong with everyone.

Meg had telephoned and asked if they wanted to come over on Sunday but Lisa had declined saying that the children weren't really up to a visit. It turned into the longest day that Lisa could remember. She was finding it hard to hide her feelings from them both and tried unsuccessfully to cheer them up. She was glad when finally they went to bed. She curled up on the sofa with Freebie and only half watched a movie. She was wishing that she had gone to Meg's it might have turned into a better day. She waited hoping that Michael would phone and when he didn't she gave up and went to bed.

Judith turned up at the shop late on Monday afternoon. After a quick run down on her last meeting with James Campbell and his lawyer, she went on to say that Jamie would have to be interviewed again.

"Is that really necessary?" Lisa asked explaining how he had been since the news of his father's return.

"Nothing's going to happen overnight." Judith explained. "We would have to have another hearing and get an extension first on the temporary order. I am presuming that you'll want to keep the children meantime. It's looking as if we are going to end up in court, but that's going to take months and we have to make sure that our case is strong." Judith wasn't feeling as confident as she was sounding. Even if James Campbell didn't win, there was no guarantee that Lisa would either but she certainly wasn't going to tell her that at the moment.

"Of course I want to keep them. How long can we get an extension?" Lisa was getting more downhearted as the conversation progressed.

"We could ask for six months that would give us some breathing space. But he's asked for access too and he may get that. But it would be supervised by one of us at the office so don't worry they wouldn't be on their own with him."

Lisa was appalled and voiced her anger as strongly as she could without sounding offensive.

"I can't believe that he would be allowed to see them. Jamie will never agree to it and I won't be trying to talk him into it either. If he says no then that's it. James Campbell can go to hell if he thinks I am going to stand back and see these kids more upset than they are at the moment."

Judith hadn't bargained for a hard time with Lisa but she was seeing a different side to her now. She was glad of that, they were going to have quite a fight on their hands and Lisa was going to be up to it.

"Let's just take it one stage at a time. I'll keep in touch." Judith said goodbye and left Lisa to think on what they had discussed.

She was angry now, so she decided to close up early and go home. She knew Jamie and Becky would be asking what was going to happen and she wasn't sure how much to tell them at the moment. She really needed someone to talk to, someone who wasn't connected to the social work department. Perhaps she could ring Josh and get Michael to phone her.

Once she had decided on this course of action she cheered up and by the time she opened the door, she was smiling.

"Hello Mrs Davidson, how are you today?"

"I'm fine Lisa. You're home early today, shop not busy?"

"No I decided I'd had enough and closed early." She fell into a chair in the kitchen and accepted the instant cup of tea that Mrs Davidson always seemed to produce with a moment's notice.

"I was hoping to have a word with you Lisa." She kept her voice low as the kids were doing homework at the dining room table, and she didn't want them to overhear.

"I don't know if this is serious, but Jamie's teacher was a little concerned about him today.

She said he didn't want to join in and was very sullen. Is everything all right?"

Lisa had tried to keep Mrs Davidson from worrying about the children's uneasy situation but she felt that perhaps the time had come to let her know exactly what was going on. She mentioned the return of James Campbell and the allegations Jamie had made and what the social work department was doing to resolve the situation. Mrs Davidson was both shocked and disgusted.

"This is dreadful. But surely if the child is so afraid no court would grant the man custody." She had always been a woman who had put her faith in the law and justice and she wouldn't like to be disillusioned now. She liked Lisa and she dearly loved these children. They had become a family and she wouldn't like to see them split up. She could see how distressing this all was for Lisa. She had no idea how she was managing to run a shop and look after these kids and keep cheerful with what was going on.

Lisa continued speaking quietly although there was little need as the homework had become a pencil fight and neither of them was listening to what was going on in the kitchen.

"We'll have to be patient with him over the next few weeks and make sure that he understands that he is safe here."

"Don't you worry Lisa, I'll help out in any way I can and I hope for his sake, James Campbell doesn't turn up at this door, I'll give him something to complain about. Now let's get some dinner and I'm sure we'll all feel better." She started lifting the lids on the pots on the cooker and tested that everything was ready.

Lisa had no doubts about Mrs Davidson coping. She only hoped that she herself would succeed in doing the same. She had promised to call into the school first thing in the morning and explain the situation to them. There was no way of knowing if Campbell would turn up there and cause any trouble. She would also need some kind of assurance that he wouldn't be given her address. She had no desire to have any kind of confrontation with him. It was a daunting thought that after Mrs Davidson had gone she would be alone in the house with the kids. Her elderly companion had been thinking along the same lines and before she left she had some advice for Lisa.

"Be careful now and don't you be answering the door to anyone after I'm gone unless you know who it is. If you're in any doubt at all don't hesitate to call the police."

"Don't worry I won't open the door to anyone. We'll see you tomorrow." She closed the door firmly behind her. She also locked it and put on the chain and then made sure that all the downstairs windows were securely fastened. She laughed at herself for suddenly becoming so security conscious but she decided that it was better being safe than sorry.

When the kids were safely tucked up in bed and she had read Becky a bedtime story, she finally sat down to phone Josh. There was no reply and she hesitated before leaving a message on the answering machine. By ten o'clock she still hadn't heard anything and as she was getting impatient she turned on the television to pass the time. It was possible that Josh may not get her message until it was too late to do anything that evening. The news was only starting. Maybe the rest of the world would be more absorbing than her own problems. It certainly wasn't any more cheerful, wars, nuclear testing, famine in Africa and a murder. As she was about to switch off, Michael's face appeared on the screen. She turned up the volume. The announcer's voice stunned her:
"Scottish Television reporter Michael Bradshaw is to join a team from ITN to report on the crisis in Ethiopia. The team will follow aid workers as they try to assist refugees fleeing the worst hit areas..."

The voice went on to outline Michael's career and all the time his face lit up the screen, smiling.

Why hadn't he told her? She felt let down and disappointed and somehow betrayed. Everything all of a sudden was going wrong. She couldn't bear the thought of him leaving her too. Her eyes filled up, tears slowly drifting down her cheeks. Maybe she hadn't meant anything to him at all. What had she done to deserve being treated like this? One minute her life had been well organised then the children arrived, then Michael. Before she was ready for any of this, James Campbell had turned up to take the children. Michael was going to Africa. Things couldn't be any worse.

The telephone rang and although she contemplated not answering it, she found the receiver in her hand.

"Darling I'm sorry the press release wasn't due to go out until tomorrow. I'm sure you heard the news tonight. I didn't want you to hear it like this."

"What difference does it make how I heard it. You didn't tell me and that's what matters. Why Michael?" Her voice was beginning to shake with anger and disappointment.

"I had intended calling you tonight, even before I got Josh's message. Kerry's making my life a misery and I believe she'll get even nastier. I don't want either you or the kids involved. When the opportunity came up to join the

overseas unit, I thought it would make life easier all round. We'll be there for a few months but we may get the chance to travel backwards and forwards, so we can't possibly see less of each other than we're doing at the moment. Lisa, I love you. I'm not leaving you I'm only going to be away a few months at the most. Please try and understand why I'm doing this."
But she didn't understand. What chance did they have if they weren't even going to be in the same country?
"Lisa, please don't cry. I'll make arrangements to see you before the weekend and we'll talk this through. I do love you and it doesn't matter how far away I am nothing's going to change that. We'll be together Lisa when this is all over, I promise."
His words meant nothing to her at the moment. When the call was over she broke down and wept. She had a feeling that her world was falling apart and she couldn't do anything about it.
She wished he had never come into her life and then regretted her thoughts as quickly as they had come.

She did love him, but she was tired of being on her own. She had wanted his support tonight and she hadn't even told him what had been happening.

She sat drinking coffee until late, mulling things over in her head. She knew exactly what she was going to do. She had survived a broken marriage, lived with little money and lived up to now with no children. She could do it all again. From now on she would depend on no one, that way she wouldn't be disappointed and if James Campbell wanted a fight then he was going to get one. And if they went to court and she didn't win, she'd live through that too. Lisa Whitford was going to be there for Lisa Whitford. She didn't need anyone else.

CHAPTER 7

The following morning Lisa made some more decisions. She would talk to Jamie first and when she was sure she had his confidence she would explain about why he had to go back and make a further statement.

She was determined that she was going to fight the access request, whether the social workers were behind her or not. And finally, she was going for custody. She was going to go to court and fight James Campbell for custody of his own children. She would give him a run for his money, if he had any. She was determined Jamie and Becky were going to stay with her and she would do whatever she had to do to make that happen.

She had no idea how much control she was going to have but she was going to push it to the limit. No one was going to get in her way, not this time.

She telephoned Meg and told her what she had decided. Meg was dumbfounded. Lisa was a strong character, but even this was beyond the bounds of comprehension.

"Are you sure you know what you're doing? Forever is slightly different to having them for a few months. Are you sure you've thought this through? Lisa you can't make a decision like this when you're in such a temper."

Meg tried to reason with her. She loved the two children dearly but Lisa's course of action did worry her.

"I've never been more determined in my life. I won't let him have them, and if it all goes wrong and I don't win, then at least I can say I tried as hard as I could. I owe Jamie and Becky that at least." Lisa didn't want to argue about it. No one was going to change her mind.

"What does Michael think about this? Surely this has to be his decision too if you intend being with him." Meg was clutching at straws.

"It's got nothing to do with Michael." Lisa replied. "Haven't you heard, he's going off to Africa for months to look after refugees. He won't be here to support me anyway, so the decision is mine."

Meg realised there was no talking to Lisa once she had made up her mind. She was the most stubborn person Meg knew and nothing would budge her, so she gave up and promised to call back later.

That same evening she sat down with Jamie and told him as much as she could. She tried not to build up his hopes. But she did make it clear that he had to tell the social workers exactly what he wanted and more to the point what he didn't want.

Two days later Lisa arranged that he make another statement, this time it was all witnessed. She also requested that the hearing be arranged as quickly as possible. She needed to know that someone was on her side and she hoped the children's panel would be that someone. Travelling home with Jamie she realised something about herself, she seemed to cope better when the chips were down. Maybe deep down she needed to fight for things and her determination to win and succeed made it all worthwhile. Whatever it was, she was happy with herself and the way she was feeling.

Kerry would never normally have visited the studio, but today was an exception. Michael wasn't getting to disappear thinking it would put an end to his troubles. If he thought for one minute she was going to let up or give in, then he was very much mistaken. Scandal wouldn't go down at all well with his superiors and although she had none as yet, that didn't mean there was none.

She was directed downstairs to editing where she found Michael and one of the technicians. She was pleased to see how uncomfortable he looked when she appeared. Before she had a chance to speak the telephone rang. He spoke into the receiver before lifting his jacket from the back of the chair. "You can wait here, I'll be back in a few minutes." He hardly lifted his eyes as he walked by her out of the room.

The technician offered her coffee and she accepted. She might as well make herself comfortable; she would probably be here for some time. Left on her own, she glanced around the messy room. She had never liked the studio or the people. It was always too hot and too noisy and the technicians who worked here were always so busy they didn't notice visitors. She wasn't the type who enjoyed being ignored by anyone.

She switched on the tape machine and watched the pictures flit across the screen. She recognised some of the stories and there was nothing current. Michael was obviously clearing up loose ends before he left. The girl on the screen looked familiar even through the grime and the smoke of some disaster and Kerry was sure she had seen her before. She had probably seen her on the news. She re-wound the tape as Michael walked back into the room.

"What do you want Kerry? You had no right coming here." His voice was cold and reprimanding.

"I wouldn't be here if you returned my calls. What do you think you're playing at?" She was enjoying her little visit all the more because he wasn't. "If you think by running off your life will be easier, then think again. I'll ruin your career and I'll make sure you never enjoy your freedom. I fully intend being Mrs Michael Bradshaw as long as I can. If you continue with this divorce I'll drag it out as long as possible and I'll make sure it costs you a fortune." She spat out vehemently. "You think about that. You are going to regret ever starting this."

"You're an evil bitch I don't know what I ever saw in you because you're nothing. Without my name and me you've got nothing and as far as costing me a fortune, it'll be worth every penny to get you out of my life. And if you're detective continues following me I'll have him arrested. Now get out of here."

He had thrown in the part about the detective to see her reaction and by the change in her expression he had been right. He was thankful now that he had taken such care. As she stormed along the corridor almost knocking the tray of coffee out of the technician's hands, she wondered how he knew about Eddie. Surely the man was experienced enough not to get noticed, or had someone told Michael and if so, who. Now she would have to watch what she said and who was around when she said it. She didn't trust many people and until this was over she could survive without trusting anyone.

Once home she called Eddie and asked him over. He may not be much use to her from now on with Michael in London or out of the country or wherever they sent him. Surely he would have some information for her. This was costing her plenty and Kerry Bradshaw always believed in getting her money's worth.

Eddie had been paying attention to the news, much more so now that he was involved in it. He cursed when he heard how Michael Bradshaw was leaving the country. He hadn't expected that his services would be terminated so quickly. There was also his employer to think of; he hadn't wanted to finish with her so quickly either. And now she had summoned him, was this the end. He was sorry because he had been looking forward to enjoying her for some time yet.

He drove out to the prestigious neighbourhood where Kerry lived. He got a certain thrill from sweeping into the driveway because he could never have afforded a house like this no matter how hard he worked. These people were a different class. Not better he thought, just different. She opened the door dressed in nothing but a bathrobe that did nothing to disguise the shape beneath it. As he entered the hall he knew he would have to play this casually because if she knew he wanted her things might go differently. He had to let her think she had the upper hand. He had nothing to lose and everything to gain by playing her little games. She poured him a drink, straight tonic, and got to the point.

"He knows he's being followed so perhaps it's just as well he's leaving. He's not stupid enough to walk into a trap. I don't suppose you have anything on him yet?" She sipped her glass of wine sensually.

"He hasn't spotted me I can guarantee you that but honestly he's as clean as a whistle, up until now anyway."

The bathrobe had slipped off one shoulder and she made no attempt to return it to its rightful position. Eddie wanted to touch the soft skin and the evenly tanned shoulder and he knew she was enjoying being admired by him. Kerry could feel his eyes burn through her robe and her body re-acted pleasurably to his gaze. She could feel herself again being seduced by this unlikely character, even though he hadn't touched her yet. She wanted him and she hated the fact that she did. She leaned forward and allowed her lips to brush against his. His hand reached for her hair, such beautiful hair. He slowly wound the long strands around his hand and on reaching her head he pulled her towards him. She was unable to pull away even if she had wanted too. He kissed her harshly whilst his rough hands found her expectant breasts, eager for his touch. She moaned and guided his hand to where she really wanted to be touched. He couldn't believe she was so ready for him. They slipped down onto the carpet and although soft and plush, it burned her back as he pushed inside her. No soft bed and no satin sheets but Kerry Bradshaw was being loved like she had never been loved before. There were no frills where Eddie was concerned, not for her anyway. He knew what she wanted and he was giving it to her as roughly as he could. Her cries encouraged him and as his body moved with hers they collapsed exhausted at exactly the same time. God she was good, perfect, in body anyway. He pulled away much quicker than she had expected and her little gasp he could have sworn sounded disappointed.

Courage and Clowns

He refilled the glasses and handed her a drink. Her hand shook as she lifted the glass to her lips and took a sip. He missed nothing, wasn't it his job to be observant? She had enjoyed it and she wasn't pleased about that. He had the power and she had realised it. He could see the anger rising in her eyes. Eddie quickly sensed he had played his hand more openly than he had intended, he had let himself get carried away. He had to redeem himself very promptly.

"I was thinking of arranging a meeting with a technician I know, just in case he's come up with anything. Do you still want me to go ahead with it?" He hoped this would work and as he watched she seemed to be calming slightly.

"Yes of course I do." He was mistaken. She was anything but calm. "This matter is far from being finished. If he is seeing someone then she's more likely to be here than anywhere else and you have until he leaves to find out." She emptied the rest of her glass in one swift gulp.

If Eddie was anything it was perceptive and he knew his presence was no longer required, for today anyway. He hadn't arranged a meeting with the technician, but there was no harm in stopping by the studios on his way home.

After seeing him to the door, Kerry poured herself another drink, a large one. She didn't know what attracted her to Eddie. He was a good lover but in no way was he going to become a companion. She had no need to depend on any man especially one like him with no money and no prospects. She wasn't winning this one and she knew it. Under normal circumstances her tactics worked very well but in this case she would have to come up with something different. Eddie Chadwick wasn't impressed with her money or her class and she knew that. She gave her problem some careful consideration and poured another drink.

Eddie was in luck at the studio. His contact was there and had some time to see him.
"Let me finish running these tapes that I've been working on most of the day because your Mrs Bradshaw turned up so I had to make myself scarce. Boy was she angry when she left. Michael's out with a unit at the moment so there's no chance of him coming in while you're here. There's fresh coffee there if you want a cup."
Eddie poured some coffee and he literally fell into a chair. He felt shattered. His little assignation with Kerry had left him drained. He smiled to himself thinking he was just a little out of practice. The screen in front of him was running news items. He watched Michael's face continually appear on the screen. Then he sat bold upright almost dropping his coffee. He

stared at the screen. It was the girl from the Saturday night get together at the sandstone villa. She was dirty and dishevelled but there was no mistaking that face. Hadn't he looked at it often enough at home? What was she doing on a newsreel? A newsreel that Michael Bradshaw also appeared on. What was the connection? He watched the rest of the film engrossed in her. Since he had taken her photograph he had become obsessed with her. He had even hung the photograph in his kitchen, sentimental fool that he was. The technician had told him he was putting together some reels that Michael wanted to keep.

When Eddie left the studio he was whistling to himself. He wasn't tired anymore; it was amazing what a little piece of information could do for you even if you weren't sure where it fitted into the jigsaw. He didn't have a name but he knew exactly where the piece had been filmed and it was more than a coincidence that the girlfriend of one of Michael's friends should appear on one of Michael's own newsreels. It was time to find out. Turning onto the motorway he headed for Stancroft.

The first few houses drew a blank. Of course it was possible that no one would know her, she could have been passing and stopped to help out. But today luck was definitely with him and when he asked at the third house the occupant remembered her. He was told that she had left with the Campbell children and that she was a social worker.

"Oh and that nice young reporter from television came looking for her too. I remembered who he was after he'd gone now what was his name…"

"Do you mean Michael Bradshaw?" Eddie held his breath this was too good to be true.

"Yes that's him, nice chap, always smiling."

Eddie couldn't believe his luck.

Mrs Johnstone closed her door. She wondered why everyone was so interested in that girl.

Never mind, she thought, it was none of her business and off she went to feed her cat.

Eddie considered phoning Kerry to tell her the good news but as she hadn't been too pleased with him when he left, he decided to keep it to himself until he knew more. With someone like Kerry it would be wise to always have something up his sleeve to draw on when the chips were down. Rather pleased with himself he decided he could afford to have the night off. He wasn't sure yet how it all fitted together but this was where his connection would be, he knew it in his bones and his bones weren't generally wrong.

Courage and Clowns

Lisa had been apprehensive about meeting Michael especially in public but he had assured her that the pub in Mineford would be quiet and he knew the owner. It had taken her about forty minutes to reach the village and there were few cars in the pub car park. Michael had told her about his meeting with Kerry earlier on in the day and as he had mentioned the detective to her he imagined she would assume he wasn't stupid enough to get up to anything and get caught. He was sick of all this cloak and dagger stuff anyway. In fact he was past the stage of caring who saw him.

Lisa saw him sitting at the bar as soon as she walked in. She couldn't believe she had thought of not coming. She had missed him so much it was good to see him. He walked towards her smiling. He kissed her cheek and even this small show of affection made her pulse race uncontrollably.

"Darling you look lovely as always." He whispered leading her to a table in the corner.

She was glad she had worn the black dress because it was smart without being too dressy and she could tell Michael approved of her choice. The restaurant was quaint and better still, quiet. There were only four other tables occupied and no one had given them a second glance. Peter the owner took the order himself.

He was tall, dark and slim with a mischievous grin. Lisa liked him and he made her feel at ease as he chatted while he scribbled on his pad. Everything was home cooked he had said and he was right. Their meal was delicious and the portions more than generous. Fabulous as it was Lisa struggled to finish her main course and declined dessert opting instead for coffee.

"Perhaps you'd like to take your coffee upstairs in the lounge." Peter suggested as he cleared the plates.

"Excellent idea Peter." Michael said as he reached across and took Lisa's hand. "Let's go the coffee will follow. The lounge is very comfortable and we'll be on our own."

They slowly climbed the stairs. At the top Michael pulled her around to face him.

"I've wanted to do this all evening." He leaned forward and gently kissed her. His arm was soon around her, drawing her closer to him.

"Michael someone will see us." She tried to pull away from him.

"Come here I really don't care who sees me, I want you Lisa."

Again his kisses found her lips and her resistance lessened. They walked into the lounge with his arm still around her, his hand gently stroking her breast. Lisa was responding pleasantly to his touch, her embarrassment totally gone. They were sitting together on a large leather sofa, when Peter arrived with the coffee. Lisa fumbled to straighten her dress but he seemed not to notice.

"If you need anything else give me a shout." He called as he closed the door.

Michael moved closer stroking the back of her neck, his hands tracing a pattern down her spine.

"I've booked a room so could you please do me the honour of drinking your coffee fairly quickly before I feel the urge to attack you where you're sitting." He smiled and winked at her.

"Michael I can't stay you know I have to get back."

"I know that, I'm not a complete idiot." He said kissing the back of her neck. "But we have at least two hours and I think I can manage to finish off you evening nicely in that time. What do you say to that?" He grinned at her discomfort.

"Michael what about Peter? What will he think?"

Michael laughed and sat back against the soft leather.

"Peter will probably think what a lovely way to say goodbye to you and he's probably a bit jealous. I saw how he devoured you with his eyes every time he spoke to you."

"He did not Michael. You're imagination is running away with you." Lisa had suddenly realised that he really was saying goodbye for the time being. She had no idea how long it would be before she saw him again. She stood up, rather abruptly, which he hadn't been expecting.

"Lisa, what's wrong, what have I said?" He was at her side.

"You've just reminded me that you are going away. So what room number are we?" He could see the mischievous look in her eyes.

"You're incredible, unpredictable and I love you."

With that he swept her up into his arms and laughing they made their way along the corridor. Outside the room door Michael fumbled to get the key out of his pocket.

"Perhaps you would get on much better if you put me down." Lisa suggested.

"No chance of that. You might escape and after the meal I've just eaten I don't think I could run to catch you. Anyway I was a contortionist in a previous life. See, I've done it."

The door creaked open into a beautiful oak-beamed room. Lisa loved it. Michael placed her on the bed and reached to undo the buttons down the front of her dress.

"Where are you going to summon the strength for this, considering you couldn't chase me?" She joked as he again fumbled, this time with the buttons.

"You let me worry about that. Now if you don't mind I could do with a little help here."
Within minutes their clothes were lying on a chair.

Michael gazed at her before pulling the cover over her nakedness. His hands were gentle as they touched and caressed her. She was gasping with anticipation and before long she was pulling at his hands to return to where her body was demanding they be.
"Calm down lady, we've got hours for this." But he knew she wasn't listening.
Her body arched as he touched deep within her. He pushed further inside and listened to the pleasant sounds escaping her lips. She was more than ready for him and he wasn't about to waste the moment. He surged home with a force that both excited and moved her to want more and more. She was pulling at the skin on his back, her nails cutting into him and manipulating him into using all his strength and determination to satisfy her. She fell back breathing heavily but before she could relax in the ecstasy she was feeling his hands were again exploring regions that were now so sensitive he had to use little effort to bring her to a climax, again and again. Finally her body couldn't take the slightest touch and he lay back allowing himself a well-deserved rest.

"Run out of energy then?" Lisa raised her head and rested her elbow against the pillow.
"No you ungrateful wretch, I was giving you a rest. I thought you needed one."
Michael rolled her over onto her back and pinning her down he kissed her until her lips ached. He noticed the sigh, she was tired.
"Who's the one with no energy now?"
He wished they could fall asleep together and waken in the morning still together. He also knew that was a wish for another day.
"You really are amazing." He remarked. "You look all prim and proper and immaculate and then when you get into bed you become someone totally different."
"No I don't."
 She was slightly embarrassed by his observation.
"Yes you do but I think it's wonderful. You make me feel very much appreciated. Will you miss me?"
Lisa sat up. "Why did you say that? I was trying to forget that tomorrow you'll be gone. Michael I don't want you to go."
She could feel the tears but she fought them back not too successfully.
"Darling don't cry. It won't be for long and when I get back my divorce will be well under way and maybe the children's case will be resolved."

She couldn't share his optimistic view and she didn't want him to remember her with swollen eyes and a tear stained face.

"I have a little surprise for you." He reached over to the bedside cabinet and slowly opened the drawer. As his back was to her Lisa was unable to see what he was doing. As he turned around he spoke more seriously.

"Lisa will you marry me?" He held out a little box, opened to reveal the most beautiful diamond ring. She gazed at the ring totally numbed by his question.

"We only have a few hours here Lisa could you answer me?" He waited.

She looked up at him. "Michael I don't think you can get engaged when you're not even divorced yet."

"Lisa, listen to me. I haven't heard any rules about being engaged and if there were any I'd ignore them. I want you to be waiting for me and I want something to come back to. I want you to wear this. Now do I get an answer?"

"Yes Michael, Yes." She threw her arms around his neck.

"Hold on we're not engaged yet, you have to put the ring on."

He reached for her hand and slid the ring onto her finger. "We are now, congratulations." He kissed her lightly.

Lisa's head was spinning. She had just promised to wear Michael's ring with all the problems that was going to bring. She hadn't liked the deception but she had no idea how she was going to handle this.

"Now," Michael continued. "The best course of action I think would be for you to tell your close friends and of course Mrs Davidson. But as far as the social work department is concerned I can understand if you want to keep it a secret until after a decision is made on the kids. I don't mind being kept in the background with them. And if Mrs Davidson knows then I won't feel apprehensive about phoning the house when I feel like it. Now, how about some champagne? I'll pull on some clothes and go find Peter. And before you tell me you can't have any because you're driving home then leave your car here and get a taxi. No arguments."

With that he pulled on his clothes and left the room.

Lisa gazed down at her finger. The brilliant stone sparkled back at her. It was the most beautiful ring she had ever seen, and it was hers, and so was Michael. The ring said forever. She still couldn't believe it. She was engaged to Michael Bradshaw. Even if it was going to be kind of unofficial she didn't care. She loved him and nothing else mattered.

Michael returned with the champagne, glasses and an enormous bouquet of red roses. He had thought of everything.

"I'm sorry this isn't much of an engagement celebration." He said. "But we'll do it all properly when I get back."

They drank their champagne and talked and planned. Lisa's face was flushed with excitement. Michael carefully lifted the glass out of her hand and lay her down across the bed.

"Now let me give you something you won't forget for a while, I hope." He smiled and let his tongue loose on a body already high on champagne and exhilaration.

They were soon engrossed in satisfying each other and when they finally lay back together they were both exhausted. When Lisa opened her eyes the room was in darkness. In panic she switched on the bedside lamp and was horrified to discover it was three in the morning.

"Michael waken up, please. I've fallen asleep and Mrs Davidson will still be at the house. God this is a mess. She'll be worried sick. Michael."

"Lisa, stop screaming in my ear." He sat up. "I phoned Mrs Davidson when I went for the champagne and asked her to stay overnight. I'm afraid I've spoiled your surprise I had to tell her what had happened. And by the way, she's delighted and sends her congratulations and she says she'll see you in the morning. So what's the problem?" He grinned at her.

"So why didn't you tell me?"

"Because you wouldn't have agreed and you were exhausted. I thought you'd sleep all night. I was wrong. Now lie down and get some sleep and stop drawing me those looks. You really don't want to get up and drive home anyway, do you?"

"No but I do like to know what's happening."

"Okay." He said turning to face her. "This is a blow by blow account of what's going to happen next. I'm going to make love to you again and after that you're going to sleep until morning. Now be quiet and come over here."

She obeyed dutifully and once more gave herself to him before falling into a deep sleep, her head resting on his shoulder.

When she woke at eight, Michael was already in the shower and after they were both washed and dressed they went downstairs to find Peter having breakfast.

"I thought that I would have to send out a search party for you two. Care to join me?" He beckoned them over to his table.

Michael laughed and pulled out seats. "Good morning to you too, and I am famished."

"I'd like to phone home first Michael." Lisa was now feeling guilty about the time.

"Sure, there's a phone over there help yourself." Peter indicated a desk over in the corner.
Minutes later she joined them and ordered some breakfast.
"Congratulations then, I hope you'll be very happy." Peter smiled and lifted his coffee cup in a toast.
"Thank you Peter but we have a long way to go yet." Lisa answered and looked across at Michael. He flashed a broad smile in her direction before asking if everything at the house was in order.
"Yes, Mrs Davidson's in her element." She replied.
"Michael tells me you're looking after two lovely kids. How old are they?"
"Jamie's nine and Becky's six. I'm sort of fostering but if things work out, who knows."
After breakfast Michael walked her out to the car park.
"I'm going to miss you." He said stroking her hair, now lying loosely on her shoulders.
"Let's not talk about it. Promise me you'll phone as often as you can?" Lisa didn't want any sad thoughts to ruin her day. It was the first day of her engagement and she wanted to be happy.
"I'm flying down to London this afternoon, and from there I don't know yet but I'll phone you

tonight." He kissed her passionately before letting her go.

Michael watched as the car drew out of the car park and out of sight. He hadn't wanted to spoil Lisa's day by telling her that he was flying out to Africa later that evening to join the aid workers heading into Ethiopia. He wished there had been another few days to spend with Lisa. There was no point in wishing. He was off tonight and if he didn't make a move he would be neither packed nor anything else.

Lisa was totally unprepared for the welcome she received. The kids were all over her asking where she had been and telling her that they had baked a cake for her coming home.

"For heaven's sake, let Lisa get settled before you ask her fifty questions." Mrs Davidson's remark fell on deaf ears. "I'll go put the kettle on."

Five minutes later they were all in the sitting room having tea and cake. Jamie and Becky were either side of Lisa and couldn't get any closer if they tried. Mrs Davidson had put the roses in a vase and placed them on the coffee table.

"Right, Jamie, Becky can you take Freebie out into the garden for a few minutes while Mrs Davidson and I have another cup of tea." Lisa lifted Becky onto her feet. "Don't look so worried Becky, I'm not going anywhere. I'll still be here when you come in, now run along."

Amidst a clatter of feet and barking dog the little procession made its way outside.

"Mrs Davidson, I'm really sorry about last night I hadn't intended staying overnight." Lisa could tell by the smile on her companion's face that any fears or guilty feelings she might have were unfounded.

"I'm so pleased for you. Though I must admit it was quite a shock when you're Mr Bradshaw phoned and told me who he was, and what was happening. But I am delighted and I'm sure when this is all over you'll be very happy."

Lisa proudly showed off her ring before going upstairs to change into something a little more practical than the outfit she was wearing for last night's dinner. She had explained to Mrs Davidson about the engagement still being unofficial as far as the social work department were concerned and also that she would prefer Michael's name not be mentioned in front of the children just yet.

Once changed, they all piled into the car and took Mrs Davidson home before calling in at Meg's to tell her the good news. Once the children were enthralled by a video, Meg and Lisa went back into the kitchen with their coffee.

"I can't believe it Lisa, you're really engaged. Can you be engaged when he's still married? God you're unbelievable. One minute you don't want a relationship and then half an hour later you're engaged. Don't you think flashing around a ring that size will cause no end of problems? Of course it does explain why diamonds are called rocks." Meg was already seeing the headlines.

"But I won't be anywhere except at the shop, where no one knows anything about my private life, at home or here. And if the social work find out, then I'll just have to brass neck it and hope for the best. Meg be happy for me at least."

"I am happy for you, of course I am. It's wonderful news but I think you're both just a little mad, that's all."

They left Meg's a little before dinner. Lisa had a lot to do tonight and she still had to get the kids bathed and ready for school in the morning.

The phone rang shortly after nine. She lifted the receiver and barely heard Michael's voice over whatever was happening in the background.

"Michael where are you? The noise is terrible."

"I'm at Heathrow we're flying out tonight, in about an hour."

"Michael no, not already, you said you'd be in London for a few weeks. Why are you leaving so soon?"

"The situation out there is getting worse and they want us there as quickly as possible. I'm sorry it's such short notice. Take care of yourself and remember I'll be thinking of you." His voice sounded quiet and sad.

"Please be careful and don't try doing anything heroic, promise me."

"Lisa don't worry I'll be fine. I don't know when I'll get the chance to phone again but as soon as I can, I will. I need to go now they're calling the flight. I love you, goodbye darling."

She replaced the receiver and fell into a chair. He was gone.

Sleep wouldn't come to her that night. She drifted in and out of dreams where Michael was sent out into the middle of a war zone and there in no-man's land, James Campbell was standing with the children. All attempts to reach him, failing. She woke up, perspiration dripping down her face. What was she thinking? Michael wasn't a war correspondent. Exhausted, she finally slept the remaining few hours until morning.

CHAPTER 8

Lisa gazed into the pine mirror above her dressing table. Her sleepless night was obvious in the dark circles under her eyes. She looked out over the blue, cloudless sky and wondered where Michael was now. Had he arrived safely? Had they got to their base? Where was the base? With no answers for any of her questions she pulled on some clothes and went downstairs.

She had promised the children they would shop today for a Christmas tree and she couldn't remember a time she wanted to do anything less. She drank her coffee staring at the phone wishing it would ring. She wanted to hear Michael's voice but she knew it was much too early to be hearing from him.

She showered and changed just in time for the children wakening and putting on a braver face than she felt they somehow managed to have breakfast without either Jamie or Becky thinking anything was out of the ordinary. With Freebie walked they were soon on their way to the garden centre for their tree.

"We always had an artificial tree at home never a real one." Jamie had said as they walked around and looked at all the different trees. "What size can we have?"

"Look for one that says it's six or seven foot, nothing bigger than that or it won't fit." Lisa advised as she and Becky looked at all the new decorations. Finally Jamie decided on the tree and Becky chose the decorations so everyone was happy. After they had been to the café they set off home.

"Are we going to put the tree up today Lisa?" Becky asked. Her little face was flushed with excitement,

"Yes we'll get the tree up when we get home and then after dinner we can decorate it. How would that suit?" Lisa was trying very hard to sound happier than she felt.

With dinner over and the tree in place they spent the rest of the evening decorating it. Becky thought it was the most beautiful tree she had ever seen. Finally they were both in bed and Lisa could relax, curled up with the dog on the sofa. She had already bought some of their presents and she had decided to keep them at the shop until Christmas. She had a skateboard for Jamie and a remote controlled car racing set, and a pram for Becky, along with another doll and a dressing up set with make up and face paints. Meg had bought them an assortment of games and new sweatshirts with Disney characters on them.

Lisa made some tea and scribbled out a list of the things she still had to buy although she was finding it hard to make time for Christmas Shopping. She still had to decide on something for Meg and her mother with only just over a week to go. She was glad the shop had done well in the past few weeks with outfits for festive work nights. People were dressing up a bit more again and that suited her, and made her some money. She had almost forgotten Mrs Davidson's present and added that to her list. Having decided that Michael wasn't phoning that night she went to bed.

Over the next week she found out more of what Michael was doing from the news reports than from his two fairly brief phone calls. They were keeping him busy and he seemed to have little time to himself. The children were busy on the last week of school before the holiday and as usual Mrs Davidson was a godsend. She was always in the right place at the right time. Becky's class did the nativity play and she was an angel with a costume that had to be made with less than a week to go because she had forgotten to tell Lisa. But between Mrs Davidson and her they had managed to put one together and Becky was delighted.

By Christmas Eve they were both hyper. Mrs Davidson had stayed a little longer before going off to help her own family. Lisa had no idea where she got her energy, but she was very grateful for all the help. At nine the kids were settled watching a video and Lisa has some time to do her final tidy up before the morning. She had decided it would be better to let them stay up a bit later in the hope that they slept until a decent hour, but then there were no guarantees that they would. At ten o'clock she made some hot chocolate and mince pies and all four of them sat at the fireside. Freebie had picked up on all the excitement although he wasn't really sure what was happening. Finally it was time for bed.
"Will Santa know where we're staying?" Becky asked as she climbed the stairs. "What if he goes to the old house and there's no one there?"
"I don't think that will happen. Santa knows where everyone lives and remember you sent him a letter from school. I think you should get some sleep and I'm sure Santa will have been when you wake up."
Lisa tucked her in and kissed her goodnight. Freebie was curled up as usual at the bottom of the bed and Lisa patted his head as she left the

room. She popped her head into Jamie's room where he was lying reading.

"How are you doing?" She asked as she ruffled his hair. He sat up and placed his book on top of the covers.

"Do you think they have Christmas in heaven Lisa?" His big brown eyes searched her face.

"Of course they do Jamie. I'm sure Father Christmas visits there too and maybe the angels help give out the presents. Tomorrow we'll have a lovely day and I'm sure your mum will have a special day too. I think she'll be watching you, in fact I think she watches over you all the time. She would want to see you happy and you and I have to make sure Becky has a lovely Christmas too. Now give me a hug because I think you're very special and I'm very pleased that you're here with me for Christmas." She opened her arms and put them around him. She hadn't realised that of course he would be thinking of his mother at a time like this.

"Lisa, I love you. And thank you for all you've done for Becky and me. And I think if mum's watching she'll be glad that we're here. You and I will make it a great day for Becky."

Lisa kissed the top of his head and tried to swallow the lump in her throat. He really was a very special little boy. "I love you too Jamie." She said as she tucked his covers under his chin.

"Sleep well, and don't get up if you hear Santa or he may not leave anything." She closed the room door.

Sitting downstairs with another cup of hot chocolate she thought about what Jamie had said. She had no idea what he was feeling, not really. This was his first Christmas without his mother and her heart went out to him. And yet he was still prepared to make sure Becky had a good day. He was the most exceptional child she had ever met. The phone rang at eleven. Meg was checking the arrangements for tomorrow. She and Keith were coming over in the morning to see the kids and then Lisa and the kids would go to Meg's for Christmas Dinner at three.

"Are they excited?" Meg asked.

"Actually they weren't too bad and they went to bed no problem. Jamie asked about whether his mum would have Christmas." Lisa tried to explain the conversation.

"Poor little might. Don't worry, we'll make sure they have a good day. They really have both been marvellous considering what they've been through. My brother's kids will be there too so they'll have some company to play with. I'll let you get to bed now and I'll see you in the morning. Goodnight Lisa."

"Goodnight Meg see you tomorrow." She put the phone back and made herself more hot chocolate. She wondered where Michael was. She looked at the clock it was eleven thirty.

She switched on the television and caught the start of a Christmas movie. Within minutes Freebie had joined her on the sofa. She cuddled her little friend and he snuggled in closer. Together in the peace and quiet they watched the movie. Something flickering at the window caught Freebie's attention; it was snowing. He ran to the back door and Lisa let him out into the garden where he chased snowflakes and bit at the snow. Lisa stood at the back door. She loved the snow and this was a perfect start to Christmas. Already the garden was covered in a thin blanket of white and she couldn't wait to see the kid's faces in the morning. This had to be a good Christmas for them one that they would all remember. She called Freebie back in and dried him off before he scampered upstairs to his bed.

She spent the next half hour laying out their presents and making sure everything was ready for the morning before going upstairs to get ready for bed. Before long she was sound asleep.

Lisa was awakened at eight o'clock by Jamie screaming for her to come downstairs and see the snow and all the presents. She pulled on her dressing gown and woke Becky before following Jamie into the sitting room.

Courage and Clowns

"Well it looks as if Santa found you. Let's have some cereal first and then we can open your presents." Lisa took his hand and led him into the kitchen. Becky appeared with Freebie at her heels. Lisa was glad to see that they were both excited at the thought of their presents and she hoped that this excitement would last for the rest of the day.

For the next hour the Christmas paper was flying. First one present then quickly the next one. Freebie made the same amount of mess opening his treats then dashing from one person to the next to see what everyone had in their parcels. He was quite attached to Becky's doll and persistently picked it up by its hair and dragged it away. Becky thought this was hysterical.

"Look," she cried out, "Freebie wants a doll too." She retrieved her doll and placed it carefully into the pram, with all its matching covers. She was thrilled with her presents. Freebie looked as if he wanted into the pram too and Lisa knew before long the doll would be abandoned in favour of pushing the dog around the house. She knew this would be right up his street. Jamie couldn't try out his skateboard in the snow but he seemed unperturbed and set up his racing cars. The last present was one that Jamie pulled from well under the tree.

"This one's for you Lisa, from Becky and me." Jamie handed the carefully wrapped present to Lisa. She hadn't been expecting this and slowly undid the silver bow on top of the parcel.
Inside she found new gloves, a hat and matching scarf and two little bottles, one with bubble bath and one with body lotion.
"Thank you so much both of you these are lovely."
"We bought them ourselves. We gave Mrs Davidson some of our pocket money each week and she told us how much we had saved and we picked these." Jamie explained as Lisa gave them both a hug.

She was touched that with the little pocket money they each received they had thought of doing this for her. How could anyone not love children especially like these two. She watched them play with their toys and laugh at each other and there was no doubt that as a brother and sister they would always be inseparable.
"Right you two run upstairs and put on some warmer clothes and we'll take Freebie for a long walk in the snow." Lisa started picking up some of the paper scrunched up and lying in colourful balls on the carpet.
 "And don't forget to put on boots instead of trainers." She called as they raced each other up the stairs.

It was a beautiful morning. The snow had stopped falling and the country road they had chosen for the walk had seen no traffic so they made patterns with their feet as they walked along. Jamie and Becky threw snowballs and Freebie raced about trying to catch them. They were all exhausted when they got home. Meg telephoned to say that they were running late and that she and Keith wouldn't manage over in the morning but that she would see them all when they got to her place later.

Soon however it was time to get ready for Meg's and while Lisa was getting changed the telephone rang.
"Hello darling, Merry Christmas." Michael's voice was crackly and uneven.
"Michael, Merry Christmas. Where are you phoning from? This is a very bad line." Lisa sat down on the bed relieved to hear his voice at last.
"We're back at base today but we're having difficulty getting phone calls out. How are you and are the kids enjoying themselves?"
"We've got snow. It started last night - it's lovely. And yes the kids have had a great day so far we're just getting ready to go to Meg's for dinner. What are you going to manage in the way of a Christmas dinner?"
"I think it is tinned turkey, tinned vegetables and tinned potatoes followed by tinned sponge

pudding and tinned custard. But when you see how little the people in some of the outlying areas have, I don't even think we should be having that. This is heartbreaking out here but I'll tell you all about it at a later date. I don't want to put a damper on your day. I miss you so much Lisa and today of all days I wish I was at home with you."

"I know I wish you were here too." Becky coming in and twirling in one of her dresses interrupted Lisa. "Hold on a second." She said into the telephone. "Becky you'll need a sweater or a cardigan with that so could you go find one and take trousers with you in case you want to play outside after dinner, and take your slippers too, and tell Jamie the same."

"Okay." Becky called twirling her way out of the room.

"Sorry Michael I'm trying to get them organised. Becky's twirling about in a party dress."

"I bet she looks like a little princess I wish I could see her. I'll let you go now. If I can get a line later this evening I'll try and phone back. I love you, take care and have a lovely day."

"I love you too and I'm sorry you're not having a proper Christmas. I'll talk to you later goodbye." She placed the phone back on the bedside table. She sat for a few minutes trying to imagine what Ethiopia was like. She couldn't ever really remember knowing very much about it apart from the few scenes she had seen on television. She picked up one of her little rag-doll clowns and fingered the taffeta of his costume. The children's voices brought her out of her daydream. She continued dressing and before long they were all ready to go.

"Jamie did you bring slippers?" She asked packing his spare trousers in the holdall.

"Do I really need them?" He replied

"Yes you can't jump about at Meg's all day in a pair of boots now run up and get them."

He went back upstairs without question and returned with the slippers. Lisa picked up the remaining presents and finally everything was ready for the car. Even Freebie, he had positioned himself beside all the stuff in the hall fearful that he might be forgotten.

"Come on then let's go before we miss the meal. Can you pick up something and take it to the car?" They each picked up a bag and a few minutes later they were all in the car and on their way.

On arrival all the kids and the dog raced upstairs to play at some game and Lisa and Meg poured a glass of wine and sat for a few minutes in the peace and quiet. The meal was all ready to serve and Marjory was fussing about putting the finishing touches to something. Keith had called hello from the sitting room where he and Meg's brother and her sister-in-law were watching some comedy on television. At last everything was ready and with the kids called downstairs everyone was soon seated at the table.

The meal was excellent and the conversation varied and amusing. It was a wonderful day and Lisa was enjoying every minute of it. Keith took the kids through to the sitting room where he played Santa as Lisa and Meg made some coffee for everyone before doing the washing up. Becky and Jamie were running in and out of the kitchen showing Lisa their new presents. There was no doubt in her mind that they were having a wonderful day too. Freebie was exhausted and fell asleep in front of the fire. He was just as at home at Meg's as he was in his own house.

At eight o'clock it was time to get ready to go home. They said their goodbyes and were home in front of their own fire by nine. Jamie and Becky had changed into their pyjamas and were switching channels on the television to find something to watch. Before long Becky's eyes were closing and the next time Lisa looked over she and Freebie were asleep on the sofa. She gently lifted her and took her upstairs and put her in bed. She woke for a few minutes to tell Lisa she'd had a great day and was then fast asleep again. Downstairs Jamie had found a movie and with more hot chocolate they curled up together to watch it.

"Thanks for all the presents we got today Lisa and it was good at Meg's. I've never seen so much food." He said in a matter of fact sort of way.

"Well I'm glad you had a good day." She replied kissing the top of his curls. She had no idea how she was ever going to let these children go. They were more than a part of her life now, they were her life. She tried to concentrate on the movie and pushed her thoughts to the back of her mind.

The rest of the holiday passed quickly and in no time they were organising school uniforms again. Mrs Davidson was back and Lisa realised how much she had missed her being around. She had become very much part of this little family. The many weeks they had to wait for the hearing had Lisa's nerves on edge and she suspected the children were feeling the same. Finally the day arrived. They were ushered into a waiting room by a friendly assistant where Judith was waiting. For the first time they came face to face with James Campbell. Becky's tiny hand gripped Lisa's like a vice. Judith did the introductions and Lisa found it hard to nod an acknowledgement. Jamie hadn't lifted his eyes from staring at the carpet and he wouldn't even speak. Becky looked petrified and wouldn't let go of Lisa's hand. Lisa hoped that Judith was taking note of all of this. The only word Lisa could find to describe Campbell was 'sleazy'. She hated him on sight. How dare he sit there and tell the children they looked great and how big they had grown. She had to bite her tongue. It wouldn't do to have words with him before the hearing even started. But there was plenty she wanted to say. She knew she would never like the man even if he had been more pleasant to look at.

"The children look well Miss Whitford. I'm really grateful to you for looking after them." He smiled at her.

Who the hell cares what you think she thought? How dare this man have the cheek to say he was grateful to her? Instead she acknowledged his comments. She was even more determined now that what she was doing was the right thing. James Campbell was never getting custody of her children. She looked at them both. Jamie's face was white and he looked near to tears and Becky was frightened. Neither child smiled back at their father.

The friendly assistant returned and announced that the panel were ready. They were all led along the corridor to the room for the hearing and once it was decided where everyone would sit, the panel introduced themselves.

There were two women, both in their fifties and one man who looked slightly older. Lisa knew that they would have been made aware of all the circumstances that had brought about this meeting, although a lot of the details wouldn't be discussed today. The panel would talk to the children, ask questions and then they would decide what was in their best interests.

One by one they asked first Jamie and then Becky, how they liked their school, what sort of things had they done before going to live with Lisa, what sort of things they did now, were they particularly good or bad at anything at school and who looked after them when Lisa was at work. Lisa was asked one or two questions. Becky was amusing despite her initial discomfort relating stories about the dog and her new bedroom. Jamie on the other hand answered only the questions he was asked offering no additional information.

The lady who was chairing the panel finally asked if they wished to be able to visit their father. Neither child replied. She then addressed their father.

"Mr Campbell, perhaps you could leave us for a moment I think I should speak to the children on their own. And if you don't mind Miss Whitford would you mind leaving too. This will only take a few minutes.

Lisa rose to her feet before saying to Jamie that she would only be outside the door. Judith was to remain.

The chair lady repeated her question. Becky was quick to say no. She didn't remember the man sitting at the other end of the table and she didn't like him, and she said so. Jamie was much more hesitant. He was frightened and he couldn't hide his terror. The tears rolled down his face and he looked around for Lisa. Judith tried to calm him and when that didn't work Lisa was asked to return to the room.

"This child's terrified, can't you see that? You can't possibly think either of them would willingly go with their father?"

"Lisa please..." Judith had interrupted before much more was said.

The chair lady spoke very gently to Jamie. "Jamie are you afraid of your father?"

The directness of the question had the desired effect.

"Yes," came the choked reply. "I'm not going to stay with him, I'm not, I want to stay with Lisa."

Lisa managed to calm him down and finally he stopped crying. James Campbell was invited back into the meeting. Each panel member gave his or her individual recommendations. The decision was unanimous. The children would remain with Lisa and access, as the children hadn't agreed to it, had to be denied. The temporary order was extended with the condition that if the children's situation changed in any way, another hearing would be called. Lisa was elated. She could tell by James Campbell's face that he was furious. Jamie was relieved and Becky was glad that the meeting was over and she could go home. Lisa was aware of the fact that James Campbell could appeal but she wasn't unduly concerned.

Judith had been surprised that Campbell hadn't brought his lawyer along but she was sure he would be reporting back to him. He wasn't the type to take this lying down. She knew there was a bigger storm ahead but withheld her fears from Lisa.

It had taken Eddie weeks but he had finally tracked down Lisa Whitford to Kilmains. He had the address and he knew Kerry would be more than pleased. He had found it much more difficult getting information out of the social work department but as he had fingers in all sorts of pies, his efforts had paid off. He left a message on Kerry's answering machine and returned to his office. He had an appointment this afternoon and he didn't want to be late.

With any luck there would be another little job coming up.

Back at his office he made some coffee and settled down to clear his mountain of filing. It had to go back at least six months. Someday he hoped he could afford some clerical help but in the meantime he was all he had. Humphrey Bogart and Philip Marlow all had female help so he was sure it was just a matter of time. His appointment was prompt and at exactly two-thirty there was a knock at the door. As James Campbell entered the office it didn't occur to him that the place was untidy or that it was in need of redecoration, it was merely an office. He sat down where the detective indicated and as yet neither had spoken one word.

Eddie could tell on sight that James Campbell was bad news. He had seen too many like him before. He had mixed with the less distinguished members of society on more occasions than he cared to remember.

"Well Mr Campbell, what can I do for you?" Eddie wasn't at all sure he wanted to do anything for him but then money was money and every client should be treated the same, in theory anyway.

James Campbell for his part wasn't sure he trusted the man sitting opposite. He didn't like his superior attitude. Policemen always looked superior and this man had that same kind of look.

"My children have been taken into care. I wasn't here you see and they're with this young girl and I want them back and I want you to help me. I have money, more than enough, so you don't have to worry."

Eddie had to be honest. Looking at James Campbell he wasn't sure that anyone in their right mind would leave kids with him. They were probably better off where they were.

"I'm not sure where you think I can help Mr Campbell. I am supposing that you mean the children are with the social work department. Is that correct?" Eddie did wonder where he might have been when the children were taken into care but he didn't ask.

James Campbell explained as best he could about the meeting and the hearing he had attended. Eddie was still unsure exactly what was expected of him.

"I think Mr Campbell if you have already involved a lawyer it might be best to leave it to him. I'm not really sure where I fit into this?"

"The girl who's looking after my kids is young and I want to know if there's anything worth knowing about her. You know what I mean?" James Campbell fidgeted in his chair and had a very annoying habit of constantly fixing the sleeves of his jacket. Pulling them down towards his wrists as if they were somehow shortening the longer he sat.

Eddie knew exactly what he meant. Dig up some dirt on her and that wouldn't be an easy thing to do. The social work didn't hand out kids to just anyone and especially not to anyone with a dubious background.

"Mr Campbell I really don't think there's much chance of coming up with something on a foster parent, irrespective of how young they are. They have to be trained to do what they're doing and I'm sure their backgrounds are fully checked out. I really think you'll be wasting your time and money." Eddie wished the man would sit at peace. It wasn't like him either to turn down money so easily. He didn't like Campbell one bit and it wouldn't surprise him to learn that he had done time somewhere. You could always tell.

Campbell continued, "Try at least for a few days. Here's her name and address." He pushed the scrap of paper across the desk in the direction of Eddie.

Life was strange, so very strange. Here he was looking at Lisa Whitford's name again and what the hell was she doing with his kids? What was she doing with Michael Bradshaw? This case was beginning to bite. Almost immediately his attitude changed.

"Leave it with me and I'll see what I can do but I can't promise anything. I'll contact you in a few days if you leave me a number."

James Campbell scribbled down a telephone number and left as promptly as he had come. Eddie swivelled round in his chair. This was becoming very interesting indeed. A foster carer or whatever you called Lisa Whitford and a television personality who had very recently walked out on his wife. What more could a man ask? His thoughts were disturbed by the telephone ringing.

"Have you found out anything yet?" Kerry's voice was its usual cold and abrupt self.

Half an hour ago he was ready to tell her about Miss Whitford but now he wasn't so sure he was ready to divulge his progress. Not just yet anyway. The last thing he wanted was Kerry knowing that someone else was heading along the same trail.

"I thought I had something but it didn't materialise. Jumped the gun a bit, sorry, but I'm still following a few leads." He could hear the exasperated sigh at the other end of the line.

"Please don't waste my time and when you have something, call me."

And goodbye to you he thought as he listened to the dialling tone. She had a habit of slamming down phones on him. He wasn't the least bit put out because at the moment he was the only one that knew he had the upper hand. He spent the rest of the afternoon making calls and scribbling notes to himself before lifting his jacket and deciding that tomorrow was soon enough to start his new lines of enquiry. Tonight was for himself with maybe a nice meal and who knows.

James Campbell turned the latchkey in the front door of his rented apartment. The smell of cooking met him in the hallway as he dropped his keys on the table and made his way into the kitchen and helped himself to a beer from the fridge. Patty was standing over the cooker and spoke to him without lifting her head.
"Where have you been? You said you wouldn't be long and you've been away hours."
Campbell slammed the fridge door shut. "It's none of your business where I've been and don't ever question me on my whereabouts." He turned out of the kitchen and the next sound she heard was the television.
She hadn't wanted to come to Glasgow. It was cold and miserable and she knew no one. James constantly left her in the flat and went off for hours on end without ever a word of where he was going. She had no idea why they were here and no idea where she would be if not here with

him. She had no life in Manchester and London had been even worse but at least before she met James she could have earned her own money. It wasn't exactly a great life but at least it had been her own. She had been on the streets since she was fourteen and knew nothing else. There had always been one or two older girls to keep an eye on her. But living in her dingy flat was depressing and the bright lights of London had offered her nothing else. James had picked her up one night and he had plenty of money and in the beginning he had seemed nice.

His temper now frightened her but then her parents had fought all of their lives and her father could be violent so she had run away and had never had any reason to want to go back. Her mother had put up with being black and blue most of her married life and Patty had always assumed that most men were the same. James was no worse than anyone else was. He had looked after her and although she had no idea where his money came from he always appeared to have enough and he wasn't the type of man you questioned, about anything. She poured the soup into the bowls and placed it on the table.

"Soup's ready." She took her place at the table and said nothing further for fear of more harsh words. He sat down without a word.

"Anyone call while I was out?" He asked between mouthfuls.

"No, the telephone hasn't rung all day." She refrained from telling him that she had gone for a walk in the park. He'd throw another fit if he had been expecting a call and she had missed it. There had been one or two calls from London since they arrived but she wasn't permitted to discuss his phone calls either. He wasn't always like this, sometimes he could be quite gentle but those occasions were few and far between. She wasn't complaining, at least she had a roof over her head and a very nice one at that.

She cleared away the plates and took the pie from the oven. The steam billowed out as she cut into the pastry. She served the potatoes and vegetables and sat down again. The rest of the meal was eaten in silence.

At seven o'clock the phone rang and he jumped to answer it before Patty had a chance. There wouldn't have been much point in her taking the call anyway, no one knew she was here.

She had liked James in London; she still liked him but he had been edgy since that night he had come home and said they would have to go away for a while. It had seemed like a good idea at the time but now she wasn't so sure. She didn't know this town or anyone here.

He spoke for about fifteen minutes and he appeared much happier when he replaced the receiver.

"Want to go out for a drink?" He asked

"Yes I would, let me get my coat." She hurried through to the bedroom before he changed his mind. The washing up could wait until later.

James was smiling as they walked down to the pub.

The news from London was promising. More money was arriving at the end of the week although he hadn't run out of the first lot yet. This was the easiest way he had ever found to make money. All he had done was pick up a container at Dover and deliver it to an address in London, a warehouse in the East End. His first payment had been waiting for him with the promise that the other half would follow.

Other jobs were in the pipeline but they had suggested he get himself out of London for a few months, until the heat died down. James had no idea what had been in the container. He hadn't asked and they hadn't volunteered the information. He was being paid for knowing nothing so what did he care.

"How long are we going to stay here James?" Sensing his better mood Patty felt brave enough to ask. She had learned quickly with James that you had to pick your moments.

"I don't know yet, another month or so probably. Are you in some kind of hurry to get back to London?"

"No not really, just wanted to know that's all." She was none the wiser but at least he was in a better mood and she intended enjoying her night out. The pub was quiet and the large windows looked out over the park where she had walked earlier in the day.

"What's the park called?" She asked as he put her drink down on the table in front of her.

"It's Queen's Park, it stretches for quite a distance. I think there's a pond in it somewhere, with boats. You could take a walk round it some afternoon." He lifted his pint glass and slowly took his first drink, savouring its taste.

Again she didn't mention that she had already done that but nodded to him. This was much more pleasant than having him scowl at her. Maybe he had business problems, which she accepted were none of her concern.

James had considered going back to Stancroft to stay. He still had a friend there but decided Glasgow would be more convenient as his parcel would arrive at a depot nearby and all he had to do was pick it up himself. He also hadn't wanted to answer a lot of questions that he was sure his friend would ask. It was through a chance phone call that he had found out about the fire and the kids. He was sorry that Eleanor had died but he hadn't loved her so he couldn't miss her. She had trapped him into marriage by getting pregnant and he hadn't got away. Everyone assumed they would marry and he still wasn't sure why he had. He really hadn't ever forgiven her for depriving him of the life he wanted, travelling the roads with maybe a girl at every stop.

He went back to the bar and collected more drinks. He had no idea why he was fighting for the kids except that no one was telling him he couldn't have them and no one was taking away something that belonged to him. He wasn't even sure what he would do with them if he got them, but he was going to give the social workers a run for their money and that stuck up Lisa Whitford. His kids didn't belong to her or her lifestyle for he imagined by the way she dressed and spoke, she moved in much higher circles than he did.

"What are you thinking about?" Patti ventured, pushing her fine fair hair out of her face and looking up at him. She was no more than a child herself and her waif like appearance made her look younger than her nineteen years.

"Nothing you need worry your little head about." He answered putting his arm around her in an unexpected show of tenderness. Patty could look after his kids, she'd be an ideal little mother and she wasn't really any trouble what with her being quiet the way she was. Now that it was settled he was looking forward to taking her home.

Eddie swung round in his chair and raised the blind on his office window. It was a miserable day, grey and drizzly. His wasn't a very pleasant job at the best of times, but much worse in rotten weather. He lowered the blind again and contemplated his next course of action. He really had no intentions of telling James Campbell where Lisa and the kids were, but he had to at least make an effort to show that he had done something to earn his fee. He didn't normally take money under false pretences, but for Campbell, he didn't think it would upset him greatly. He knew he wasn't going to find anything dubious in Lisa's background or she wouldn't be in the position she was in, but her present situation interested him no end. Was she Michael Bradshaw's other half? He wasn't going to catch them together at least not at the moment with Michael away, but maybe if he could get closer somehow, he could confirm his suspicions. Although what he was going to do with the information once he got it, he had no idea. It was early afternoon and he decided to take a drive out to Kilmains. He had some shopping to do, and that was as good a place as any.

Eddie had days when luck seemed to run with him. Of course he had even more when it didn't but today he couldn't have asked for more. As he was parking in the multi-storey whom did he spy but Lisa and the kids coming out of a dark blue Granada. The kids were excited and jumping about. He quickly locked the car and followed them downstairs to the shopping mall. There were enough people milling about to ensure that she would never know she was being followed. He couldn't think of a better way of spending his afternoon. As they moved from shop to shop he even managed to pick up his own bits and pieces. They had been shopping for clothes for the children, fancy clothes obviously for a special occasion. At last they made their way into one of the mall cafes and again with luck on his side, he had acquired the table next to them. He ordered a sandwich and a coffee and listened while they ordered burgers and milk shakes. It wasn't long before their table was cluttered with their order and not very long after that, a milk shake toppled off the table and emptied at his feet, covering his shoes in chocolate bubbles.

"I am so sorry, I hope it hasn't stained your suit. There isn't much room on these tables and the glasses are rather tall for children." Lisa was very apologetic and luckily there seemed little damage. "Becky you must be more careful in future. Now I think you should apologise to the gentleman."

"I'm very sorry, it was an accident." The little face looked at Eddie sorrowfully.

"Don't you worry little one, at least it was a chocolate milk shake that doesn't show up on my shoes. Now had it been strawberry that would have been a different story. Can you just imagine me walking around with pink shoes?"

Becky and Jamie both laughed and Lisa was relieved he was taking it in such good humour.

"It's very kind of you to pretend it doesn't matter, but I'm sure your shoes will be ruined." Lisa could see the milk already staining the shoes.

"Nothing of the kind," replied Eddie. "Who ever heard of milk shake disintegrating brown leather?"

The children laughed again. He couldn't believe it, he couldn't have wished for a more opportune accident.

"Now let's find a waitress and get you another milk shake young lady, another chocolate one is it?" Eddie beckoned for a waitress.

"There's really no need, I can get this." Lisa had the money ready when the young girl brought the drink over but he insisted saying that in case Becky decided to throw another drink over him he wouldn't feel quite so bad if he'd paid for it.

He continued chatting to them throughout the rest of their meal. Lisa found him both amusing and mannerly. He insisted on buying her a coffee while the kids went to throw coins in the ornamental fountain in the centre of the mall.

"You have lovely kids, they're a credit to you. So many children now are either too noisy or too cheeky. How did you manage it?" Eddie hoped she would admit they weren't hers.

"It's kind of you to say, but they really are just normal kids and they can be extremely noisy." Lisa replied, she felt no need to tell a stranger any more.

He had been careful not to suggest that he might know anything and she certainly wasn't giving anything away.

"I really must go now, thank you for the coffee and it's been a pleasure meeting you Mr.."

"Chadwick, Edward, and the pleasure was most definitely mine. Say goodbye to the kids and perhaps we'll meet again. Good bye."

He strolled off leaving Lisa to gather her parcels and go in search of the children. Eddie was extremely pleased with himself. He was sure she hadn't suspected anything and she was everything he had imagined her to be. He was slightly besotted with her. She was classy and intelligent and she was flashing the most amazing diamond engagement ring. It had to have cost the earth and certainly the kind of gift Michael Bradshaw would probably bestow on his beloved. Could they be engaged? He wished it could be the sort of information he could pass on to Kerry Bradshaw, just to see her face. She most certainly couldn't handle finding out that her husband was already planning another wedding before his first was over. Of course it was possible there was another explanation. She could be engaged to someone else. The kids had said they were going to a wedding, but whose wedding? If it was Lisa's wedding then she wasn't marrying Michael Bradshaw, not so soon. He would worry about it later. One thing was certain, James Campbell didn't deserve such nice kids and somehow they suited Lisa. He wanted it to work for her.

He drove slowly back towards the city, his thoughts elsewhere. Years before he remembered the feeling of belonging. He hadn't thought of his wife in a long time and he was sure her thoughts were very seldom of him. She must have really hated him in the end. Never home and when he was, he was usually drunk. He had blamed the pressures of his job for changing him dramatically over the years. When he had first joined, the police were to be respected. Even the villains had some sort of code of practice, and it had been a good job. Then all the college graduates had arrived and policing had become all computers and stress. More stress than he could handle. The officers in charge were getting younger and had their own ways and somehow Eddie began to feel old and out of touch. Maybe he should have stayed in uniform but he had been ambitious in his younger days and was in CID in his mid twenties. In those days he knew most of Glasgow's illustrious criminals and life had been good. How had he let all of those years slip away.

His thoughts again returned to his wife. He had once loved her more than anything. Maybe he should give her a call. No, maybe not. She probably didn't want to hear from him. For all he knew she could have re-married or she may not still be in the area. But the thought wouldn't leave him. When he got home, maybe he would give her a call. However once he was at home he had picked up the phone at least three times and then replaced the receiver. He looked around his flat. It had never really been a home. It was partially furnished when he moved in and he hadn't been enthusiastic enough to finish it off. He didn't know why suddenly having a home was so important to him. Maybe he was cracking up in his old age. He picked up the phone again and this time he allowed the number to ring. Before he could change his mind it was answered.

Her voice was unmistakable.

"Val, it's me Eddie."

There was more than a moment of silence before she spoke and when she did he could hear the slight tremble in her voice.

"Eddie, you were the last person I was expecting. This is a surprise."

"More of a shock I'm sure. I had this urge to phone and see how you were. Are you annoyed?"

"No I'm not annoyed, but like I said, it's a bit of a surprise. How are you?"

"I'm okay. It's nice to hear your voice again. I thought you might have hung up on me."

"It's been almost four years Eddie. Why did you call me?"

"I told you I just wanted to hear your voice and now that I have, I'm pleased I made the effort. There's no more drink Val. I haven't touched a spirit in over three years. Can't even remember now what it felt like to be drunk."

"You let it all go. You wasted half our life together. And then when it suited you, you just gave up on everything."

"I'm not looking for forgiveness. I know how much of a mess I made of my life and I'm sorry I hurt you. I couldn't see what I was doing."

"It's all in the past Eddie. It was nice to hear from you. Look after yourself."

"Don't hang up yet, I wondered whether you might have dinner with me sometime soon?"

"I don't know Eddie, I must go now. Maybe you could give me some time to think it over and you could call me in a few days."

"Ok, I'll leave it for now. Nice to talk to you again and I'll speak to you soon."

He was physically shaking when he put down the phone. Why had he phoned her after all this time? Once he had made some coffee he had calmed down sufficiently to think straight. Yes he was glad he had called and he was going to call her back in a few days. Maybe he should leave it for a week. Whatever, it didn't matter. She had at least said he could call again and that pleased him.

Now it was back to work. He was about to do something he had never done before. He was going to follow his client, James Campbell. Eddie was good at his job and his instincts were seldom far off the mark. Background was the obvious place to start and he made a call to his old department where he still had some contacts. If there was some reason for Campbell being in this area then it was most probably not to reclaim his kids.

CHAPTER 9

Michael settled down shortly after take off to study his notes. He was glad he had reached Lisa before he left, because although he had told her he would telephone, he had no idea how good or bad the phone lines would be where he was going. He hadn't wanted to leave her at all, but this was for the best. If he was out of the way they couldn't be connected and this opportunity had come up out of the blue. His instincts told him that James Campbell would cause trouble and he was worried. Surely she would phone Josh if she needed any help.

He glanced back at his folder. The very short briefing prior to leaving Heathrow hadn't been long enough for them to learn anything substantial, but the bulky folders each had received would presumably contain all the background they would need.

There were seven of them travelling on this flight. The most experienced and well known was Gerard Knight of ITN. He would be the anchorman and responsible for holding the whole thing together. Michael had liked him immediately. He was sitting across the aisle from him at the moment looking nothing like the debonair newsreader the country watched on news at ten. His casual travelling gear consisted of dark blue sports trousers and a blue and yellow rugby shirt. He could quite easily have been a rugby player as he was broad shouldered and six foot four in height. His thick mop of greying hair was today untidy and curly. The experienced face was full of character. Michael knew that they were going to get along.

Charlie Carr from Central News was sitting two rows behind Michael and he was already chatting up the stewardess. He had met Charlie before but this was the first time they had worked together. There were two cameramen whose names escaped him and a girl from the studio in London who would be doing some kind of continuity work. She had arrived at the airport too late for any introductions to be made. Last, but not least, the researcher, Daniel Booker.

It was going to be a long flight. As Michael flipped open the first page of his folder the friendly face of a stewardess appeared and offered him a drink. He opted for coffee and unclipped his little tray to accept his drink. He read for over an hour, unable to comprehend how the situation had deteriorated to this level with only the surface being scratched by the world's media. Now that the story had broken, national news teams from every country were converging on Ethiopia.

"Making headway with your background material?" The voice was that of Gerard Knight.

Michael looked up and smiled across at his colleague.

"I'm getting there. I had no idea it was this bad already."

"None of us did until the last reports came through, now, there's a mad panic to get us there. Thousands are dead already and the aid agencies are working flat out, without much success at the moment. Our contact and travelling companion on the ground will be a chap called Chris Newman, a Boston graduate who runs the American voluntary agency called Africaire. He's an incredible guy. Stands no nonsense from anyone and has a way of getting round all the bureaucracy. He's arranging our travel permits to get us to Korem, where I believe they've already started to set up our base."

"Are we travelling there straight away?" Michael asked.

"No, much too late for another journey. We'll stay one, maybe two days in Addis Ababa and then depending on what's been arranged, we'll either have another flight or we'll have to travel hundreds of kilometres overland. But we'll find out soon enough. Chris is meeting us at the airport."

They were interrupted by the stewardess serving dinner and the conversation moved on to more everyday subjects as they ate their meal. Michael hadn't been wrong in his initial liking of Gerard. He proved to be amusing company and was a mine of information on any topic under the sun.

Bole airport was quieter than Michael had imagined it would be. But then it was almost midnight and there couldn't be many more flights coming in at this hour. In no time at all they were through customs and had collected their luggage. Chris was soon bustling around arranging taxis. Both Michael and Gerard travelled with Chris in his car back to the hotel. They were checked in swiftly and arrangements made to meet back in the bar in twenty minutes. Chris was nothing if not organised. On their return he launched straight into their itinerary.

"Sorry you won't have much time to rest, but I've managed to arrange a flight for us tomorrow to Assab. That's the port where the aid food arrives and if you'll look at the little map I've drawn up, you'll see it's on the Red Sea coast. I thought you would get a better insight into what we're doing here if you followed the food route to see where the aid is going. Unfortunately we'll have to split into two groups for travelling. The second flight doesn't leave until tomorrow afternoon. So if you don't mind I would suggest that three of you travel with me in the morning. You can decide who travels with whom, but you'll need to be ready the flight leaves at six. Any questions?"

"Who'll be travelling with the second party, I mean none of us speak the language." It was Charlie who had spoken. He had already decided that he would travel with the second flight.

"We're picking up one more passenger at Assab, his name's Kabay, he works for us but he's a local. No one here speaks all the languages; there are at least seventy of them spoken as mother tongues. Thirty per cent of the total population consists of the Amhara whose native language Amharic is also spoken by an additional twenty per cent of the population as a second tongue. Amharic is Ethiopia's official language but there will be times when even that won't be of much use to us. We're only splitting up for the flights, we'll all meet up in Assab before splitting up again to travel to Makalle and from there we go overland to Korem where there's no airstrip. Now I suggest if there's nothing else you should all get some sleep, we've a long day ahead of us." He spoke for a few minutes more and answered one or two questions before bidding them all goodnight.

Shortly before six the following morning they were boarding a single-engined Cessna. Daniel Booker was on the early flight with Gerard and Michael and one cameraman, Drew Webster. Conversation was difficult so Michael contented himself with trying to see what he could from his window. It wasn't much. His only visible landmark was the Awash River, if of course he was reading his map correctly. As they neared Assab the landscape changed. Michael imagined this was what the moon must look like, parched and pitted. An unparalleled landscape of long dead volcanoes.

They landed in a fierce dust storm, whipped up by the giant turbo-propellers on two transporter aircraft. They turned out to be RAF Hercules C130's on loan from Britain. The first thing to hit Michael after the dust was the heat. He struggled to remove his jacket, although lightweight, it was still too heavy. Assab had to be the hottest place on earth. No wonder their flight had been so early in the morning.

"Most of the work here had to be done either very early in the morning or just before dusk. I should have mentioned the heat but we're all so used to it now. Firstly let's get to the hotel and then I'll give you the grand tour of the port."

Once again Chris seemed to be on top of everything and it wasn't long before Michael was sitting in the shadiest corner of the small hotel lounge with a cold drink.

"I feel soaked already and it's still early in the day. I'm getting too old for heat like this." Gerard's voice seemed very loud in the quiet confines of the lounge. He threw himself into the chair next to Michael. "Chris has gone to let them know the rest of our group are arriving later in the day and also to see if he can arrange a meal for us before we go back out into the furnace."

Michael sympathised with him. Daniel and Drew had gone out to have a quick look around on their own. Neither appeared daunted by the heat. Michael had been scribbling some notes before Gerard had joined him and writing a short message on the back of a postcard he'd picked up in the hotel in Addis Ababa. The card was of a little girl; her long black hair had been divided into sections and arranged in tiny plaits all over. She was resting her arm on a wall and her head was using it as a pillow. She was a beautiful child and except for the darkness of her skin, she could have been Becky. The unfortunate title of the postcard was "Smiling Ethiopia". There wasn't much to smile about at the moment. He wondered where she was now, the little girl who had posed for the photograph. He wrote Lisa's address on the card and stuck it into his pocket until he could find somewhere to post it.

Lunch was more than adequate but no one seemed to have much of an appetite because of the heat and they were soon heading down to the harbour. They spent the next few hours talking to ship's personnel and watching the unloading of the bulk commercial wheat. These first reports were put on camera and would be ready for transmission the following day in Britain if they could get the tapes on the first flight out. They walked back to the hotel in the middle of the afternoon.

"Who were you writing the postcard to this morning?" Gerard wasn't being inquisitive, merely making conversation and before long Michael had told him about Lisa and the kids, and the divorce.

"We've all been there, not very pleasant, but at least you have something to look forward to afterwards."

They walked the remainder of the journey in silence. Gerard constantly mopped his brow with a now saturated handkerchief. He was looking forward to travelling north, where he was assured it would be a lot cooler.

On arrival at the hotel they were informed that the rest of the party had arrived and had also gone towards the harbour. But as they hadn't met it was assumed they had wandered down different back streets. It was easier to eat later in the day when it was cooler and the party complete again, spent a fairly relaxing evening in the bar. Michael had managed a very quick call to Lisa merely to say they were there and heading out to their base.

The following morning they boarded the aircraft again heading for Makalle the regional capital of Tigre. Their flight went north first before heading west across the featureless Danakil Desert. The landscape changed dramatically from very flat to barren grey highlands. The airport stood on an exposed plain on the outskirts of the old city and thankfully for Gerard in contrast to Assab, the air here at above two thousand metres was cold. There was a Hercules unloading and the recipients of its cargo were two Soviet MIL-6 and MIL-8 helicopters.

"I hope you're ready to rough it tonight, we're camping out. Your first night of many from now on." Once again Chris had taken care of the airport formalities and before long they were driving into the old town, where they picked up supplies before continuing on to one of the semi-permanent shelters and set up camp along side the Red Cross and UNICEF. Michael stepped down from the Land Rover and surveyed the straggling, tented, camp area.

"Drew, how about grabbing your camera and we'll go for a walk?" Michael had already lifted a hand held tape recorder. "Does anyone mind if we go have a look round?" His question was aimed at Chris more than anyone else.

"No, that's what you're here for, just don't get lost. It's easy to lose your bearings in the middle of these camps until you get used to them."

Luckily they bumped into a girl who worked for the Catholic Relief Services and she wandered with them for quite a way. Her name was Julie Ann Aylward, and she proved to be fairly knowledgeable informing them of the resettlement areas in the south. Michael's eyes were opened to the true horror of the situation. Women and children predominantly inhabited the camp. Those who weren't lucky enough to have tents had scooped out hollows in the ground. Some of these people had walked over two hundred kilometres looking for food, Julie explained as they moved from one sad band of refugees to another.

"How long have you been here?" Michael wondered how anyone could walk through here showing the calm indifference that Julie Ann did. "I know what you're thinking Michael. You have to learn to cope with what you see here. I've been here almost three months and in the beginning I couldn't walk amongst these people without sobbing my eyes out. But we're here to help them, so we have to at least look as if we can handle it."

"I'm sorry I hadn't meant to upset you. I didn't realise."

Drew was filming everything he could. No one would believe this until they saw it with their own eyes and he was making sure he missed nothing.

It was a more subdued party eating dinner than they had been the previous evening. Michael couldn't finish his meal thinking about all the people out there who were starving. They had lost everything. He excused himself from the table in the tent that served as a canteen and walked out into the cold evening.

The camp was uncommonly hushed except for the faint cry of a child. Maybe he wasn't the right person to be doing this. He had come for his own reasons but now he was deeply moved by the plight of these people. Charlie joined him. They hadn't had much chance to talk since they had left Addis Ababa.

"Not at all what we expected, is it?" Charlie lit a cigarette and blew the smoke upward into the cold air.

"We spoke to a girl today from one of the relief services and she says it's much worse where we're going though I can't envisage anything worse that what I've seen today." Michael's voice was strangely quiet.

Charlie continued enjoying his cigarette. I'm walking into town later to try and get a call home from the press offices here. Why don't you come along, take your mind off things."

"Thanks Charlie I'll do that. I've only managed a couple of very quick calls since I left Glasgow. I wouldn't mind getting another try. What time are you leaving?"

"In about an hour, I'll give you a shout. Kabay says he'll come with us in case there's a problem." Charlie disappeared back into the canteen.

Michael went to find a sweater and was back at the same position when Charlie returned an hour later.

The makeshift press office in Makalle was noisy and stuffy considering how cold it had become outside. They waited for hours, passing the time chatting to an American news team who had been in Makalle for over a month. Finally Michael was summoned to a desk and his connection put through. Lisa's voice crackled at the end of the line. They had managed calls back to the UK during the day but purely to the network stations. Only at night when the lines weren't busy could you place a call home for a chat. It was good to hear her voice. He hated being away from her, but as Gerard had said all the more to look forward too afterwards. Before long he was given a signal that brought his call to an end.

"Right, ready for the walk back?" Charlie's voice had brought him back to reality.

The following morning they were on the move again. The last flight was to Alamata, where they wouldn't be staying long before the road journey to Korem. They left Alamata behind, a town once again crowded with drought refugees.

It turned out to be more of an expedition as they wound their way up a mountain road to travel the twenty-five kilometres to Korem. On this road it seemed a much longer journey.

If Michael had thought Assab and Makalle were bad, then Korem resembled the end of the world. There were children grubbing for a few grains of corn that had fallen on the ground. There were at least thirty thousand refugees who had no shelter in the main camp. Some had no blankets and at night the temperature could fall below freezing.

If this wasn't the end of the world then it had to be near it. It took them at least two hours to set up camp. Again they had joined forces with the aid agencies and would share their facilities.

Chris held another of his little get togethers, explaining how the system operated and where, on the reporting side, the most good could be done. The following morning a small convoy was expected. The mountain trail they had followed today could be treacherous for the trucks. On some occasions the sacks of grain had to be rescued and lugged up by cart. They would be permitted access to everywhere, except the makeshift hospital where the risk of infection was too great.

There were timetables in the office area, yet another tent, and these should be checked every morning so as not to get in the way of the relief workers.

"Surely there's something we can do to help. I can't imagine trailing about behind aid workers and doing nothing myself." Michael's comment had received a resounding 'hear, hear' from the rest of the crew.

"All help would be greatly appreciated and it's kind of you to offer. Perhaps we could add your names to the roster and then everyone would know where they should be at any given time. If you agree that is?"

"No problem for me," replied Michael and confirmation was soon given by his colleagues.

Courage and Clowns

He felt better knowing that he was doing something, no matter how little, to help out here. It had been a long, tiring day and much sooner than normal they were all ready to turn in. Michael was exhausted and before long he had drifted into a dreamless sleep.

The morning started early at Korem and by six o'clock Michael could hear movement outside. He quickly dressed and made his way to the canteen where Gerard was already having coffee. "Apparently I'm in the supply tent this morning. You've got distribution. I've never felt so humble as I did last night. Makes you really sit up and take stock of things." Gerard helped himself to more coffee.

Chris and one of his colleagues, another American, Peter, joined them.

"How did it ever get to this?" Michael asked. "Surely there has to be some kind of warning. I mean this didn't all happen overnight."

"In theory there is a warning system that feeds directly into a relief action system. Meteorological information is collected from relatively few weather stations. There is crop forecasting, which is based on limited information and concerns itself with on farm produce. Starting with a centralised system puts Ethiopia at an immediate disadvantage. It is unable to react to the localised nature of famine and cannot draw upon the wealth of local knowledge to react to and cope with it."

"I'm sorry you must get sick of people saying the same dumb things." Michael apologised.

"No, it's a fairly logical question. The same system works in Botswana and India and there famine has been averted." Peter explained.

There was no more time to talk as people began to surface and the day's work began.

CHAPTER 10

Standing outside his old home was strange for Eddie. The garden had a few more plants than he remembered but then Val had always been the gardener. Somebody had to make time for it she had said and he was never there. He pushed the reminiscent thoughts to the back of his mind and rang the doorbell. He was slightly nervous about tonight and he had been surprised when Val had actually agreed to have dinner with him. He had thought that when he had phoned back she would have made some kind of excuse. But she hadn't and here he was.

He had been keeping an eye on James Campbell this past month and Campbell in turn had been following Lisa Whitford. What was he up to? When the door opened he was miles away and Val's voice made him jump. She stepped back to let him enter.

"I'll only be a few minutes so go in and have a seat." She made her way back upstairs leaving Eddie to wander into the sitting room.

It used to be his sitting room but it wasn't any more. The carpets were different and the suite was new and there was a cat curled up in one of the chairs. He didn't like cats. Strange creatures that jumped about from place to place and looked at you as if they knew something you didn't. The cat however paid him no attention whatsoever, and for that he was grateful.

He was still standing in the middle of the room when Val returned. She looked lovely. Her dark hair, almost black with still no hint of grey and her tall slender figure hadn't changed at all. She was wearing dark blue and it suited her. It made her look quite sophisticated. He hadn't remembered her looking sophisticated but then maybe he hadn't really paid enough attention.

"The house looks lovely and I'm glad you're doing okay. I didn't know you liked cats?" He said.

"Neither did I until he turned up on the doorstep and decided he was staying. He's good company."

Eddie thought the cat looked too lazy to be much company but he refrained from saying so.

"Ready then."

Val had already put on her coat.

If he had been more attentive he would have done it for her, but perhaps she hadn't noticed his lack of manners. He would have to try harder for the rest of the evening. He wanted it to be a success.

The little restaurant he had chosen was Italian and it was quiet. Their meal was delicious and on more than one occasion he had succeeded in making her laugh and that could only be a good sign. She had been promoted at work and had a lot more responsibility and she seemed to be enjoying it.

"How's your work faring?" She asked as the waiter poured their coffee.

"Not bad. Well that's not strictly true. I've had a very slow few months, then all of a sudden two cases at once. Only trouble is they're connected and it's becoming a little awkward." He had never really discussed his work with Val before.

"Do you want to talk about it? I was always good at listening but you never seemed to confide in me."

Eddie realised he had a chance to step up another rung on his ladder to forgiveness and saw no harm in outlining his cases.

"That's a real mix up. Tell me, why are you following that man Campbell, you've just said he's a client. What are you up to Eddie?"

"I don't know yet. I feel that if I don't keep an eye on him I'm going to regret it."

Val liked what she was hearing. There had been no one in her life since Eddie. In the end though he hadn't been the man she had married and when he decided that she would be better off without him she had seen no reason to prevent him from going. He looked older than she had remembered and he had gained a bit of weight. But then the drink had probably caused both of these changes. Without the drink he was very much the old Eddie she had known, one that she would never have let go.

"So the girl with the kids is having an affair with Michael Bradshaw?"

"I've no proof, never saw them together but my instincts tell me I'm right."

They ordered more coffee and continued their conversation.

"Then why haven't you told Bradshaw's wife about her?"

"Because I don't like her and the more I meet her the less I like her and she isn't the type you would tell anything to, without being absolutely sure of your facts."

Val laughed. "You won't be a very successful Private Investigator if you end up investigating your clients and not telling them things. Are you mellowing in your old age?"

"Maybe I am. A few months ago I wouldn't have batted an eyelid. I'd have made out my reports, took their money and moved on. But recently I've begun to think that there's no point in doing this if it doesn't feel right. So until I know what I'm doing with these cases, I'm saying nothing. I'm hoping it will all work out in the end."

The waiter brought them their coffee and the conversation changed. It was almost midnight when Eddie dropped Val off at the house. He declined her offer of more coffee because he wasn't sure he could handle what might come after the coffee.

"No, I don't want to overstay my welcome. It's been a lovely night Val and I'd like to do it again."

"Give me a call." She reached across and gave him a little kiss on the cheek. He could smell the sweet perfume. "Goodnight Eddie thanks for dinner."

The car door closed and the sweet smell of the perfume had gone too. He sat for a few minutes before driving off. The evening had been a success and he was looking forward to their next date. He drove over to Frank's for a chat and a coffee. He had just left the stall and was sitting at traffic lights when he glanced into the car opposite. It was Campbell and he had a young girl as a passenger. When the lights changed Eddie managed to change lanes and turn right. Well, there was no point in missing an opportunity and for him the night was still young.

The car stopped outside a club in the centre of town. There was no chance of Eddie going in. Apart from the fact that he hated the noise, it wouldn't do for Campbell to spot him. So he settled himself in the car with yesterday's newspaper and a clear view of the door ready for when Campbell re-emerged. After only an hour they came out and they were arguing. The girl was being pulled roughly over to the car. Campbell fumbled with the keys and pushed her inside before the car sped off with Eddie following at some distance. It took only fifteen minutes to reach the flat.

Eddie parked a little way up the street but he could clearly see the parking bay and James Campbell get out of the car. He didn't wait for his young passenger to alight but stormed round to her side and pulled her out. She struggled with him and broke free, heading back along the street. Campbell went after her, screaming some words of abuse and at the same time he lifted his arm and with his full strength brought his fist down on the side of her head. She staggered and fell. Eddie felt sick, but if he went to her aid, he'd blow the whole thing. Campbell didn't wait around. He left her lying and went through the door into the apartment block. Without hesitation now Eddie ran over to where she was attempting to get up.

"Take it easy now." He said gently. There was blood pouring from the side of her face and she was already badly bruised.

"I'm fine, please go away. You'll make my husband worse if he comes back."

Eddie knew there was little chance of Campbell coming back to see how she was so he helped her to her feet. She had used the word husband although Eddie suspected that was far from the truth. She couldn't be more than twenty and a frail looking little thing she was.

"He can't get away with that maybe we should have you checked over at the hospital?"

She looked horrified and frightened.

"No, I'll have to go in. He'll cool down soon. Thanks for your help." Patti was feeling kind of dizzy and she was grateful for the strong arms supporting her. But it would be better if she got rid of him in case James came back.

Eddie watched as she made her way into the building using the wall the support her. He went back to his car. What he wanted to do was go right up there and beat the hell out of Campbell. Instead he went home and soaked in a hot bath. Physical violence had always been part of his job but what he had seen tonight left a sickening feeling in the pit of his stomach. In the morning he'd call Campbell and tell him there was no point in continuing with his case. He'd lie and say that extensive enquiries had brought up nothing on Lisa Whitford. With this thought in his mind he fell into bed and tried hard to bring back some of the pleasure of the evening prior to his last encounter. But all he could see was that young girl's bruised face. He wondered how James Campbell had known where to find Lisa for he was sure the social workers wouldn't have given him that information. Maybe it would be wise to continue watching Campbell. There was no knowing what he was capable of.

The months passed quickly. James Campbell's appeal had been turned down and Lisa had been given another extension to the order. There would follow a court hearing to decide who should have permanent custody of Jamie and Becky and a date had yet to be decided. The children were now very settled into their life with Lisa and Mrs Davidson and although Judith had explained on a number of occasions that the court would decide on custody she felt that Lisa had been lulled into a false sense of security. The court could still quite conceivably award custody to James Campbell as he was still the children's father. But Lisa was determined and would not accept that she would lose. Judith had no doubt in her mind where the children would be better off, but the decision wasn't hers to make. She only wished that Lisa would at least consider the possibility.

Michael remained in Ethiopia after his initial three-month period was over because he and his colleagues had felt that if they all left at the same time the aid agencies would suffer and the world would once again sit back and forget. Most of them had returned to the UK in the early months of the year and some had come back again in the spring. The work they were doing was continuing day by day. There were many weeks when he was in outlying areas where there were no telephone lines and he was unable to speak to Lisa but he had assured her that by autumn he would be home.

Final arrangements for Meg's wedding were under way and the children were excited at the prospect. Keith's friend Andy would be home on leave from the RAF and Lisa had met him before and was looking forward to seeing him again. There was a time that Meg had thought he and Lisa would have made a lovely couple.

He sun was shining brilliantly through the gap in the bedroom curtains causing a beam of light to fall across the pillows. Lisa opened her eyes and sat up, puffing up her pillows behind her. It looked as if Meg was going to have a beautiful day. She picked up the phone from the bedside cabinet and dialled the familiar number. Meg's voice was anything but sleepy.

"Hello Lisa, looks like I was up before you this morning."

"How did you know it was me, and I'm not up yet I'm still in bed but I am contemplating movement. How are you, feeling nervous yet?"

"Nervous, I don't think I slept for more than two hours at a time last night and I've been up for almost an hour."

Lisa glanced at her bedside clock. It was half past seven, a time rarely seen by Meg unless she was going to work.

"You've got a beautiful day, how did you manage to arrange brilliant sunshine?"

"I don't intend counting my chickens this early it could still rain by three. In fact knowing my luck we could even have the first recorded snow fall in July. Listen, why don't you come over for breakfast. I don't have to be at the hairdresser until ten. Please come and keep me company until then or I'll go mad."

"Okay, but only if we can have pancakes."

"I'll never fit into my dress if I eat pancakes this morning. Why can't you eat a normal breakfast like other people, sausages or eggs or even toast?"

"Pancakes, and I'll see you in less than an hour."

Lisa swung her legs out of the bed and put her feet into her slippers, and then instead of reaching for her robe, she slipped on jogging trousers and a top.

She would get the children up before she washed and changed to go to Meg's.

They had already heard her and they were both awake. She stuck her head round the door of Becky's room.

"It's today the wedding, it is today isn't it?" Becky's voice was full of excitement. She had never been to a wedding.

"Can I put my dress on now?" She asked bouncing up and down on the bed.

"No you certainly can not. In fact if you're very quick we can go and have breakfast with Meg before she goes to the hairdresser. Jamie, time to get up."

Jamie appeared already dressed.

"You are supposed to get washed before you dress Jamie." Lisa said as she lifted Becky off the bed before she did some damage.

"I am washed. I did it while you were on the phone, I could hear you talking."

"Take the dog downstairs for me then and I'll get Becky washed."

Jamie raced away with the dog at his heels.

"Come on Becky, let's get you organised."

Becky appeared at the door of the bathroom, her face was flushed and Lisa hoped she wasn't going to make herself sick with excitement.

"Will I see Meg's dress when we go the house?"

"No, you don't get to see the dress until Meg comes to the church so you'll have to be patient a little longer. Now stand still."

Becky's hair had a will and a life of its own and it seemed to grow at an alarming rate.

"Run along and put on a jogging suit for now and then get downstairs and have a drink."

Lisa tidied the bathroom and went downstairs to make some tea.

Both kids were sitting outside in the garden and Lisa lifted her tray and went to join them. It really was a glorious day.

Drinks finished, they locked up and drove over to Meg's house. They could smell the pancakes.

"I'm sure someone was supposed to make my breakfast this morning. I mean I am the bride after all." Meg was piling pancakes on to a serving dish.

"I think you've made enough for a regiment. Right kids tuck in."

Lisa poured the tea and then sat down at the table.

"What's your dress like for today Becky?" Meg said pouring maple syrup on her pancake.

"It's a secret, you can't know until we get to the church." Becky said with her usual charm and diplomacy.
"Oh I see it's a secret like mine."
"Yes, but I'll tell you what colour it is if you want to know." The little one continued.
"I wouldn't dream of asking. I'll just have to wait until I get to the church."

After they had eaten their fill of the fresh pancakes, Meg gave Jamie a copy of a new video release and for Becky she had a little silver dolphin on a chain. Lisa fastened the chain around her neck and they both disappeared into the sitting room to watch the video.
"Meg you must stop buying them little presents. Remember you'll soon be a married lady and you won't be able to throw your money around like that."
"I like to spoil them. Anyway until I have some of my own I'm allowed to spoil other peoples." She made another pot of tea.
"Have you heard anything from Michael?" She asked as she brought over some clean cups.
"Not a lot over the past few weeks. One or two very brief calls and I scan every news channel at night. They are somewhere north of the capital but I can't remember the name of the town and the reports are so brief. He's only on screen for a few minutes, and then he's gone."

"Perhaps if there's no phone where he is he'll write to you. You could hear something in the next few days."

"Yes maybe. I just wish he hadn't gone at all. That's pretty selfish isn't it?"

"No considering he just gave you an engagement ring, I think it's fairly normal to expect him to be around."

Lisa wanted to change the subject. "Have you spoken to Keith this morning?"

"He won't even be out of bed yet. He'll phone while I'm at the hairdresser, because he'll have forgotten what time I'm going."

As they drank their tea Lisa told Meg that Campbell's appeal had been rejected and that they were now both fighting for custody.

"Does that mean going to court?" Meg asked.

"Eventually, but Judith's gone on holiday and I couldn't get a hold of anyone else. So I don't know how long that will take. I'm not giving these kids up. I don't care what the court decides - even if I have to run away with them."

"Do you think you could delay any rash decisions until I get back from my honeymoon? I don't want to come back and discover that you're a news item yourself."

"Meg, I don't know what I'd do if they change the order and give him access or worse still custody."

"Well we're not going to worry about it today."

"No, this is your day and I intend to enjoy it as much as you do."

"I wish you had agreed to be matron of honour. It's going to be strange not having you right there beside me."

"Bridesmaids are supposed to be young and pretty, your niece will look much better and I will be there sitting at the front beside your mother. Now if we don't get a move on none of us will be at church."

They said their goodbyes and headed off in different directions.

Becky looked stunning in her ballerina length dress with its little bolero jacket. It was the softest shade of lilac, fairy lilac Becky had called it. If Lisa had a daughter of her own, she couldn't have wished for a more beautiful one. Jamie was looking very superior in his first ever suit, with collar and tie. Finally they were all ready. They were at the church with fifteen minutes to spare and just enough time for Lisa to say hello to everyone before they took their seats. The organ music changed and heads started turning as Meg walked down the aisle.

"She looks just like a fairy princess." Becky's little voice carried across the church. Meg smiled at her and winked.

There was at least an hour of photographs before they moved on to the hotel for the reception.

"I believe you're the young lady who'll be seated next to me at dinner."

Lisa looked up into the smiling face of Andy, in full RAF uniform.

"Andy, it's lovely to see you again and say hello to the children. This is Jamie and the one who can't sit still is Becky. This is her first wedding and she's afraid she'll miss something."

"You look lovely as ever Lisa, and that colour really suits you." He was charming as always.

Lisa's outfit was a much deeper shade of lilac. She had wanted to wear blue but didn't want to clash with the bridesmaids.

Andy organised drinks for them and tried to keep up with Becky's constant chatter throughout the meal. Andy was good company and the evening passed all too quickly.

Meg and Keith had stayed until the end of the reception. As Meg said, it was her wedding and they were staying overnight in a hotel, so why leave early. Lisa stood outside with all the other guests and waved them off in their taxi. It had been a lovely day with no hitches. Andy had offered her a lift home and looked slightly put out when she admitted she had brought her own car.

"Why don't you come and have dinner with us before you go back to your base? That's if Becky hasn't bored you to tears already."

"I'd like that and you're very lucky, she's charming. I'll give you a call tomorrow and we can arrange something. Goodnight Lisa, it's been lovely seeing you again."

"Goodnight Andy, I'll speak to you tomorrow."

Lisa went off to round up the kids and get them home. They didn't seem to be the least bit tired although it had been a long day.

On the drive home however, Lisa noticed that Becky was struggling to stay awake. As soon as they got in she checked the answering machine. But there was still no message from Michael.

There was a note from Mrs Davidson to say that the dog was fed and walked and she had left some sandwiches in the kitchen in the event of them being hungry when they got back, as usual she had thought of everything. Lisa began to wonder how she had managed before Mrs Davidson arrived. She certainly couldn't survive without her now.

After a drink and something to eat the children were more than ready to fall into bed. Jamie very carefully put his suit back on the hanger. He had felt very special today.

"I had a lovely time at the wedding Lisa and thank you for my suit."

"You looked fabulous in it, very grown up. Maybe you're too grown up for a goodnight hug."

He laughed and threw his arms around her neck. "I'm glad we live with you Lisa. No one will take us away now, will they?"

"No Jamie, no one is ever going to take you away. I love you more than anything in the world. Now head down and get some sleep." She tucked the covers under his chin. Becky was already sound asleep when Lisa went in to put the light out. Her dress had been very carefully placed on her chair.

Lisa finally changed and sat down in the quiet of her sitting room with her usual cup of tea. She was half way through her second cup when the phone rang. It was one thirty in the morning. It had to be Michael.

"Hello. Hello." There was nothing but the sound of crackling and then finally, she heard his voice.

"Lisa can you hear me, this line is dreadful."

"Yes Michael I can hear you."

"How are you? Both the kids well?"

"Yes we're fine. It was Meg's wedding today so we've only come in. Where are you? I can't work it out from the news reports."

"Tonight I'm in Makalle but our base is at Korem in the mountains. It's too late tonight to travel back so we'll stay here and make the journey in the morning."

"How bad is it over there? The little we're seeing at home looks bad enough."

"It would break your heart if you could see what's happening. Outside our base, there's a field with sixty thousand camped out and the numbers are growing daily. Those who don't die of starvation are dying of a multitude of diseases. I could never have imagined it being this bad. Within the next few days the real shock will hit home. We've put together a film and it shows everything. We need the rest of the world to sit up and take notice. These people are dying in their thousands every day and irrespective of what's done now, it will still be too late for more than half of them."

"How long will you be there Michael? It's already been months longer than we expected."

"I know Darling but time doesn't have quite the same meaning out here. I'll be at least another month anyway. How was the wedding?"

"Becky talked the hind legs of everyone and Jamie wore a suit for the first time and he was quite the little gentleman. And their father's appeal was thrown out. Now we have to go to court."

"I suppose we should have expected that. Don't worry Lisa, I should be home before then and I don't think he has any chance at all and promise me you'll be careful."

"We'll be fine. The kids are on holiday from school and Mrs Davidson's here with them every day. She'll keep an eye on them."

"You know Lisa I should be at home right now buying you flowers and giving you presents. We only got engaged for god's sake. What am I doing out here? I should have stayed and fought Kerry, instead I ran away. I came here for all the wrong reasons."

"Michael I think the carnations and clowns can wait. We have plenty of time ahead of us. What you're doing at the moment is worthwhile. You had a choice and it took courage to stay when you could have come home. I'll still be here when you get back. I love you Michael."

"I love you too. I'll be home in just over a month and then I'll buy you thousands of carnations. Listen, I have to give up this line now. Take care and I'll speak to you soon."

There was so much she felt she wanted to say, but there was never enough time it was just so good to listen to his voice.

The line went dead.

Lisa swallowed another mouthful of tea. It had gone cold.

Courage and Clowns

It was a Sunday, supposedly a day of rest. The kids were out playing and Lisa was struggling with a pile of ironing. How she loathed ironing.

It had been a few weeks now since she had spoken to Michael. She knew it was difficult for him but she wondered why he hadn't ever written. Thinking of this she decided that she could drop him a line if she could find out from Josh where to send it. Cheering up, she called Josh and not only was he pleased to hear from her he suggested her coming over for dinner that week. Everything decided, she made a note of the address he had given her and returned to her ironing. She would write tonight when the kids were in bed. She had arranged to meet Meg, now returned to normal life, at one of the local garden centres. It was actually a country park where there was an activity area for the children and a lovely coffee shop. With half an hour to spare she quickly tidied the kitchen and called the children.

Lisa couldn't see Meg's car in the car park but as she was normally late they decided to go through to the garden centre and buy some plants. Jamie was interested in building a rockery in the garden and had been spending at least an hour every day collecting large stones and trying to build up the soil. He had continued with his visits to the library and on his last trip had come back armed with gardening books. He had a list of what plants he wanted to buy and before long they had purchased much more than Lisa had intended.

"There's Meg," gasped Jamie as he tried to lift a fir tree that was much too heavy for him. By the time Lisa looked up, Becky had already run to meet her friend. Meg was still tanned from her holiday and was making the most of it by constantly wearing brilliant white tee shirts. With the trolley finally loaded they made their way into the coffee shop.

"I saw the man from the café looking at plants." Becky had been trying to attract Lisa's attention.

"What man Becky?" Lisa had no idea what she was talking about.

"Remember I dropped chocolate milk shake on his shoes, that man."

"Yes I remember now. I expect he was buying plants for his garden."

Lisa paid no more attention to Becky but heard her try to explain to Jamie that it was the same man.

It was good having Meg home again. Although she had been busy over the past few weeks she had missed their little chats and there was no one else she could phone at any hour of the day or night.

"Who's going to be busy then?" Meg passed her gaze over the assortment of plants and small shrubs.

"I'm going to build a rockery. I got this book from the library and it showed me how. It's going to be the best rockery ever. You can come and see it when I've finished." Jamie explained to Meg.

"Can we go out and play on the climbing frames?"

"Yes Jamie but watch Becky and make sure she doesn't fall."

Lisa had really no need to say that. If Jamie was anything at all, it was protective of Becky.

They watched them run off.

"Did you manage to see Andy when he was home?" Meg asked

"I had invited him over for dinner, but he was called back before we could arrange anything, but it was lovely to see him again."

"What's the news on the children's saga?"

"Well the good news is Campbell had his appeal denied."

"That's great news. You must feel a lot more settled now."

"The funny thing is, I don't. The man isn't going to just disappear into oblivion. If he's gone this far he's not going to simply give up."

"What have the social work department said?"

"They seem to think we have a good case, but no one knows how the court will make their decision. I've applied for permanent custody and he's not going to take that lying down."

The door of the coffee shop burst open and Jamie ran in with Becky sobbing close behind him. His face was flushed and he was out of breath.

"Jamie, what's happened? Did Becky fall?" Lisa bent to examine Becky for cuts and bruises.

His little voice was trembling. "My dad was out there watching us. And then Becky saw him and started crying. I made her run all the way back here."

Lisa started gathering up their belongings. "Right let's get out of here. Meg can you do me a favour and bring the trolley." She picked Becky up and took Jamie securely by the hand.

"We're going straight to the car. When we get there you lock the doors as soon as I put you in. Do you understand?"

Jamie nodded. He was near to tears. They hurried out of the coffee shop and crossed the car park.

With the plants loaded and the kids safely inside, she turned to Meg.

"Can you get in the car and stay with them."

"Where are you going? Lisa just get in the car and let's go home."

"No he's standing over there, enjoying every minute of this. If he thinks he's frightening me then he's made a mistake. I'll be back in a minute."

"Lisa, this man's crazy. Why can't we just get home and phone the police?"

But Lisa was already on her way. He had to know she wasn't afraid of him. She was shaking with anger.

He smirked as she approached.

"I suppose you think you're very amusing, frightening two little children. I want you to stop following me. If you don't, I'll call the police." She was still shaking.

He laughed and pushed his hair back with his hand. "The police and what exactly are they going to do? I'm not doing any harm. I just wanted to see my kids. I don't think there's a law against that."

"Yes there is when you terrify the life out of them. You need to accept that you won't get these kids back and leave us in peace."

By now Lisa realised that she was shouting and people were beginning to stare.

"Listen Miss high and mighty, just because you have money doesn't make you any better than me. They're my kids and I'll get them back."

"When hell freezes over. You are disgusting. Stay away from me, or you'll be sorry."

He wasn't smiling when she walked away. She wasn't accustomed to such a confrontation and she was shaking from her head right down to her heels. When she got back to the car she slid into the driver's seat. She knew what she had done wasn't clever but one look at the kids had told her he couldn't get away with it,
"Thanks Meg, will you follow us home?"
"Of course I can. I'm parked over there so I should only be a few minutes behind you." Meg jumped out of the car and Lisa watched as she got into her own vehicle.
"Right then let's go. It's all right Becky, everything's fine."
Becky remained unconvinced and sobbed all the way home. Once inside Lisa called the police and it was at least an hour before they arrived by which time both Jamie and Becky had calmed down.
"What do you mean you can't do anything?" Lisa's remark was aimed at the elder of the two constables.
"We can put in a report, but as he hasn't actually done anything, there's nothing we can charge him with." The officer was sympathetic.
Lisa wasn't going to be fobbed off. "Well then, you can find something. These children were terrified. I take it you're going to wait until he does do something. How comforting."

When Lisa was angry there was no calming her down.

"Miss Whitford, I appreciate how distressing this must have been but I suggest the best course of action is to take out a court order to keep him away from the children. The social work department would back you up I'm sure and they can be granted quickly." He was genuinely sorry but there was nothing he could do.

"That's fine, so it's entirely up to me. I have to protect these children on my own. And what do I do if he turns up here?"

"If he turns up and causes a disturbance, then we can do something."

Lisa saw them to the door. "I'm sorry I'm not normally quite so rude."

"I understand Miss Whitford. If you need us to come back, then please call the station."

She closed the door.

"How to win friends. Well done Lisa." Meg knew there was no reasoning with Lisa when she was like this.

"Meg I'm not going to sit by and let this man walk all over us. And the police, some help they turned out to be."

"What are you going to do?"

"First of all I'm going to phone Judith and find out how he knew where to find us. They promised me he wouldn't be given this address.

And if he hasn't been following us how did he know where we would be today. He hardly looked like he was interested in gardening."

When Meg had gone, Lisa called and left a message for Judith.

While she was making dinner she decided what she was going to do.

Her first call was to Emily Forbes. Emily had done some part-time work at the shop when Lisa had first opened.

Her next call was to Mrs Davidson. With everything arranged, her little family sat down to dinner.

"How would you like to go on an adventure?" She asked them both.

"What kind of adventure? Where to?" Jamie's face was full of excitement.

"That's where the adventure part comes in because it's a secret until we get there."

"When is the adventure?" It was Becky's turn to sound excited.

"Tomorrow morning, very early. So what I need you both to do is have your baths early and get to bed, so that I can arrange everything and we'll be ready to leave in the morning."

"What about all of my plants?" Jamie asked.

"If you're very quick with dinner we could plant them tonight and then when we come back you'll be surprised how much they've grown."

Jamie was eager to help the situation along. "We could plant them now and have dessert later." He suggested.

"That's a good idea." Becky had already jumped down from the table.

Before long the plants were all in and Jamie was delighted with his garden. True to their word they were both in bed shortly after eight. Lisa set about packing. It could get cold where they were going so she had packed some sweaters and warm trousers as well as plenty of summer clothes. They had to take plenty because she had no idea how long they would be away. When she was satisfied she hadn't missed anything she packed the dog bed and some toys and with everything ready in the hallway, the car could be easily loaded in the morning.

Feeling quite pleased with herself she got ready for bed. She would get at least five hours sleep and then she was putting some distance between them and James Campbell. And there they would stay until somebody convinced her they were safe.

CHAPTER 11

James Campbell wasn't at all happy when he came home later that Sunday afternoon. Patty wasn't in a particularly good mood either. She had wanted to go out that afternoon but James had disappeared as usual and left her at the flat. She desperately wished she had never come with him but she had no money left and no option but to stay until he decided they were leaving. He hadn't spoken a word since he had come in and when her offer of tea was refused she carried on with her preparations for dinner.

James looked out over the park. The social work department was going to suffer for what they were doing and as for Lisa Whitford – no woman spoke to him like that especially in front of other people. He could hear Patty clattering about in the kitchen and he was beginning to find her irritating. He was wishing he had left her in London. He picked up his jacket again and made for the door.

"Where are you going James? I'm in the middle of making dinner."

"Out," he shouted as the door slammed behind him.

It was Monday morning, the start of a new week and Eddie was contemplating his next move. He wanted a meeting with Campbell but when he telephoned the girl had said he was still sleeping and that she would get him to call when he got up. He had also tried to contact Kerry, but no luck there either.

He had been amazed at Lisa Whitford's outburst in the garden centre yesterday. She had guts; he had to give her that but she had no way of knowing how vicious Campbell could be. There was no doubt in Eddie's mind that Campbell wouldn't let her get away with it. She had stood up to him and that thought alone convinced Eddie that she was quite capable of taking care of herself. He only hoped she wouldn't ever be in a situation where Campbell had her on his own. The consequences didn't bear thinking about.

He had followed Campbell after the incident but he had made no attempt to go after her. Instead he had gone home briefly before spending the rest of his evening in the pub. At closing time he could hardly walk and Eddie had to feel sorry for the young girl who would have to put up with him when he got home. It was hardly surprising he was still asleep this morning.

He pulled his jacket from the back of the chair and picked up his car keys. He was going to warn Lisa Whitford. He had an awkward moment yesterday when the little girl had recognised him but now it didn't matter. After today James Campbell wouldn't be his client so he wasn't doing anything unethical, well not exactly.

Eddie might be a lost cause in some respects but he wasn't going to sit around and see any harm come to two innocent children. And then of course there was Lisa. He didn't want anything to happen to her.

It wasn't long before he was parking at the back of Lisa's shop and he did notice that her car wasn't there. The little overhead bell chimed as he entered. He loitered in the background while the woman behind the counter dealt with the one or two customers and when she finally raised her head and spoke to him he walked over to the counter.

"I was looking for Miss Whitford."

"I'm sorry she's not here today. Can I help?"

"No it's a personal matter. I'll try and contact her at home. Thank you." Eddie had turned to walk away when she spoke again.

"She isn't at home, she's actually gone on holiday." The woman looked apologetic. "Are you sure there's nothing I can help you with?"

"No I'm sure thank you. She didn't mention a holiday last time I spoke to her. Gone off somewhere exotic has she?" Eddie was hopeful of a little more information.

"I've no idea. I think it was a last minute decision."

"Thanks anyway I can give her a call. Any idea when she'll back?"

"Not exactly, she said a few weeks."

Eddie thanked her and left the shop. There was a café opposite and he decided to treat himself to breakfast. As he sat and waited for his order he pushed this new information around in his head. It was obvious no one running a business left suddenly on holiday, so Lisa Whitford had done a runner. Good for her. He hoped she was far enough away that Campbell wouldn't find her. Comforted by this new development, he tucked into his bacon and eggs.

He had almost finished his coffee when he spotted Campbell. He looked rougher than normal and Eddie fervently hoped that he had one hell of a hangover. He paid for his meal and was back in his car before Campbell came out of the shop. He was blazing mad and in Campbell that wasn't hard to detect. He drove off almost hitting a bollard at the entrance to the car park. Eddie followed.

It was obvious that Campbell had just been the recipient of the same news Eddie had been given an hour before. Here he was out for blood, and his prey had flown. Life did have its compensations. Eddie was still gloating when he realised that not only had Campbell headed back into the city but he was making for Eddie's office. Thinking quickly, he turned down a side street hoping to miss the traffic lights up ahead and with luck he could be at the office before Campbell got there. It worked but only just. He had no sooner sat down when Campbell barged into the office. He didn't look as if he had calmed down any.

"You're supposed to be watching that woman and she's disappeared with my kids."

"Mr Campbell I called you this morning to tell you that I've come up with nothing on her and I'd be wasting your money if I said I had any more avenues to check out. Give it up, there's nothing wrong with her and certainly nothing you'd be able to use against her to get custody of your kids."

"I want her found Chadwick. That's what I'm paying you for. Now are you going to do something?" Campbell was stabbing the desk with his finger.

"No, I'm not. Leave the girl in peace. Walk away from this one."

"If you're not going to do anything I'll find them myself. How much do I owe you for nothing?"

Eddie gave him a figure and Campbell threw the money on to the desk. Eddie wished he had an excuse to take a swing at him and give him the hiding he deserved, but Campbell walked out of the office. Eddie looked at the money lying on the desk. He didn't really deserve payment for the job, but he was taking it anyway. He made himself a coffee and dialled Kerry Bradshaw's number.

The Granada rolled off the ferry and within a few minutes was clear of the pier. It had been a long journey and they had made more stops than Lisa had envisaged meaning they had almost missed the two o'clock ferry from Malaig. She was more relaxed now but her lack of sleep and the driving had left her shattered.

She turned in the direction of Portree and followed the road for a few miles before turning to her companion.

"How long now Mrs Davidson?" The children had enjoyed the ferry crossing but Lisa knew they were tiring of being in the car for so long.

"It's less than an hour, the cottage is this side of Portree. You must be exhausted my dear, but we'll soon be there."

"It's very kind of your sister to take us all at such short notice, I really appreciate this." Lisa had no idea what she would have done if Mrs Davidson hadn't suggested the holiday.

"Not at all, she was delighted. It's been two years since I've been here and don't worry there's plenty of room. And if it hadn't been for you I doubt I would have visited this year. Now that I see the old place I'm glad I'm home. It's times like this I realise I don't visit often enough."

Mrs Davidson had been very upset when Lisa had told her what had happened with Campbell and readily agreed the children's safety had to come first. She hadn't hesitated in offering a solution and had phoned her sister to make the arrangements. Lisa couldn't take the children out of the country without their father's consent, so travelling south had been out of the question too. Coming here had solved the problem quickly. The children's excited chatter hadn't halted the entire journey. Lisa tried to enjoy the beautiful scenery. She had never been to Skye and was looking forward to exploring what appeared to be a beautiful island. Bringing your own home grown guide was a stroke of genius.

At the brow of a hill they turned on to a small track that continued to wind it's way upward. The last bend opened out into a courtyard and there stood the most beautiful cottage Lisa had ever seen. Mrs Davidson's sister was sitting outside in the front garden. She rushed forward as the car drew to a halt.

"Jane, it's lovely to see you and this must be Lisa. I've been hearing all about you. And Jamie and Becky and this little chap must be Freebie. I'm Grace and I am so looking forward to this you can't believe. Now let's get you all inside and get you settled." She led the way through the honeysuckle and roses growing over the doorway.

"The house is beautiful Grace. I had no idea it was going to be this big. Mrs Davidson said a cottage." Lisa was overwhelmed by what she had seen so far.

"Wait until you see the rest of it. My son's a builder you see. It used to be two cottages and a couple of outhouses and he joined them all together to make it into a bed and breakfast. But I only do that when I feel like some company." She continued chatting in her jovial manner. Lisa felt quite at home and as usual Mrs Davidson was organising the children.

"Are you putting the children in the attic bedroom Grace?"

"Yes I thought they'd like that."
"In that case I'll take them up and show them and then I'll put the kettle on and meanwhile you can show Lisa where everything is."
Mrs Davidson went off with the children who were shrieking and giggling with excitement. Lisa only hoped they calmed down soon. She thought they would all benefit from this break. She followed Grace through a large farmhouse kitchen into a conservatory and into the garden. It was breathtaking. Freebie was already running about sticking his little nose into everything. Lisa called him over.
"He's fine." Grace assured her. "There's plenty of room for him to run and he can't get out of the garden."
"Who does all the gardening, it's absolutely beautiful?" Lisa asked. The lawns were expertly trimmed and the large flowerbeds looked like a lot of work.
"I do most of it myself but my son comes and cuts the grass and helps with some of the heavy work." Grace replied as they wandered along the gravel paths.
"How much ground do you have here?"
"I think it's about three acres and you needn't worry the dog won't get lost. There's a six-foot stone wall surrounding the entire area. It's very safe."

"It's so peaceful I love it already." Lisa said honestly as they worked their way back to the conservatory.

"I usually have breakfast in here, it catches all the morning sun."

"It really is so beautiful and look at that view." Lisa gazed out over the water. She couldn't imagine waking up and looking out over anything more splendid.

"Come and I'll show you upstairs." Grace continued with her tour.

There were two staircases one at either end of the house leading to three bathrooms and six bedrooms. Lisa had been put into a huge double-bedded room overlooking the front and the sea, it was absolutely beautiful.

When they came back downstairs Mrs Davidson had already set up a table in the garden and the tea tray was ready. Lisa was glad to sit down and relax. The sun was still warm and she turned her face to feel the rays touching it. If the weather lasted this would be a fabulous holiday. She gratefully accepted her tea and helped herself to a sandwich.

"You must try and have a rest here Lisa. You haven't stopped since the children came to live with you and with the shop you never seem to have a minute." Mrs Davidson was doing her usual trying to look after everyone.

"You work twice as hard as I do Mrs Davidson. I never have any housework to do any more."

"I think you should call me Jane. I never really thought to mention it before. Are you going to call the social worker and tell them where we are?"

"Not today, in fact I may leave it for a few days. They won't be very pleased with me anyway."

"I see you're engaged Lisa. When are you getting married?" Grace asked.

Both Jane and Lisa laughed and then tried to explain briefly what was so funny about Lisa's engagement. Grace was tickled to death with their story.

"I like a little bit of intrigue and I promise I won't breathe a word to anyone."

Lisa took herself back off down the garden in search of the kids and the dog and to give Jane and Grace a chance to catch up on family news. The garden was a maze of paths going in every direction but eventually by following the noise she found them. There was a summerhouse amassed with roses and clematis and the children had found a swing that someone had rigged up from the branch of an old apple tree. The dog was jumping up and down underneath the swinging children. This was idyllic. Lisa took a seat on an old rustic garden bench that had seen better days but still served its purpose. The warm sun was beating down, but inside the summerhouse was cool. Lisa closed her eyes for a few minutes and for the first time in months she felt as if she hadn't a care in the world. When she opened them again it was quiet. The children had gone. She hadn't been aware of any movement and wondered if she had actually dozed off. She found her way back to the house where preparations were well under way. Her offer of help was refused and she wandered into the sitting room. From where she sat she couldn't see into the kitchen but she could hear the children rattling away nineteen to the dozen. She thought about James Campbell. How could anyone harm two little children? Perhaps that was unfair. He hadn't actually tried to harm them yesterday, but he did have a sinister presence about him. She knew Judith would probably be annoyed that she had removed the children, but then James Campbell hadn't confronted Judith. In fact, he hadn't even confronted Lisa; she had gone to him. And when Judith read the riot act she would simply have to face the music.

Her eyes fell on a bookcase in the corner and when Jane called to say dinner was ready, she had already flicked through the titles and picked out two books on the island. One was full of myths and legends of the highlands and she thought it might make good bedtime reading for the children. She left the books lying on a chair and wandered through to the conservatory. The sun although beginning to set, was still shining through the windows and the setting was picturesque.

Jamie and Becky continued their endless chatter throughout the meal. They wanted to know if there would be other children for them to play with and they were delighted to learn that Grace had six grandchildren who would all be visiting within the next few days. Grace had a son and a daughter, both married, and they still lived on the island. In appearance Grace and Jane were very alike. Both wore their white hair in similar styles, both had glasses and both had the same cheery disposition. The only apparent difference was that Jane was slightly taller.

Later in the evening when the children were in bed, Lisa sat with the sisters drinking sherry and chatting. Lisa wasn't much of a drinker and after only a few glasses she began to feel light-headed. She used that as her excuse and said she was tired and needed her bed. After a long soak in the bath she slept soundly until morning. The house was strangely quiet when she got up and after she washed and dressed she went downstairs and found Grace in the kitchen, baking.

"I hope you slept well. If you give me a minute I'll put the kettle on." Grace began cleaning her flour-covered hands on her apron. The smell of fresh baking was all over the kitchen.

Lisa lifted the kettle from its stand. "I think I can manage to make some tea. You carry on with what you're doing. Where is everyone?"

"Jane took the kids and the dog for a walk over the hill at the back. They shouldn't be very long."

Lisa enjoyed her breakfast of hot, freshly baked, buttered scones and tea. She had no sooner finished when Jane returned with the kids. Although they all had breakfast earlier they were soon tucking into the scones.

Later in the morning Lisa and the kids decided to take a drive into Portree. There were one or two things that hadn't been packed, like the camera. Lisa couldn't miss out on all this fabulous scenery. Jane gladly accepted a lift into the small town but she intended visiting some old friends. The journey didn't take long and they soon found a parking space near the harbour. They parted company with Jane and easily found the shop that Grace had suggested. Lisa purchased a camera and a few rolls of film. They strolled back to the harbour and took some photographs of Portree Bay. Lisa had no pictures of the children yet so she managed to get them to stand still for one or two shots and a kindly passer-by took one of the three of them. The town was very picturesque and they spent a lovely afternoon browsing. Most of the shops were privately owned and each one asked if they were on holiday and how long they would be staying.

"Why do all the people talk differently to us? Are we still in Scotland?" Jamie wasn't sure whether being on an island meant he had left his own country.

"People in the Highlands and Islands have a much softer accent than we do, but they are still Scottish." It hadn't occurred to Lisa that they might not have known the islands were part of Scotland.

They found a little gallery and spent more than an hour looking at the paintings. Most of them were scenes of the island with its beautiful bays dominated by the Cuillin mountain range.

The owner was very informative and spent some time explaining where the places were and how to get there in order to be able to enjoy the views in the paintings. Lisa thanked him and promised they would return. He was very taken with Becky and suggested she should sit for a portrait. Lisa was flattered that he had asked but assured him Becky couldn't sit still at the best of times.

They had lunch in a little tea-room overlooking the bay and afterwards they headed back to relieve Grace of the dog. Jane was making her own way back later in the day. They spent the rest of the day lazing around in the garden. Lisa had bought some writing paper and envelopes in Portree and she settled down to write to Michael. It was so easy to talk to him and before long she had written pages and pages. She didn't mention her encounter with James Campbell and merely said they had gone on holiday. She enclosed a couple of postcards of the island. Grace said there was a post box about half a mile along the road next to the bus stop. She picked up Freebie's lead and off they went. She wished she'd had a photograph developed and she could have sent it but that would keep for another letter. She had said in the letter that they would be staying for a few weeks or maybe a month and hopefully if he had time to write back he would use this address. She wished their troubles were all over and that Michael was home. Less than a year ago her priorities had all been so different.

That evening after dinner Grace's son visited with his wife and family. Their children were a few years older than Jamie and Becky but they all seemed to get along fine. When they left shortly after ten they promised they would arrange a day together at one of the beaches. The change of air was making Lisa very tired and once again she apologised to her hostess for not being better company. Grace and Jane didn't seem to mind although Lisa felt she was being slightly rude. She had only been on the island two days and she was in bed again before midnight.

Their days passed very quickly. They had been on nature trails and visited Dunvegan Castle. They had been to the south of the island where the scenery was even more spectacular and they had taken a boat trip. There was certainly plenty to do and the kids were enjoying every minute.

Today however they had both gone off with Grace's son Robert and his three kids to see badgers somewhere on one of the nature trails. They had been on the island two weeks now and Lisa hadn't felt this relaxed in months. She was sitting in the garden enjoying the heat of the day. Jane and Grace had gone off to visit friends. It had been difficult to convince them that she was perfectly happy to have a day to herself and that they weren't to worry about her. However now that everyone had gone the house seemed strangely desolate. After a few hours she decided to drive into Portree. She had seen one or two things in the shops and she hadn't had a chance to shop on her own. She parked fairly close to the little gallery and she thought it would be an ideal opportunity of purchasing one of the paintings to take home. The little wind chimes jingled as she went in. Her elderly friend, the owner was delighted to see her again.

"Come over here I have something to show you." He said excitedly leading Lisa through to the larger of the two exhibition rooms.

Facing Lisa as she entered the room was the most outstanding portrait of Becky. She had been caught unawares and for a few minutes she was speechless.

"I hope you don't mind but I bumped into the children with their Grandmother down at the harbour one day and I did a rough sketch while we were there." He said apologetically.

"I don't know what to say except that it's beautiful."

He had somehow caught the mystical expression Becky often had when she was daydreaming. There was no doubt it was a true likeness.

"Did Becky know you were doing the sketch?"

"No, she was sitting listening to her grandmother talking to some fishermen and I just saw an opportunity. I hope you're not offended?"

"Good gracious no. I'm thrilled with it. Please say it's for sale because I must have it to take home."

There was no price on the painting.

"I'm sure we can come to some arrangement. But I do hope you aren't going home already. You see the portrait is creating a lot of interest locally. I've been extremely busy since I put it on display and I was hoping I would have it at least another week."

"That's not a problem. I have no idea at the moment when we're going home. Could I ask something though?"

The old man looked hesitantly at her.

"It's nothing serious. I only wanted to ask if you could keep Becky from seeing it at the moment if she happens to come in with her grandmother."

She had used the same familiar term for Mrs Davidson rather than have him feel he was being corrected. He assured her that should the situation arise, he would deal with it accordingly. Lisa looked once again at the portrait.

"You're daughter is one of the most fascinating children I have ever come across. She's going to be a real beauty. You're very lucky to have such an adorable child."

"Thank you. It's very kind of you to say." Lisa made no attempt to correct his second assumption. She was proud of Becky and she wished she were her own daughter. She said goodbye to her friend and made her way to the tea-room. This had become another of her favourite haunts.

While she waited for her order she thought back to her conversation with Judith. She hadn't called for three days after they arrived. Judith had just about blown a gasket.

"Do you realise what you've done. James Campbell is threatening to sue the social work department for negligence. His lawyer has been on the phone demanding to be told where the children are. And what could I say, I don't know? I've been hauled over the coals for this one. We are responsible for these children and for three days we haven't even known where to find them."

Lisa had apologised and said she thought she was doing what was right for the kids.

"Lisa we're trying to get a custody order and you do something stupid like this. I really can't believe it. You do realise James Campbell is entitled to know where his children are."

At this point Lisa had ended the call before Judith had added anything else.

It had been another two days before Lisa had relented and told Judith where they were. Judith had phoned Campbell's lawyer and he appeared to accept that they were simply on holiday. He still persisted that the Social Work Department was negligent. The whole thing was growing into some kind of monster. Lisa should have been more distressed by all the trouble she was causing but contrary to her upbringing, there was a devilish satisfaction to be gained from going against the establishment.

"Could I have another pot of tea please?"

"Are you enjoying your holiday?" The young girl asked.

"I'm falling in love with the place," replied Lisa. "I won't want to go home when the time comes."

The girl stayed and chatted during Lisa's second pot of tea. She suggested some places the kids might like to visit if they hadn't done so already. Lisa thanked her and left to continue her shopping. She was making her way back to the car when someone rushing out of a shop ran straight into her and sent everything flying. Her assailant turned out to be rather charming and walked her back to her car with all the shopping.

There was a pile of mail waiting behind the door as Kerry entered the house. She pushed it out of the way with her foot and put her suitcase down in the hall. She heard the taxi wheels crunching on the gravel driveway on its way out. What she needed was a drink. She kicked off her shoes and walked barefoot into the kitchen. The tiles were cold against her tanned feet. Italy had been wonderful and she was glad she had gone. She mixed her drink and returned to the hall picking

Courage and Clowns

up the mail on her way, and settled herself in the lounge to flick through it. She could see nothing pressing amongst the envelopes. She reached over and activated the answering machine button. The little machine sprang to life and the messages recited forth as if in staccato. Eddie Chadwick had left more than one message and she lifted the phone and dialled his number.

While she waited for him to arrive, she thought of Richard Miller. She couldn't believe her luck in meeting the American film producer on holiday and there was no mistaking he was besotted by her. He hadn't wanted her to leave but that was usually the best time to go. Kerry had played all the games before and she was an expert. Richard Miller would be quite a catch if she played her cards right. She decided to get changed before her grubby little detective arrived. She had only stepped out of the shower when the doorbell rang. She cursed everyone in the world who was punctual and wrapping herself in a robe, she padded down to the door. It wasn't Eddie. The courier handed her an envelope, which she signed for, and gazing at the unfamiliar handwriting, she closed the door. The letter wasn't signed but the photographs told their own story. She felt sickened. How could he do this to her? She picked up the photographs again. She was very photogenic but the explicit nature of the shots meant not only was she being followed, but whoever it was knew his stuff. The only one of her recent amours not to be photographed was Eddie Chadwick. She contemplated ripping them up but decided against it. The details of the letter were as explicit as the pictures. If she continued with her harassment of Michael, he would divorce her on grounds of adultery and the proof of the claim was enclosed.

She was in a filthy temper when she opened the door again fifteen minutes later. This time it was her expected visitor. Eddie didn't need to be a mind reader to tell he had caught her on one of her off days. She slammed the door and led him into the lounge.

"I don't suppose there's any point in asking if you've come up with anything." She asked in her usual sarcastic manner.

"I've talked to everyone I can and there's nothing to tell. All your husband does is work and sleep and now he's out of the country. This really is a waste of time." He refrained from mentioning Lisa. He didn't even know where she was but wherever it was, she was out of harm's way.

This woman had everything he thought, and it wasn't enough for her. The phone rang and she reached back on the sofa to lift the receiver. The robe spread out to reveal her long shapely leg.

Eddie felt a sudden urge to stroke the soft skin but he pushed the thought from his mind. He could hope but he wasn't taking anything for granted.
"Richard darling, how nice of you to call." She smouldered down the phone.
He had no idea who 'Richard darling' was but he cared even less.
"Florida, I'd love to when....sounds divine"
She had only come back from somewhere because he had tripped over the suitcase in the hall and it looked as if she was off again. Some life thought Eddie.

Her call ended, she replaced the receiver in its little cradle and turned back to Eddie. She was more charming than she had been prior to the call. Eddie was thankful to Richard darling whoever he was.
"I've decided I won't need your services at the moment, but would it be acceptable if I changed my mind to call you?"
"You certainly can although really I think you'd be wasting your money."
"You let me worry about that. Now you must excuse me I need to dress for dinner. Thank you for at least trying. Send me an account of your charges and I'll get the bank to settle up with you."
She walked him to the door.

Eddie felt as if he had escaped rather than being set free. The feeling was good anyway even if it had left him a little frustrated.

Kerry had watched him drive away. She could quite happily have spent a relaxing few hours with him but she had no desire to add any more fuel to the already smouldering fire. If Michael was going to play her at her own game he still had no chance of winning. He wasn't good enough. Richard wanted her to join him in Florida at the end of the month and she didn't want anything to rock that particular boat at the moment.

She was meeting friends for dinner and was looking forward to showing off her tan and making them envious of her next trip. Richard Miller's name would add to the conversation and bring back some of her credibility, which had been slightly lessened by Michael leaving. Richard was worth more millions than she could count. She was back on top and she liked the feeling. It was where Kerry believed she belonged.

She knew she couldn't contact Michael by phone but she could write. She completed two pages telling him how despicable she thought his actions were and how she didn't think he had the guts to go ahead with his plan. She certainly wasn't rushing to the divorce courts but she thought he could at least have done all of this when he was at home and not miles away. She scribbled her signature and addressed the envelope, c/o his lawyer and slipped it into her handbag. She would post it tomorrow when she was shopping for her trip to Florida. Kerry didn't think Americans had much dress sense so there was really going to be no competition but she had to impress Richard.

Eddie was particularly cheerful this morning. Last night he had another night out with Val. He had the feeling she was about to ask him to stay overnight but she hadn't. He knew that she had considered it. He wasn't going to rush her because if there was any chance of getting her back, nothing was going to mess it up. He had plenty of time and he had another few cases to work on and that would keep him occupied.

The phone on the desk rang loudly. He had looked a couple of times for the volume control on the telephone but as he wasn't good with equipment he had given up. If it was there it was disguised as something else. The voice on the other end of the line was a blast from the past.
"How are you doing Eddie? Long time since we've spoken."

Eddie was caught off guard. The voice belonged to George Barrowman. They had worked in the same division at police headquarters and as Eddie had lost touch with most of his old soul mates, he was more than surprised to hear from George."
"Yes it's been a long time."
"Look the reason I'm calling, is to see if we could meet for an hour this morning?"
Eddie was even more surprised but agreed to meet him at a pub in the city centre in an hour. He replaced the phone and tried to finish off some paper work. But his lack of concentration made him get up and pull on his jacket. He would walk over to meet George. It was a nice enough morning and the exercise would do him good.

He reached the pub a good ten minutes before George and ordered a beer. He hadn't gone off drink completely, an occasional beer he could handle. He sat at a table in the corner and watched the door. He hadn't been in this pub for years, sober anyway, and he didn't remember it being this dingy. He remembered it looking a lot better through the bottom of a glass.

George hadn't changed except that he looked older. Must be the job thought Eddie. They all aged before their time.
"Good to see you Eddie. How long has it been?"

"At least three years but no one exactly tried to keep in touch so I don't know why you sound so surprised."

Eddie had always thought he had good friends on the force, but when he was at his lowest they all seemed to disappear into the woodwork.

"Eddie you didn't want to see anyone. Can't you remember? It was everybody else's fault you lost your job."

"Funny I don't remember it that way. But then there's almost a year I don't remember at all so maybe you're right."

They chatted for a while and Eddie caught up with the promotions and the gossip. George had always been good at his job and Eddie had no doubt he deserved his title of Inspector.

"What are you working on at the moment Eddie? Anything exciting?"

Eddie laughed. "You know I'm hardly likely to discuss my cases with you George so what prompted this little get- together. It wasn't for old time's sake. So what's on your mind?"

George had to watch what he was saying. He couldn't disclose any details of his own case.

"We're working on something at the moment and the lads keep bumping into you. Wherever we go you seem to be there too. We don't want anyone interfering and messing up what we've got so far."

Eddie hadn't seen any signs. Either they were getting better or he was getting worse.

"I'm not working on anything big enough to be of interest to you. Mine are mostly domestic matters. So where do I fit into this?"

"I need you to stay away from the container base in Bridge Street."

"Is that all. No problem. It isn't connected to what I'm working on anyway. I think one of my clients is trying to get a job there."

"Do you miss the job Eddie? Twenty years is a long time."

"I suppose I did in the beginning. But now there are other things in life. Trouble was it took me years to find that out."

"It doesn't get any easier. I've only five years left until I retire but I honestly don't know how I'll handle that. This job's been my whole life."

"I used to think that too, but you'll find something else. Maybe I'll need a partner by then."

George laughed. "I might take you up on that. I need to make a move Eddie we've a lot on at the moment. It's been nice seeing you again. Keep in touch."

"Sure George." Eddie stayed and finished his beer before driving over to James Campbell's place. Campbell had been to the container base on at least four separate occasions and Eddie's instincts had told him that he was up to something. The police had confirmed it and Eddie wanted to know what.

He waited almost an hour before Campbell appeared. He turned left out of the building away from the car park. It looked like the container base again because it was one of the few places he ever went on foot. Eddie held back at the last minute. He didn't want another visit from the police so he looked around for somewhere to wait for Campbell's return. He was never in longer than fifteen minutes and the bookshop was an ideal vantage point. The base was at the end of the street opposite and Eddie would have a clear view of Campbell coming back.

He waited for over half an hour and apart from the guy in the bookshop giving him peculiar looks nothing else was happening. Something wasn't right about this visit. He left the shop and hurried across the road and down the street in time to see Campbell drive off in a unit with a forty-foot trailer. Damn it. Eddie's car was back at the flat. He had lost him for the time being. He walked back to the car and drove to the office. He would take a run over to Campbell's tonight and check if he had come back. He didn't want to lose track of him just as things were beginning to liven up.

CHAPTER 12

The unit picked up speed as it moved along the slip road leading to the motorway. James Campbell was doing what he liked best, driving, on his own, with only the road in front of him. He enjoyed the weight and power of the vehicle. Something you didn't get from driving a car. His money had arrived without incident at the base and they had suggested if he kept in touch another job might come up. They had been right.

This load was on its way to Leith and he was promised another run next week. The money was more than he had ever earned before and he wasn't going to refuse it.

If it weren't for that stupid girl, things would be working out for him. When he got back from this run, he was sticking her on a train back to London. He had enough problems at the moment without her falling pregnant. She had only told him last night and she was very much mistaken if she thought her condition would make him stay with her. She was trying it on with the wrong man. That's how he'd got trapped before and it wasn't going to happen again. He was bored with her anyway.

The other fly in his ointment was Lisa Whitford. It seemed some woman was always ruining his life. She wasn't getting away with making him look a fool. He knew she hadn't simply gone off on holiday and they had been away three weeks now. No, she was making sure he didn't get near the kids. Not that he particularly wanted them, but no one was telling him he couldn't have them, not the social workers and certainly not Lisa Whitford. He would sort her out in his own time. First of all he had to get rid of Patty. She had been whining about going back to London for weeks so she could hardly complain if he put her on a train. He switched on the radio and put his foot down.

He had landed lucky with this outfit and what if he didn't know what he was carrying. It was only another container. In less than an hour he would be unloaded and heading back. He could get home by six at the latest and if he was lucky enough, maybe he could get her on a train tonight.

Eddie had returned to the South Side shortly after six and had only to wait forty minutes before Campbell appeared. It was after ten when he re-appeared carrying a suitcase. He slung the case onto the back seat and drove off with Eddie following some distance behind. Was he doing a disappearing act? Campbell parked his car outside Central Station and made his way inside. Eddie swore under his breath. Why was there never a parking space when you desperately needed one? He found a meter at last and ran all the way back to the station in time to see Campbell coming back out, but minus the suitcase. Eddie wondered what he was up to. If he was planning to get away, why the train? He had a car and where did he intend going?

Eddie followed him back to the flat and waited another few hours. He had convinced himself nothing else would be happening and was about to start up the engine when Campbell appeared again. This time he looked up and down the street before putting a second suitcase in the boot of the silver Peugeot and speeding off. Eddie should have given up at this point and concentrated his efforts on a case for which he was being paid, but something made him continue. The two cars sped along the motorway towards Greenock. Eddie had no idea where they were going in such a hurry. He was even more surprised when the car in front took the turn off for the Erskine Bridge, and the road north. It was rather late to be taking a scenic drive up by Loch Lomond but that was exactly the route Campbell was following. Almost an hour later, the Peugeot pulled into a hotel car park. He took the suitcase out of the back of the car and went inside. Eddie was thankful he had decided not to travel any further that night. These roads were difficult enough in daylight but trying to follow someone at night was virtually impossible. The numerous bends and blind spots made it easy to lose your prey if he turned off suddenly.

There was still something about tonight that was making Eddie uncomfortable. He couldn't work out why the first suitcase was presumably deposited in left luggage. If Campbell was running, where was his girlfriend? Something in Eddie's gut told him there was something wrong. He drove back to Glasgow a lot faster than he had left it and before long he was back outside the flat. All the lights were still burning although it was after two in the morning. Eddie's gut was still churning. He entered the apartment block. He had seen Campbell at his window on a previous stake out so he knew the flat was on the second floor and it faced the park. He made his way slowly upstairs. The whole building was deathly quiet. Well it would be wouldn't it, everyone was in bed. He had no idea what he was doing, but he kept going. On the second landing he studied the doors and by a process of elimination he worked out which flat was Campbell's. There was no sound from within. The poor girl had probably fallen asleep with the lights on. He was beginning to feel as if he was barking up the wrong tree when he heard a strange bump like something falling inside the flat. The second thud was a lot louder and Eddie couldn't mistake the sound of a body crashing to the floor. He knew a flat like this would have a supervisor but he had no idea where to find him. He raced back downstairs and checked the names at the door. There was nothing there to help him. He was about to try the building next door when he heard laughter from outside. Three people were coming in and thankfully Eddie met them in the hallway. They pointed out the caretaker's flat and Eddie wasted no time in rousing the man from his sleep. He was not happy at being roused in the early hours and even less happy with Eddie persistently telling him there was something wrong.

Michael had never worked so hard in his life. They were all up at six every morning and they didn't normally finish until it was time for dinner. The last few hours of the evening became a time for counting off the minutes until bedtime.

The refugee camp was growing in size and the supplies coming in weren't enough to cope with new additions every day. But there were now more people dying of disease than malnutrition. It was hard to watch the children growing weaker as time went on.

Another Red Cross team had arrived yesterday with the convoy and most of them had worked overnight in the makeshift clinic. Everyone helped where they could, but at times Michael wished he had some form of medical knowledge.

"There are two letters for you this morning Michael." Chris's voice had lost some of its earlier enthusiasm. "But I've forgotten to lift them. They're over at the supply station. Sorry about that."

"I've finished breakfast anyway, I'll walk over and pick them up before I start."

"There's another band of refugees in the north on the mountain road, about sixty kilometres from here. I'm thinking of taking a truck with some supplies and driving out to meet them. They'd have more chance of getting here with some food inside them. I wouldn't mind another pair of hands if you fancy making the journey with me.

Although I should mention the road north is worse than the road back to Makalle."

"If you give me some time to finish off with the Red Cross, I'll gladly come with you. How soon did you expect to be leaving?"

"Not much before midday. There's nothing loaded yet and first of all I have to go fight for a truck. How about you meet me back here at the canteen at twelve."

"Twelve's fine. Good luck with the truck."

Michael didn't have any doubts that Chris would acquire some form of transport and went off in search of his mail.

He collected the two letters. One was from Lisa and the other from his lawyer. He was tempted to open Lisa's letter straight away but instead he put both envelopes in his pocket for later and made his way over to the Red Cross station. He worked until late morning sorting and recording the medical supplies that had arrived with the convoy. He finished his lists and stored the medicines with just enough time to get back to the canteen to meet Chris. An hour later they were on their way.

They had anticipated that their journey would take two days or possibly more on the difficult terrain. The trucks were practical but not the most comfortable mode of transport and the bumpy road made for an unpleasant ride.

Michael reached into his pocket for his letters and opened the one from Lisa first. The letter was long but in parts very amusing. He glanced at the postcards of Skye and marvelled at how beautiful it was. He had never been there. She was having a lovely holiday and he was thankful that they were all well. It wouldn't be long until Christmas and he would be going home. It was only three months longer than he had intended staying when the summer started but he had made his mind up this time. He wanted home to Lisa.

He gazed out over the barren countryside and thought of home. It seemed as if he had been away years.

"Good news then. Not often you look like the cat that's got the cream."

"Yes, it's from Lisa. She's taken the kids on holiday to one of the islands. She's incredible Chris and I miss her so much. You'll have to meet her someday."

"Tell me about her. I could do with something to take my mind off this road. How did you meet her?"

Michael chatted on at length and it was apparent to Chris that his companion dearly loved the girl he had left at home.

"What on earth possessed you to come out here then? Shouldn't you be playing happy families?"

Michael recounted the trials and tribulations of Lisa's situation coupled with his divorce saga and then remembered he still had his other letter. He ripped open the bulky brown envelope. There was a letter from his lawyer and one from Kerry. He opened the first envelope; it simply said there was a letter enclosed from his wife and if there were any instructions to be followed, could he write by return. He couldn't make sense of Kerry's letter. He had no idea what she was accusing him of and he really didn't care. She was a vicious woman and he really had no interest in anything she had to say. He crumpled the letter and threw it out of the truck window where it lay with everything else in the desolate landscape.
"Well, that must have been really good news," said Chris. "And do you have any idea how litter messes up the countryside. I should make you go back and pick it up, but I think the possibility of stopping here would be a trifle difficult."
Michael Laughed. "Just another little note from the ex-wife and of no consequence." He folded Lisa's letter and put it back in his pocket. He reached into his bag and lifted out a notepad. It would be sensible to keep a log of their journey. He felt around behind the seat for his jacket. There should be a pen in the pocket. Besides the

pen, he pulled out the postcard he had been meaning to send to Lisa. 'Smiling Ethiopia'. He had been in Makalle twice and had forgotten to post it both times. He gazed again at the smiling face of the innocent child. He hadn't seen many faces like that since he had arrived. He put the postcard back into his pocket and began making notes.

"Would you like me to take over Chris? You've been driving for hours."

"Can't do much more tonight anyway. The light is beginning to fade and travelling any further I think would be dangerous. We'll have to look for somewhere to pull over, with enough space to camp safely. If we get to sleep early we can set off at dawn tomorrow, and if you want, you can take over the driving for a while."

It took them almost an hour to find a suitable place and after they had something to eat, they both got their heads down. Dawn would come around four in the morning.

After a very quick breakfast of bread and coffee, they set off again with Michael in the driving seat. The truck was really struggling on the climb. Most of the next hour it travelled in second gear. Michael was anxious to keep a steady pace, but he wasn't the expert Chris was on these roads. And it was tiring. His arms ached with the weight of the steering wheel and the constant need to keep your vision glued to the path made his eyes sore. Chris made this look easy. By the second evening there was still no trace of the refugees and again with light fading, they had to camp. They had left it later than last night to stop and their task was much more difficult. Eventually Chris told him to pull over.

"This should do, right here."

There was little room, and the tent had to be pitched right up against the rocks and wedged in against the side of the truck. Michael had no trouble falling asleep and was thankful that Chris would be driving the following day.

Halfway through their third day on the road, there was still no sign of their stray band of travellers.

"I reckon we should have bumped into them by now. We've travelled more than sixty kilometres now, and if they kept coming towards us, we should have met them by now." Chris's American drawl spun out the words as he gazed across the landscape. They had a short plateau to cross before their journey climbed again.

"We could have missed them on that last plateau. It's possible they decided against travelling to Korem. Though God knows where they're headed. I'm for turning back. What do you think?"

Courage and Clowns

Michel was hardly going to disagree with Chris's judgement. If Chris didn't think there was any point in going on, then turning back was the only option.

"We'll camp here and head back in the morning." Chris pulled the creaky machine to a halt.

There wasn't the same urgency to set off early the next morning, and it was after seven when they started their descent back to Korem. Michael had driven for the first part of the day, and he decided that coming down was much harder than going up. The wheels of the truck slipped constantly on the rough track, making the inward journey much more hazardous than the outward. It was late afternoon and Chris had taken over. They were chatting about the rest of the people they worked with and laughing at some of the misfortunes that had befallen them since they had arrived. Like Charlie, deciding he could survive on the rations that the refugees were getting, and vomiting violently for days after his attempt. Or the bad cases of diarrhoea that weren't funny, unless they were happening to someone else.

They were coming up to a particularly bad bend where the road veered sharply to the right, when the truck wheels slipped. Chris fought to correct the slide, but it was too late. The front wheels rolled off the track and the truck somersaulted over the edge, crashing against the rocks, before falling through the air for the last few hundred feet. As it hit the rocks at the base of the mountain, it came to rest. Moments later, it burst into flames. The charred remains soon melted into the background of scorched foliage.

"Could you hurry up and get the door opened?" Eddie was losing his patience with the caretaker.
"I have to be convinced that there is a good reason to open this door. I don't hear anything."
"If you don't open the door, I'll call the police."
The caretaker didn't particularly want the police all over the apartments. These were executive flats and the people paid plenty to live here. They didn't like disturbances. He opened the door.

The flat was in disarray. So many things had been tipped over; it would have been easier to say what hadn't been. Over by the window and half hidden by a chair, Eddie found the frail little body of Patty. Blood had been oozing from a gash in her head all over the biscuit coloured carpet. He knelt down beside her and realised she wasn't dead.
"She's still breathing. Call an Ambulance." He screamed at the caretaker.

Her face was swollen beyond recognition and congealed blood was set all over her hair. Her arms were badly bruised and so too were her bare legs. She wore nothing but a thin nightdress. And Campbell was getting away. Eddie grabbed the phone from the caretaker who was still mesmerised by what he was seeing. He remained motionless, with the receiver still in his hand after calling the ambulance. Eddie dialled the police number and asked for Barrowman.

"What's up Eddie, can't you sleep?"

"George, is James Campbell part of your investigation by any chance? He's a driver – took a container out of the base this afternoon. Is he connected in some way?"

"We're watching all the containers leaving the base. Name doesn't ring a bell, but we don't have any details on three drivers at the moment. They must have been clean up to now. What does he look like?"

Eddie described Campbell and suggested George might like to come over to the apartment. Barrowman recognised the description. They'd followed that driver to Leith today. Now he had a name.

"I'll be there in ten minutes. Stay put. Have you called this in yet?"

"Yes, about five minutes ago. We're waiting for an ambulance. The young girl's in quite a state."

"We'll be there as quickly as we can."
Eddie hung up. Moments later the sound of heavy footsteps announced the arrival of the ambulance and the uniformed police. The two officers took down what details Eddie could give them, and it wasn't much. He didn't even know her name. He should have done something the first time he had seen Campbell beat her, but then he couldn't have known how it would turn out.

The ambulance left and one of the young officers took the caretaker back to his flat. Eddie took the opportunity of following the other officer as he inspected the rest of the flat. They found nothing to identify Campbell's girlfriend. In fact they found nothing at all. All the drawers were empty. There were no clothes in the wardrobe. It was obvious Campbell had no intentions of returning - at least not to that address. He'd left the girl for dead.

George Barrowman arrived with two younger detectives.
"I've sent someone to the hospital. Do we have a name for her yet?"
"Nothing." Eddie watched as the two younger men re-searched the flat. They had the same result as Eddie.
"Right Eddie, how do you know this man Campbell?"

"I've no idea where he fits in with what you're doing George. But I was working on a custody case. His kids are in care and he wanted them back. I don't know anything else about him, except that I didn't trust him, and decided to keep an eye on him."

"I don't understand how he expected you to get his kids back." George said puzzled as he scribbled something in his notepad.

"No, he wanted me to come up with something on the girl who's looking after them. He's a nutcase. Complete waste of time."

"When did you see him last?" George continued as if he was interrogating a suspect.

"He's in a hotel at Loch Lomond. I followed him there a few hours ago. He's probably still there." Barrowman indicated that one of his detectives should follow up on that and Eddie passed on the details.

"I'm going over to the hospital now to see if the girl's regained consciousness." Barrowman prepared to leave.

"I'll come with you if you don't mind. I'd like to make sure she's all right."

They both left in separate cars and met up again in the hospital car park. As they were walking towards the entrance, Eddie remembered about the suitcase Campbell had left at the station.

"Well that could turn up something. I don't suppose you know exactly where he left it?"

"No, he went in with the suitcase and came out without it. Left Luggage was the only thing I could think of."

They were fairly near the ambulance entrance when the doors burst open, and two nurses came out followed by the detective who had been sent by Barrowman. On the trolley behind them, was Campbell's girlfriend.

"What's happening?" George asked his younger colleague. "Where are they taking her?"

"Neurological Unit at the General. They're concerned about her head injuries."

They both returned to their cars and followed the ambulance through town and out to the west. Over an hour later, they were still waiting in the rest area of the intensive care unit.

"She's not more than twenty, poor mite. I wonder how she came to be involved with Campbell." Eddie somehow felt responsible for her. If he had done something the first time, then maybe this wouldn't have happened.

"Do you know anything else about her Eddie, anything at all?"

"No, I only spoke to her once. She's English. Not southern, maybe midlands, I'm not really sure. That's all I know. Except that I did witness

Campbell taking a swipe at her before in the street, and leaving her there, outside the flat."

The door of the rest area opened and a middle aged doctor appeared. Both men rose from their seats like expectant fathers waiting for news.
"How is she?" George was first to speak.
The doctor's expression gave nothing away. "She's still unconscious but there's no brain damage. We're going to keep her in intensive care for the time being. Do you have a name for her yet?"
"No, I'm sorry we have no idea who she is. I'll arrange for one of my officers to stay with her. Thank you very much doctor."
The doctor left to return to his other duties and George and Eddie remained in the rest area. George put in a call to the station and arranged for someone to come over to the hospital.
"Can you describe the suitcase Campbell left at the station? I suppose that's our best bet at the moment."
"It was one of those tapestry ones. It was late and I couldn't see very well, but I'd say it was dark in colour. That's about it." Eddie ran his hands through his hair. He had been up since early this morning and he was beginning to need some sleep. He wasn't as young as he once was.
"Well, it's something at least. I'll go check it out. Are you staying here Eddie?"

"No, I'll go and get some sleep. I'll stop in tomorrow and see how she is. I'll speak to you later. Goodnight George."
"Goodnight Eddie."
Eddie sat for another ten minutes. Where was Campbell going? Maybe he wasn't going anywhere in particular. He could just be on the run.

Tired and hungry, Eddie went home and after making a quick sandwich, fell into bed. It was almost lunchtime when the sound of the telephone ringing, woke him.
"Eddie, it's George. We missed Campbell at the hotel. He left well before six this morning.
Any ideas where he might be headed?"
Eddie rubbed the sleep from his eyes.
"I've no idea. Did you come up with anything on the suitcase?"
"We've got that. But there were only some clothes and personal items, no identification, and I've been to the hospital and she's still unconscious. What about Campbell's kids? Where are they at the moment?"
"I'm not sure. In fact, they're away at the moment, and I don't know where. But you could find out something from the social work department. They came from Stancroft and live in Kilmains with a girl called Lisa Whitford."
"Thanks Eddie. Speak to you later."

Eddie was already out of bed now. He thought Lisa was safe, but if Campbell knew where she was, then maybe he had gone after her. He wasted no time in phoning his new contact at the social work department. He had no luck with her. He asked for a supervisor. He was put through to Judith Webster.

"How can I help you Mr Chadwick?"

"I know this is very irregular," started Eddie. "But I need to find Lisa Whitford."

"I'm very sorry Mr Chadwick, but we don't give out any information on our carers."

"Listen, she could be in danger. James Campbell's on the run from the police and I think he may go after Lisa. Now, he's headed north. If she's gone somewhere other than that, then you don't have to tell me. I'm a private investigator, not a mass murderer. I've already spoken to the police and I'm sure they'll be calling you next. But I've met Lisa and the kids and I want to help. You have to believe that. Now has she gone north?"

Judith was now worried. Although Lisa was in Skye, she didn't know where. She passed on this information to her caller. Somehow she had been impressed with his conviction to help and she felt she could trust him. She put down the phone and hoped beyond hope that she had done the right thing. She then called the inspector, as Mr

Chadwick had suggested, at police headquarters in Glasgow and told him what she had just told Eddie.

Eddie didn't waste any time. He quickly found the photographs of Lisa. He washed and packed a bag and before long he was heading back up the loch side, following the same route he had done the night before. He stopped at the hotel where Campbell had stayed, but like the police, he had come up with nothing. He then phoned the hospital, but there was still no news. If he kept going at this speed, he could make the seven o'clock ferry from Mallaig. He had no idea where to start, but if Lisa were still on the island, then he would find her. He only hoped that he would find her before Campbell.

The silver Peugeot slipped down the runway of the lunchtime ferry. It had been busy and Campbell didn't have a reservation. At the last minute there had been a cancellation. His first stop was at the tourist information office. He needed accommodation and that would be difficult because it was still the height of the season. But luck seemed to be with him. The girl showed him some details on a property at the north of the island. It wasn't very luxurious and it was out of the way, which was the reason it was harder to let. It was on the shores of Loch Dunvegan and it was very secluded. It was exactly what he needed.

He set off on his drive north. No one knew where he was going but it paid to be careful. The cottage was miles from anywhere. He had contemplated changing the car, but he should have done that in Glasgow before he left. Unfortunately he hadn't thought of it there.

If it hadn't been for that stupid girl expecting him to look after her, none of this would be happening. When he had told her she was going on a train back to London, she had gone crazy, saying he had a responsibility to look after her. Well, not him. He was responsible for no one, only himself. She had hit him with a lamp and he'd lost his temper. He hadn't meant to kill her, just teach her a lesson. No one told him what to do, especially not a slip of a girl.

He followed the road as far as Sconser and then turned off the main road towards Dunvegan. He reached the loch side and took out the directions the girl at the tourist office had given him. It didn't take long to find the cottage and get himself settled in. He had picked up some groceries at Broadford so there was no need to go out anywhere tonight. Tomorrow morning he would start. He made himself a meal and studied the map of the island. It was bigger than he had expected. He folded the map again and opened a can of beer.

George Barrowman didn't have much to go on. The social worker had been as helpful as she could be. But she had no idea where Lisa was staying on the island. The island police would be unable to cover the whole area, so it looked as if he would have to send some people. And then of course there was Eddie. What the hell was he doing? Unless he knew something George didn't. He needed Eddie on his side but he hadn't waited around long enough to be asked. Eddie had the advantage of knowing what she looked like. The island was going to be full of mothers and kids at this time of year. Slightly despondent, he called the local island police and said they would be arriving later that evening and arranged a meeting. He left a description of Lisa Whitford and the two kids.

The officer was very helpful. "If you like, we could check out some of the larger hotels and guest houses this afternoon?"

"That would be a great help, maybe someone will remember seeing her. We'll check with you when we arrive. And one more thing, can you arrange accommodation for two of us."

The young officer was more enthusiastic than George had expected.

"No problem. My own family has a guest house. I'll book them in there. Can I do anything else?"

George was impressed. He always thought that the police in places like this would be laid back because they couldn't have very much to do. Maybe he was wrong.

"No, nothing else at the moment. My officers will call in and let you know they've arrived and you can point them in the direction of the guest house. And thanks for all your help."

He then called in two of his colleagues. He gave them their instructions and the brief descriptions he had and sent them home to pack. He was unable to go himself because of the ongoing investigation. They were getting pretty close. They knew the goods came in at Dover, and then on to a warehouse in London. The Metropolitan police had traced the other base to Glasgow, and that's when he had become involved. The operation was massive; stolen antiques and works of art from the continent. They finally left the country again from Leith, and after that, he didn't know. But it was a big operation, and he didn't want any mistakes on his side of the border. Campbell seemed to be the only suspect who was going off the rails.

He telephoned the hospital again, but the girl was still unconscious. He called his wife and told her he would be late again. There was another shipment due in tonight and they had to record it and report back to the Met. He picked up his jacket and went off to the canteen to round up his troops.

CHAPTER 13

The little band of refugees, now only thirty in number, made their way around the outskirts of the camp at Korem. They had been walking for almost three weeks across the mountains with no food and very little water. Eventually noticed by an aid worker, they were led into the administration unit, where they would be registered.

Those in need of immediate first aid were taken over to the clinic. They were in a worse condition than the aid worker had seen in months. They had tried to survive out there on their own, but had eventually given up. There were some stragglers, still crossing the mountain path and it could be weeks before they arrived.

Charlie was assisting in the administration section today, and Kabay, as usual, was on hand to interpret. The interpreters were always kept busy and Kabay in particular was always in demand. The long process of translating began in an effort to establish the original size of each group and their origins.

"Kabay, can you ask them if they saw the truck?" Charlie had been expecting Chris and Michael to return for almost a week.

"Charlie, can that wait? These people are in need of food and sleep. Now can we get on with this please?" The administration supervisor had only limited time to gather the required information before this group got lost in the sea of waiting people already in the camp. They were trying to keep the records as up to date as was humanly possible under the circumstances. But Charlie was persistent.

"Kabay, please ask if they saw the truck. They've travelled the same road. Maybe it broke down. They might know something."

Kabay dutifully translated, but with difficulty. He was far from fluent in their dialect, but eventually he managed to make them understand. He turned to Charlie.

"This man is most definite that he passed no one, and he has not seen a vehicle in over three weeks."

Charlie knew now that something was far wrong. Chris wouldn't stay out there if he thought he had missed the party somewhere. He would have come back by now, and if need be, gone back out to search a different route. But if the truck had broken down and this party had found another way down, then Chris and

Michael could be stranded. They could be waiting for some help to arrive, or maybe expecting the group to have passed by and brought a message to the camp. He could do nothing until his duties were finished. They were short-handed enough without him rushing off and leaving them to attend to this lot.

It was almost an hour later when he made his way back to the canteen. He found Gerard having coffee with some of the Red Cross personnel. His agitated arrival left them in no doubt that something was amiss.

"God Charlie, what's wrong? Here have some coffee." Gerard poured the hot black coffee, but Charlie made no attempt to drink it.

"There's a group just arrived from the north. They've come on the mountain path, and they haven't seen any sign of the truck or of Chris and Michael. It's time to do something."

Gerard's expression changed. They had been discussing for two days, the lateness of the truck's return. But they had all been hoping that each day it would arrive, and this recent news wasn't good.

It was possible they had taken a different route, but he had to agree with everyone else that Chris wouldn't stay away from the camp this long without checking whether the refugees had maybe arrived.

"Let's go find the rest of our team. We can make a start today. We've plenty of light left and it shouldn't take long to get organised." Gerard knew he would have no trouble in getting support for the search.

It wasn't support that was the problem. There was no transport today. The Red Cross had sent two trucks to Makalle yesterday for supplies, and they wouldn't be back until tomorrow. Chris and Michael already had one of the spare trucks and the rest of the transport was tied up until later in the day. Many had volunteered to join the search party but the feasibility of this was soon knocked on the head. It was finally decided that, first thing tomorrow the party would consist of Gerard, two members of the Red Cross, should medical attention be required, and one volunteer from Chris's own agency. The only addition to this would be supplies and first aid equipment. The fewer people they carried would make the going much easier, and only one vehicle could be spared.

The news had spread like wildfire and the atmosphere in the canteen during the evening was far from optimistic. They hadn't, until now, had any casualties amongst the workers since they had come to Korem and they hoped that they wouldn't have any now. But it was difficult to believe that all was well.

Later that same evening, Gerard and Charlie stood outside gazing towards the mountains. There was a definite chill in the night air, but neither seemed to notice.

"Where do you think they are?" Gerard broke the silence.

"I wish I knew," Charlie answered. "I also wish I was going with you, but I suppose the make-up of the party is vital. Depending on what you find out there."

"Let's hope some of the personnel won't be needed. But either they've broken down and don't want to leave the truck fully laden, or perhaps one of them is injured and can't be left. But then if that was the case, they could simply have driven back. There were other scenarios he didn't want to contemplate."

He looked out over the now darkening sky and sought in its depth, the answers to his questions.

By five the following morning, they were almost loaded.

"Right, we're all agreed. Three days out and three days back, and if need be, we go back out again. Now we have to be clear on this, there's already one truck and two passengers missing." Gerard was adopting the position of leader of the group. Everyone nodded his agreement.

They gathered for coffee before leaving the camp a few minutes before six.

For the first few hours of the journey there was very little conversation. The driver, Matthew, had suggested that the first day they should put as many miles behind them as possible. His theory being that if Chris and Michael had gone off the track somewhere searching for the refugees, then the first day wouldn't have brought either of the parties close enough together. It seemed the most reasonable assumption.

By the afternoon they had relaxed more and the reason for the journey wasn't a subject of conversation. Unknown to them they had chosen exactly the same spot to camp, where days before, Chris and Michael had done the same. Unfortunately for the second party, the first had left no trace of their encampment.

Gerard had insisted he was part of the search party. He felt responsible for Michael and apart from that, he liked him. He was hoping that when this was all over he could have convinced him to move south, where Gerard had no doubts that he could get a position with the network.

But he had to find him first. They all turned in early, not because they were particularly tired, but they needed an early start in the morning. It would be the second day, in the six they had allowed themselves. Like Gerard, none of them slept well.

Courage and Clowns

On the second day, they travelled a little more slowly, looking for tracks going off the main route and searching out the few that they found. They reached the first plateau and spent the whole morning, and part of the afternoon searching. They found nothing.

Matthew had really thought that by the second night they would have found them, unless they had gone over the side. A thought he was trying to keep to himself.

The third day they reached the second plateau and again, their search was fruitless. Neither Gerard nor Matthew believed that Chris would have come any further. He had said originally that he would be away four days. Six would have been his limit. After tonight, they would have to commence their return journey. On the way back they would again search each day in the hope that something had been missed the first time.

The entire journey back, they stopped and checked possible locations where the truck might have gone over, but still they found no trace. By the end of the sixth day, they were skirting the camp at Korem.

Gerard knew that it would be his responsibility to report back to London with the news that Michael Bradshaw was missing and must be presumed dead. He would travel to

Makalle tomorrow, but tonight, sad and disheartened, he tried to sleep.

The following morning there was a large gathering in the canteen. It seemed that everyone was up and about, whether they were on duty or not. Another search party would be assembled, and this time, they would be equipped for a longer spell in the hostile terrain. There was no doubt in anyone's mind, that if they were still alive, they were ill-equipped to survive in the vast wilderness plateaux that couldn't even afford life to its own people.

One hour after the search party left, Gerard and Charlie took a land rover, and headed into Makalle.

The natural hubbub of loud voices and laughter soon ceased as the news spread around the press building. Uncommonly, any amounts of lines were now available out of the country. Gerard lit the cigarette he was offered and accepted the glass of whisky, both of which he didn't normally touch, but today he felt the need. He called his producer in London and again, he could hear the voices stilled as the news was repeated back to him, in the event that perhaps they had misheard. He spoke for only another few minutes before hanging up.

He looked around for the procurer of the whisky and allowed his glass to be refilled. By dinner time, he was unusually sozzled, but at least he would be able to sleep.

The following morning they made their way back to Korem. Gerard's head was pounding and he felt a sudden urge to vomit, and motioned Charlie to stop. Kneeling at the side of the road, he didn't know whether the feeling in the pit of his stomach was too much whisky, not enough food, or the deaths of Chris and Michael. Whatever it was, he knew that whatever time he had left here, wouldn't be quite the same.

Two weeks passed, and everyone scanned the horizon every day for the return of the second search party. On the sixteenth day an excited shout brought everyone to the edge of the camp. They were in sight. Fifteen minutes later they entered the camp. All of their worst fears had been realised. The truck had indeed gone over the side, and there was very little left of either the vehicle or its occupants. They had what they thought were the remains of one body, but well beyond recognition and they had collected some articles that had been thrown into the brushland as the truck broke up on its way down. It was an arduous process assembling the personal items and trying to decide what had belonged to each of their colleagues. Inside a jacket pocket, Charlie found the postcard, addressed to Lisa and he handed both to Gerard. He would take these to her personally. The items were boxed and tagged and left with administration, and arrangements made to send the human remains to Addis Ababa, where hopefully they could be identified.

Gerard left the confines of the administration block and went in search of Charlie. At the last minute, he changed his mind and went for a long walk. He couldn't believe they were both gone. He had thought they would find them and everything would have gone back to normal. He had watched as people died out here every day, but it wasn't the same. He hated thinking that way, but it was true. These people weren't his colleagues. He didn't know anything about them. Michael and Chris had been different and they didn't deserve to die not when they were only trying to help. He knew he'd had enough and he wanted to go home. He wanted Michael to be going home with him, but that wouldn't happen now.

They held a short service at daybreak, out of respect for their colleagues, and there was a stillness and a silence around the whole camp for the rest of the day.

"Chris's parents are flying in today." Charlie volunteered his information to anyone who might me listening. Some of them already knew and no one was looking forward to having to face them. It was hoped that within a few days they would have some results on the body. Presumably if it were Chris, they would want to take him home to be buried.

The official police land rover arrived two days later and everyone waited anxiously for the results of the tests. Gerard was present in the office, he had insisted. He needed to know. The police officer read out a long-winded report on what they had found, and then summarised.

"Unfortunately the skull was crushed and we have been unable to positively identify it as either victim. I'm very sorry."

After he had gone, Matthew was the first to speak.

"Irrespective of who it is, I think that a burial should take place, here in Africa. Does anyone have any objections?" His question was directed towards Chris's parents.

His father spoke. "We had already decided that we would like Chris to be buried here. This is where he wanted to be. So we certainly have no objections as long as it's a proper Christian burial."

His wife continued sobbing quietly as he passed on their thoughts.

It was agreed that the body should be returned to Makalle and buried there. Matthew would see to the necessary paperwork and the transportation. The funeral was held two days later. A very sombre procession returned to Korem later that day. They had to survive their last few months at the camp as best they could, before another news team arrived, full of enthusiasm, just as they had been.

Josh Ridley put down the receiver and continued to stare at the phone. Michael was dead. He'd just received a call from the International News office in London. What the hell had gone wrong? He had been there simply to report on the famine, and somehow he was dead. He pressed the intercom on his desk and asked his secretary to come through. He gave her a list of station personnel and asked her to arrange a meeting in fifteen minutes. He picked up the phone again and dialled Lisa's number. What was he going to tell her? He listened to her voice on the answering machine. He left a message for her to get in touch with him urgently. He then called Michael's lawyer and asked him in turn to contact Kerry.

The meeting went ahead as planned fifteen minutes later, and a statement prepared.
"I don't want any of this released until I say so. Do you all understand? I don't even want it

discussed in the station. I don't want it on air until I'm ready. Meeting's over."

The members of the newsroom dispersed, numbed by the shocking news.

Josh didn't think he could have continued any longer anyway. He could feel the lump in his throat. He and Michael had been friends for a long time and he found it hard to believe that he was really gone. He then called his wife and left it up to her to call their close friends. He waited all day for Lisa to return his call, and when she didn't, he continued trying her number from home during the evening. By the following morning there was still no word. He waited all day. When he had still heard nothing by five that evening, he authorised the release of the statement on the six o'clock news. His heart went out to Lisa, whom he hardly knew but the last thing he would have wished was that she should find out this way.

Lisa was surprised to find two strangers sitting having tea with Grace and Jane when she returned from her walk with the children. One look at Jane's pained expression and she knew something was wrong. When Jane suggested the children take the dog out into the garden, her suspicions were confirmed. Grace was first to her feet.

"Come along and I'll get you both a biscuit and a drink. No, Jane you stay with Lisa. Right you two let's see what we have in the kitchen."

Grace left the room with the dog and the children following at her heels. Lisa could hear Jamie's excited chatter as he recounted their walk.

"What's wrong?"

Jane was at her side. "Lisa I think you should sit down."

She did as instructed and the first of the two strangers spoke.

"I'm Detective Sergeant Vickers, and this is Detective Constable McLean, of Strathclyde Police. We have reason to believe that James Campbell's on the island. As yet we haven't been able to confirm it, but it looks as if he's looking for you."

"We came here to get away from him. What makes you think he came here?"

"He's wanted by the police in Glasgow and he's on the run. The last report we had is that he was heading north and the most likely destination is here. Miss Whitford, it didn't take long for us to find you. The only trouble we have with him is that he's in hiding so few people will see him. But that doesn't mean he won't find you. I have to advise you that he is dangerous."

"I've no illusions about James Campbell. I've already had one run in with him and I don't relish the thought of another. What exactly are you going to do?"

"We'll continue making enquiries and with the help of the local police, we'll find him."

Grace interrupted the conversation by appearing with another tray of tea, which her new guests were only too eager to enjoy. There was also a selection of her home baking.

"There now, help yourself lads, there's plenty more in the kitchen." Grace fussed around and made sure everyone was sampling her scones and cakes.

"Come on Lisa, have something. It won't do to not eat." She insisted.

"I think I've temporarily lost my appetite. Anyway I'll just go and check on the kids. It might be safer to bring them indoors." Lisa got to her feet. Now that their holiday was completely ruined, maybe it was time to go back home. She didn't know where they would be safer.

One of the officers followed her outside.

"Miss Whitford, I know how difficult this is but best thing is to try not to alarm the children. By the looks of things they always have the dog with them. If anyone got into the garden the dog would let us know. Now why don't I stay with them for a little while and you go back and sit down."

Lisa was more than happy to accept his proposal and returned to the sitting room. This time she accepted some tea and cake.

"Are you at liberty to tell me why the police are looking for Campbell, or is that top secret, Sergeant Vickers?"

"I can't say what we're working on at the moment. But Campbell was living with a young girl and she's been found badly beaten. She's unconscious and is still in intensive care, so we haven't been able to confirm that Campbell was responsible. I'm only telling you this so that if you see him, you don't confront him. I think it might be best if you and the kids stay close to the house for the next few days. Stay away from the town and any tourist attractions. Those are the most likely places for him to be looking for you."

"Thankfully, we've done most of our sightseeing, and I don't think the kids would notice anything untoward if we stayed around the cottage for a few days. The only problem would be walking the dog. He's used to being out two or three times a day."

Jane was quick to offer her assistance. James Campbell didn't know her, so she would be safe, and the chances of him being around the hills at the back of house were pretty remote. She assured the young policeman they would be able to cope.

"I'm sure you will, you just need to take a little extra care."

Lisa was wondering whether maybe they should consider going home.

"We've put you to so much trouble Grace, and now this. I am sorry, perhaps we should go."

Both Grace and Jane immediately shot down Lisa's suggestion. They were much safer if they remained here. At least for the moment he didn't know where they were.

"Now, not another word." Grace commanded. "I'll get my son and son-in-law to call round every day and maybe if Campbell does find out you're here, the sight of two men about the place, might make him think twice about starting any trouble."

The young officer had to agree. They were safer where they were, and he was sure that Campbell would be apprehended within the next few days. There were enough people searching for him. After that, they could continue their holiday undisturbed.

"Now here's the number of the guest house we're staying in, and the number of the local police. If you need us at any time, please call." Detective Sergeant Vickers rose to leave as the children returned with his colleague.

Lisa accepted the little piece of paper with the telephone numbers and thanked him. The detectives took their leave.

Left alone, the three companions talked over what they had just heard.

"Imagine him beating up some young girl." Grace was horrified at the thought of any such man being around Lisa and the children. "I'll telephone my son and ask him to call in tonight. I'd rest a bit easier if I knew he was going to be about." And off she went to make her call. Jane disappeared upstairs with Jamie and Becky to get them washed, ready for dinner, leaving Lisa alone with her thoughts. Although she had known that her fight with Campbell over the children wouldn't be pleasant, she had never really thought that they were in danger. When she heard Grace banging pots about in the kitchen, she went through to help with dinner. It would at least keep her mind occupied. When they eventually sat down to their meal the tension had lifted slightly and, with the children's constant chatter, it was hard to tell that they were in the throws of a trauma.

After dinner Grace's son Robert appeared, visibly agitated at what he was hearing. He didn't want his mother's life in danger, nor that of her guests. He suggested that perhaps he should stay over for a few days.

"Nonsense Robert, we'll be fine. Those two police detectives will be calling in and so will the local police. In fact there will be way too many people as it is. If you wouldn't mind, you could call in after dinner each evening, that would be enough."

His mother wasn't the sort to worry. She certainly didn't appear as if this recent development was getting her down. If truth be told, Robert actually thought she looked quite excited. He stayed for over an hour and satisfied himself that the house was securely locked for the evening, before returning home.

Lisa had tried to watch television for a little while, but found that she couldn't concentrate. She eventually picked up one of the books she had chosen earlier, and was soon engrossed. When it was time for the children to go to bed, she took them upstairs herself, armed with another book she had found in the bookcase. It was about Dunvegan Castle, and the myths and legends surrounding it. She read some of it to the kids as a bedtime story and Becky was enthralled to learn the castle had fairies..

"Can we go back to the castle again, now that we've heard the story?" She asked innocently.

"Maybe in a few days time, because I thought we could stay here for the next couple of days and keep Grace company, instead of leaving her everyday when we go exploring. What do you think of that?"

Jamie didn't seem the least bit put out about staying around the cottage.

"Maybe we could help her with her garden because it's awfully big. I could pick some weeds and help keep it tidy. Do you think she'd like that?"

"I'm sure she would appreciate your help very much Jamie. And what would you like to do to help Becky?"

Becky's voice was sleepy as she said;

"I'll help her with baking. I like her baking and I like the smell when things are in the oven."

With that, the little eyes closed and she was fast asleep.

"Trust Becky to want to help with the food. She's eaten so many cakes here she'll be fat when we go home."

Jamie's comment was meant more as a joke than a criticism. He hadn't done too badly himself at eating cakes and scones. And he was very partial to the jam tarts. Before he fell asleep, he was thinking that helping in the kitchen wasn't a bad idea.

Lisa made her way back downstairs to discover that the television had been switched off and Grace was again making tea.

"How do you fancy a game of cards Lisa?"

Courage and Clowns

Jane was rummaging around in a drawer until she eventually found a pack.

"I don't play very often, but I could manage a game of rummy."

"Gosh and here's me thinking you were a poker hand; just goes to show you, appearances are deceptive. Rummy, I can understand, so that will do nicely."

They were both laughing when Grace returned with the tea. They spent an enjoyable two hours playing, with Jane winning every hand.

"I got the impression you weren't very good," rebuked Lisa to her elderly friend.

"I lied. My husband and I used to play for hours on end. I didn't win very often against him, but it was the trying to that gave me most enjoyment."

"Well I'm glad you didn't suggest playing for money. I'd have been broke early on."

At last it was time for bed. All three checked the windows and doors again, and when they were satisfied with the security, they went upstairs. Lisa checked on the children, before settling herself with a book.

The following day passed much the same. The children were taking their roles seriously. Every time Grace moved to do something, they moved with her. Jamie, true to his word, had weeded some flowerbeds and Grace was impressed with how well he had done. Becky had made some cakes of her own, and everyone had to sample them with tea in the afternoon. Apart from the sponge being slightly soft, they were very good for a first attempt.

Jamie had again surprised everyone by offering to read a story while they were all sitting out in the garden.

"That would be lovely," said Jane. "What are you going to read to us?"

"It's a story I've written myself and you're all in it."

He raced inside to get his story and with everyone settled, he began. There wasn't a sound as Jamie read page after page of his story about coming to an enchanted island, where fairies lived and protected the children so that they came to no harm. As his story progressed, Lisa recognised parts of the legends she had read to him and she was startled by the way he had wound them into his story. His fairytale ended by the evil king being spirited away by fairies, and the children living happily ever after. They all applauded in earnest. The story was very good and Lisa couldn't remember him ever writing anything before, although he did love reading.

"Jamie, that was excellent. How long did it take you to write?" She asked.

"Quite a long time. Did you really like it?"

"Like it, I thought it was wonderful. You're very clever."

No one had ever told him he was clever before and he was very pleased with himself.

The two detectives arrived later in the afternoon to check that everything was in order and again stayed for tea. The younger one spent most of his time kicking a ball around with the kids and the dog.

"One of the local officers has volunteered to give up his afternoon off, tomorrow, and if you need to go into town for anything, he'll gladly go with you."

Lisa was quite touched that someone was prepared to do that. Two local shops had already delivered their papers and milk this morning. News travelled quickly around the small community and people wanted to help where possible.

"Why don't you both stay for dinner?" Grace said on the spur of the moment. "We have more than enough to go around and I'm sure Lisa would enjoy some young company. Or maybe you have something more pressing to do?"

John Vickers was more than delighted to be asked to stay.

"We'd love to. If you're sure it's no trouble. Now, would you mind if I called the guest house and let them know, just in case they prepare something for us."

"Not at all. I think we could all go inside now and I think we might be able to find you a drink of some sort. Are you allowed to drink, or are you still on duty?"

"We aren't officially off duty at all while we're here, but I think we could manage one anyway."

Grace liked the young detective. He was very pleasant and rather good looking.

Lisa was pleased that they had decided to stay. It would be nice to have some different conversation, although both of her companions were excellent company in their own right. The younger man, Phil, was very taken with the children. He was already playing a board game with them through in the dining room. Lisa, Jane and John Vickers were enjoying a drink. Jane poured another sherry.

"I'll take this through to Grace and give her a hand with dinner." She left the younger couple to enjoy their conversation.

"How long have you been fostering? You don't look like a foster mum."

John's observations brought a burst of laughter from Lisa.

"That's the first time I've seen you laugh. I know you don't have much to laugh about at the moment. But it's good if you can still do it."

"This is my first time fostering. Up until now I've only worked on voluntary projects, and that led to this. And what exactly should I look like?"

"I'm sorry but you know what I mean. You look more like a career girl. Do you work as well, or is your time spent looking after those two?"

"No, I work as well. I own a shop, although I haven't seen it for weeks. Jane looks after the kids until I get home. In fact she's much more than that. She's become part of the family. She and Grace are sisters; that's how we ended up here. How about you, do you have any children?"

"No, I'm not married. This job doesn't give you much time for a social life."

Lisa poured him another drink.

"I see you're engaged," he continued. "Where is your fiancé at the moment?"

"He's out of the country and the engagement's supposed to be a secret, so I'd appreciate if you didn't mention it in front of the kids. The ring doesn't mean anything to them. I wanted to have custody of them before anyone finds out. It would make things a lot easier and believe me there are enough complications."

John Vickers was easy to talk to, and Lisa felt as if she had known him more than a few days. Before long Phil and the kids were thrown out of the dining room and came through to join them.

Dinner was a great success. The atmosphere was much happier than it had been the previous evening and when Robert arrived to check on everyone, he was taken aback by the hilarity. Grace introduced him to the two detectives and after staying only twenty minutes or so, he decided they were safe enough and went home. Everyone had enjoyed their evening, and when it was time for the visitors to leave they were all just a little disappointed. Lisa finally got the children settled and went to soak in a hot bath before falling into bed. She had hoped she would have heard from Michael by now. It had been weeks since she had written. There hadn't been any new reports on television, so she had no idea where he was now. She missed him so much. In Michael, she had found that there was something very special in having someone to share things with, even if they weren't together at the moment. Some day soon, they would be. With that thought, she fell asleep.

The following day, she decided she was going out with the kids. It wasn't fair ruining any more of their holiday. Jane was very concerned about her decision.

"Maybe this is the best way. If he sees us, and the police are doing their job, they'll catch him."

"At least phone the police and say what you're doing." Jane suggested.

Lisa eventually phoned and left a message to say that she was taking the children to Dunvegan.

They set off in high spirits. Jane had decided to come with them and Grace had packed a picnic. It was great to be out again. The weather was beautiful and the scenery superb.

"I'd feel much more comfortable if our friends were here too."

Jane had purposely not mentioned the word police, because the children still didn't know exactly who John and Phil were.

"Maybe they'll stay in the background and use us as bait."

Jane's horrified expression soon changed when she realised Lisa was pulling her leg. She certainly hoped they weren't going to be used as bait.

They parked in the main car park and wandered around the grounds before going back to have another look at the castle. Becky had a million and one questions about the fairies. They eventually came back outside and searched for somewhere to have their picnic. It was more like a three-course dinner. There was melon, roast chicken, salad, trifle and hot and cold drinks. And for Freebie, there were corned beef sandwiches and dog biscuits. They had a wonderful day. Jamie had taught Freebie a new trick. As he held a piece of the sandwich in his hand he asked Freebie for a high five. The little dog raised himself up and hit his paw on Jamie's hand. Becky thought this was hysterical. Everyone thought it was pretty damn smart for a little dog.

While they had been enjoying their day out, they were unaware that they had passed James Campbell on the road. He had spotted them. He doubled back and followed them to the castle. Eddie Chadwick was following him. The only people missing on the day out were the police.

They were packing up to leave when Becky screamed. Turning round, Lisa saw him running towards them. She lifted Becky and called for Jane to get Jamie. They picked up the bags, but before they could get to the car, he was there.

"So you thought you were smart. Thought you could disappear." He screamed at Lisa.

Her heart was pounding. Coming out was obviously not a good idea. She wished the police were here. Her voice was shaking as she spoke.

"Why don't you leave us alone? The police are looking for you. So if you're smart you'll get out of here."

She tried to push by him, but he pulled at her arm, almost causing her to drop Becky, who was still screaming.

"You're frightening the children, you idiot. Let go of me."

Lisa tried to break free of him. She wasn't watching his other hand. His clenched fist swung round and hit her fully in the face. The force of the punch knocked her to the ground and she could hear Jane cry out for someone to help them. Jamie had also started screaming.
"Leave her alone." The child lashed out at his father, only to be knocked to the ground by a blow to his head. And then, Lisa saw Campbell struggle. As she got to her feet, she realised that someone had come to their aid. He had a heavier build than Campbell and was getting the better of him. The thudding sound of the punches was making Lisa feel sick.

She grabbed Becky and Jamie and shouted to Jane to get back to the car. Once they were all safely inside, they locked all the doors. Jane had gone into the back of the car with the kids and was trying to calm them down. Jamie's face was bruised and tomorrow there was a good chance he would have a black eye.

She looked across the car park to see that another two men had appeared and the fight had stopped. Campbell was being dragged over towards the castle, still struggling with his captors. The man who was walking towards the car looked familiar. He reached the car and Lisa rolled down the window barely enough to hear him.

"The castle staff are calling the police. If you follow this road through the courtyard, they'll let you wait inside until they arrive. And we'll find someone to see to your cuts and bruises."

He walked away in the direction he had indicated to Lisa. She couldn't remember where she had seen him before. She turned the car and headed back to the castle, parking at the back through the courtyard. The kids were hesitant about getting back out of the car, but Lisa assured them the police were coming and everything was going to be all right. Once inside the vast kitchen, a kindly housekeeper prepared some tea and arranged for someone to call a doctor. Only then did Lisa realise that she had blood trickling down her face. Her eye hurt, and so did her cheek. Her nose was bleeding and it hurt when she tried to wipe some of the blood away. Becky's screams had now turned to sobbing. Jane was shaking and was grateful when someone handed her a cup of tea. It was very sweet, but she gulped it down and accepted another.

It didn't seem that long before John and Phil arrived, along with a local constable and a police doctor. A photographer had been called as well. John was very quickly at her side and Phil had lifted Becky from her lap and was comforting her at the other side of the table.

Courage and Clowns

"We were on our way here, when the local lad caught up with us and told us what had happened. Campbell's safely locked away now, so he can't cause you any more trouble. Now, let's get you both examined by the doctor and unfortunately we need some photographs of your injuries, which will all help when Campbell's charged. Sorry about all of this but it is necessary."

The doctor was elderly and very kind and as he attended Jamie. Lisa could hear him saying what a brave lad he had been.

Her face ached and as the doctor dabbed at her wounds, she flinched. He smiled a kind of fatherly smile at her.

"You're going to look a handsome pair in the morning. I should think you'll both have black eyes."

The thought of having a black eye seemed to appeal to Jamie.

Everyone was beginning to calm down and with the doctor and the photographer gone, they accepted another cup of tea from the housekeeper.

The door of the kitchen opened again and this time she did recognise him. He was the man with the chocolate milk-shake shoes.

"Mr Chadwick, I'm sorry I didn't realise it was you. How on earth did you come to be here?"

"Well, it's a long story. But if you offer me a cup of your tea, I'll tell you."

Lisa poured another cup from the pot and handed Eddie his drink. He rambled through his story.

"So the day we met you in the shopping mall, wasn't an accident. Campbell's been following us all that time."

Lisa realised the implications of this and shuddered at the thought of the times she had been wandering around on her own, or even the times the kids had been out.

Campbell could have made his move any time and any place.

"So really, we've had our own private detective on the case all this time. Well I never."

It was the first words Jane had spoken since the ordeal began.

John took charge from then on.

"Let's get you lot home." He turned to Becky. "And you can tell Grace all the excitement she's missed today."

Jamie looked at his new friends. "Are you real policeman?"

"We're real detectives Jamie, like you see on television."

Well now, thought Jamie. Imagine him having two friends who were detectives. Wait until he told his friends at school.

Courage and Clowns

Finally everyone was bundled back into the car. John leaned over and spoke to Lisa through the driver's window.
"We'll get Campbell back to the local station and get him charged, and then we'll call in and see that you're okay. We'll have to leave on this evening's ferry and get him back to the mainland. Now I suggest you all go home and get hot baths and some of Grace's home baking. You'll be right as rain in no time."
Lisa wound up the window and the car tyres crunched on the gravel as it made its way down the drive.

John had phoned Grace and prepared her for their arrival. But when she saw them, they were much worse than she had expected.

She had made sure there was plenty of hot water and left Jane and Lisa sitting in the lounge in front of a roaring fire. It was the middle of summer but they were both cold and shivering. The smell of the peat fire was both warming and soothing.

Grace brought the kids back down, dressed in their pyjamas and dressing gowns. They were just bathed and looked a lot happier. Poor Jamie's face was a mess.
"I hear you were very brave today Jamie." Grace said as she handed the youngster a hot drink and a scone.

"Will my dad go to prison now Lisa, for a long time?"

"Yes Jamie, I expect he will."

"That means that we can stay with you, can't we? They can't take us away now."

"No Jamie they can't. No one's ever going to take you away."

The little boy ran into her arms and held on like he never wanted to let go. Lisa kissed the top of his curly head. She could feel the tears coming. The relief of knowing that Campbell couldn't get the children hadn't really occurred to her until now. They were all safe and still together.

They sat down for an hour before Grace left the room to go and start dinner. Jamie and Becky offered their help. Jane switched on the television.

"Let's see what's on, it might take our minds off things."

The six o'clock news was just starting. When Lisa looked up, Michael's face was on the screen and she only vaguely heard the voice say…missing presumed dead – before the floor rose up to meet her.

CHAPTER 14

When Lisa came to, everything was quiet. She couldn't quite remember what had happened or where she was. She tried to sit up but fell back against the pillow. Why did her head ache so much?

"Now you lie there and keep still. You've had a terrible shock and the doctor's on his way."

She heard the sound of voices and the tiny prick of the injection. She could hear Jane talking to someone. There had been James Campbell, and then she remembered Michael. Michael was dead. She remembered the news item before the drug took its effect and she drifted off into a deep sleep.

When she woke again, Jane was still by her side.

"I've brought you up some tea. Let's see if you can sit up and drink it."

Her head still ached as she sat up and allowed Jane to prop up her pillows. She took a sip of the tea. Her face was badly swollen and her lips felt

as if they were twice their normal size. With difficulty, she managed to drink the tea. Her mind was fuzzy, but she could remember James Campbell, and the fight. She remembered the man with the chocolate milk-shake shoes and the kitchen of the castle. It was all coming back. And Michael...
"Jane help me up. I have to phone someone."
"Not at the moment young lady. The doctor recommended a day in bed, and that's exactly what you're going to do. Now lie back and I'll get you another drink."
"No, I have to find out about Michael."
Jane had anticipated this and had collected the morning papers.
"I've picked up the papers, shall I get them for you."
It was already the following morning. What had happened to last night?
"Yes, I must see them."
Jane returned a few minutes later and lifting the tea tray, she left Lisa alone to read the front page story.

Lisa folded the paper and let it fall to the floor. Michael couldn't be dead. He was coming home for Christmas. That was only a few months away. She lifted her hand to her face and traced the swelling. She reached for a hand mirror. She looked at the swollen, bruised mess that yesterday had been her face, and reached for the painkillers that Jane had left on the bedside table.

She picked up the paper again and looked at the picture of Michael. He was smiling and she could imagine his blue eyes, staring out of the paper at her. She felt the tears start and soon her body was shaking in violent, tearful spasms. The rest of the day she slept, she sobbed and she took painkillers. She remembered Jane being in and out of the room. She slept fitfully through the night.

The following morning the sun was streaming in through the bedroom window. She had to get up and see the children. She glanced at her face in the dressing table mirror. It was still as swollen as it had been the day before. The bruising was darker and more noticeable. Her nose and her eyes still hurt.

As she was pulling on some clothes, she saw the bruising on her arms and legs. No wonder she was aching all over, she must have fallen a lot harder than she'd realised. Slowly she made her way downstairs. Grace met her at the bottom.

"Are you sure you should be up Lisa. Maybe I should give the doctor another call?"

"No, I'll feel worse if I stay in bed any longer. Where is everyone?"

"Jane's taken them out for a while."

Freebie had come running through on hearing his mistress's voice. Lisa picked him up and it was obvious he was delighted to see her.

"Why don't you take the dog outside and I'll make some tea and toast."

Lisa promptly opened the door and Freebie ran the full length of the garden before coming back to lie at her feet. She took some time to settle herself on a lounger. It took some time to accommodate her aches and pains, but at last she was comfortable. She would have to make some phone calls today. Meg would be going frantic, because she had no number to reach her, and then she would phone Josh. She thought back to John Vickers arriving on that first night and wondered how he had traced her. But thinking more on it, they would know that Jane was with her, and it probably hadn't been hard to trace her through her family. She would have to phone Judith to let her know that the children were safe and well, if the police hadn't already done so. Now that she had something to occupy herself for the afternoon, she left Grace in the garden and went inside.

She called Meg first.

"Oh Lisa, when I heard the news. I didn't know if you would know, and I didn't know where to phone. How are you? I'm so sorry. I still can't believe it."

"No, neither can I. We had a run in with James Campbell as well. The past few days have been a nightmare. But it's all over now. He's been arrested and I shouldn't think there will be any problem now getting a permanent order."

"Well at least that's something. When will you be coming home?"

"Probably next week. I'll call you and let you know when."

She finished her call and rang Judith. Thankfully the police had already been in touch. Judith's voice was full of sympathy.

"It must have been awful for you and of course for the children. How are they coping?"

"Remarkably well under the circumstances. We should be home next week. I'll call you when we get there."

She replaced the receiver again. Now for her last call. It was going to be the hardest one of all. She rang the television station and asked to speak to Josh. Rather quicker than anticipated, his voice was on the other end of the phone.

"Lisa, I am so sorry. I take it you saw the news. I tried to get you for two days before I released the story."

"It's all right Josh. We came on holiday and no one really knew where we were. What happened Josh? How did Michael die?" She was amazed with herself for sounding so calm.

Josh went back over the story in more detail. It was a patrol to meet some refugees, when the truck went over the edge on a mountain road and burst into flames. The remains of at least one body had been found and buried out there. They had found nothing else despite two search parties covering the terrain over a matter of weeks. Lisa couldn't continue the conversation.
"I'll call you when I get home Josh, goodbye." She put the phone back and wiped the tears, now streaming down her face. She and Michael had so little time together. Life was so unfair. They had loved each other and should have had the rest of their lives together. Instead some freak accident had taken Michael from her. Now there was nothing. She still had the children, but she had wanted to share their growing up with him. She had thought he would always be there. She felt the tears start again. She hurt so much at the thought of never seeing Michael again. Why did this have to happen to her? Other people had husbands and families, so why couldn't she?"

She wiped her eyes and composed herself before going back out into the garden. Grace rose from her chair as she approached.
"You poor child. Most people don't go through what you're going through in a lifetime." She put her arm around Lisa and tried to comfort her.

Lisa knew in her heart that it would be long time before the pain went away.

"Why don't you go and lie down for a bit. I'll call you when the children get back."

"Yes I think I will, thanks Grace. I'll see you later." Lisa and Freebie wandered back inside.

Back in her room, she lay on top of the bed with Freebie tucked in at her side. She stroked the little dog's head and he sighed with contentment. She wished she could feel so content. She thought about returning home. In another few days the bruising would have gone down enough to be concealed with make-up and they could travel back. She would speak to Jane in the morning. Before long she and her little companion were sound asleep.

Lisa woke to find the sun still streaming in through the window. She glanced at the bedside clock. They had slept all afternoon. She had a shower and changed her clothes and went back out into the garden, just in time to see the children return.

"Look Lisa, we've bought you a present. It's a surprise." Becky was dancing around in circles.

"Well, it isn't a surprise any more, because you've just told me." Lisa picked her up and plopped a kiss on her forehead.

Undaunted, Becky continued. "But I haven't told you what it is, and that's the surprise."

Jamie handed Lisa the little package.

"It's very special. Becky and me picked it ourselves. We wanted to make you feel better, so you won't be sick any more. Open it."

Lisa untied the little ribbon and undid the wrapping paper. Inside, lying on a bed of tissue paper, was the most adorable little rag-doll clown, all dressed in tartan.

"I love it. Thank you very much. I think I'm feeling better already. Now come and give me a hug, both of you."

"Now, how about some ice cream?" said Grace invitingly. "Would anyone like to help me with it?"

The two kids were already halfway across the garden towards the house. Jane had been very concerned about Lisa yesterday, but thankfully today, she was looking more like her old self.

"How are you feeling today? You certainly look a lot better."

Lisa laughed. "Look at my face, and you're telling me I look better. I think you need new glasses Jane."

"I suppose it's also about time we were thinking about getting home." Jane sighed.

"Yes, I was thinking the same. Are you sad to leave?" Lisa asked.

"No, on the contrary, I've had a lovely holiday, but it's always nice to get home."

The ice cream arrived and the conversation was put on hold.

"Oh, I forgot to mention, John and Phil did call in to say goodbye the other day. They were nice lads. John said he might give you a ring at home sometime, to see how you're doing. I hope you don't mind, I gave him the number."

Jane gave Lisa a sideways glance as she spoke. John Vickers could be good company for her, and he might help her get over what had happened.

Lisa had forgotten she hadn't said goodbye. "No, not at all." He probably wouldn't remember anyway.

The following day Lisa drove down to the gallery. She sat for a few minutes staring at the portrait, when a voice startled her,

"I'm going to be sorry to lose her. It isn't often I paint something and then don't want to part with it. But I'm sure you want to take her home." He said wistfully.

Suddenly, it wasn't quite so important to own the portrait. She had Becky after all, and perhaps the painting belonged here on the island.

"If I did leave it, you would have to promise me that you wouldn't sell it to anyone else."

The old man could hardly believe it. Was it really possible she wouldn't insist on her purchase? The painting had been drawing people in all week.

"She'll never leave here, until I do. And then she'll be yours. But I would mention, I don't intend going anywhere, for a long time to come."

"Then it's settled." Lisa said, standing up and turning to face the artist. "We're leaving tomorrow, and it would be nice to know that we're leaving a little bit of us behind. Something tells me we'll always be drawn back to the island, and it will be lovely to know someone will always be waiting."

She said her goodbyes and went for a last walk around the harbour. She was going to miss all this.

The following morning with the car all packed; she said goodbye to Grace.

"I can't thank you enough for all you've done. We've really enjoyed being here and I hope you'll come and visit us soon." She kissed her friend and slipped into the driving seat.

Grace said goodbye to the children. "It's going to be very strange with all of you gone. The house will seem very quiet. Now hurry up or you'll miss the ferry."

There were tears in her eyes as she waved the car goodbye. Lisa loved those kids and if anyone deserved to have them, it was she. She could only hope that from now on everything would be plain sailing. It was a comfort to know that Jane would be there for them, no matter what.

She went back into the house and noticing the books Lisa had been reading, she picked up the one on top of the pile. It was called, 'Island Myths and Legends'. Maybe it was time she refreshed her own memory on the mystical island that she called home.

A few weeks at home and things had almost returned to normal. Lisa was working long hours at the shop, trying to catch up and organise the stock for winter. The kids had gone back to school last week and seemed none the worse from their ordeal on holiday. Jamie had written a very dramatic account of what had happened. It had taken Lisa a good while to convince him that it was perhaps not the kind of story his teacher would be expecting, when she had asked them to write about their holiday. Eventually she had persuaded him to write about the island and all the things that he had seen.

The custody hearing was arranged for after Christmas. There was no necessity to rush anything now. James Campbell couldn't get custody now, and as there was no one else fighting for it, it was merely a formality. Everything was working in her favour now. She felt in control of her life again and she was working hard to build up the shop. She had continued to employ Emily Forbes two days each week, and that allowed her some free time for herself and the children.

It was on one of her days off that she bumped into John Vickers in Glasgow. She had been visiting the warehouse and was having a wander round the shops.

"Hello there Lisa. It's lovely to see you. Recovered from your holiday?"

"The holiday seems a long way off now. I'm sorry I wasn't around when you left and I didn't have a chance to thank you for all you did."

"Well, we could remedy that right now. How about a coffee?"

Lisa was only window shopping, having completed most of the work she had come to do.

"Yes that would be lovely."

He walked her a little way along the street before stopping outside a coffee shop. He held the door open and Lisa walked into the quaint little café.

"What would you prefer, tea or coffee?" He asked.

"Tea please."

He steered Lisa over to a table in the corner and ordered their drinks.

"So, how are you?"

"I'm fine. Busy getting stock ready for Christmas. You know the kind of thing."

"And the kids?"

"They're both well and back at school. They've never mentioned what happened that day. Except that Jamie wanted to write it as a school essay. He really has a flair for writing, maybe he'll be an author when he grows up."

"Or a reporter, like Michael."

No one had mentioned Michael's name to her in weeks.

"How did you know about Michael?"

"I was at the house that evening, to say goodbye before we left the island. You had said your fiancé was out of the country. I got there just after the news report. Who do you think carried you upstairs?"

"I didn't know."

"I'm sorry Lisa; I shouldn't have brought it up. It was thoughtless."

"It's strange. Everyone else avoids mentioning his name."

"I'm a good listener. If you want to talk about him, it's okay."

Before she knew it she was telling him how they had met and, why he had gone out abroad. John was easy to talk to and Lisa was glad to be able to talk about it all.

"Well, I really must be making a move. It's been lovely seeing you and thanks for the tea."

"Maybe we could have dinner some night, as friends?"

"Yes I'd like that."
They said goodbye and he watched as she walked away. He knew he wanted to be more than friends with her, but maybe in time.

The first place Eddie had gone on his return from Skye, was to the hospital. He really wasn't sure why. The young girl had regained consciousness and had been able to give the police a statement. Campbell was going to be charged with attempted murder and along with his assault on Lisa and the transporting of stolen goods, he should be put away for a long time. Long enough for all of his victims to recover.

He checked with reception and was given the ward number. She had been moved out of intensive care, and now began the long process of healing her wounds. Eddie knew that a hospital ward wouldn't heal all the wounds that Campbell had inflicted on this poor girl. The duty sister pointed him in the direction of the correct bed. He really wasn't sure what he was going to say to her, but somehow he still felt responsible for what had happened. Her name was Patty Conlan. As he approached the bed, she was still virtually unrecognisable. Her battered face, neck and shoulders, all too clearly visible.

She looked up when she realised someone was standing at her bed.

"Hello Patty, my name's Eddie Chadwick. How are you doing?"

"You're the man who called the police. They told me your name. Do you know James?"

"Thankfully I can say he's no friend of mine, but I had met him. You needn't worry, I won't be running back to tell him where you are."

"I lost my baby. Did they tell you that?"

"I'm sorry Patty, I didn't know you were pregnant."

He wondered if perhaps that was why Campbell had finally blown, and why this poor child was lying here. His heart went out to her.

"Do you know anyone here Patty, or is there someone I could call in London?"

"No, there's no one. They say I'll be out of here in a couple of weeks and I should be able to travel back. I don't have a lot to travel back to, but James paid six months rent on my flat, so at least I have somewhere to stay. It's very kind of you to come and see me. I don't get any visitors, but the nurses are all very nice and they come and chat to me. What do you do Mr Chadwick?"

"Call me Eddie. Mr Chadwick seems a bit of a mouthful. I'm a private detective." He saw the worried expression on her face. "It's all right, I'm not working at the moment. This is purely a

social call. I just wanted to see how you were doing. Patty, don't you have any family I could call? You shouldn't be here on your own."
"I'm fine honestly, I just need to get better and get back to London."
"Is there anything I could bring you? I mean, do you need anything at all?"
Eddie wondered why he hadn't thought of bringing her something today, some fruit or a bottle of squash. But he had to be honest; it hadn't even crossed his mind.
"No, not really. But if you do have time to come back some other day, it would be nice."
Eddie wondered where she actually came from, it certainly wasn't London. She was most likely a runaway. One of the many thousands who still thought the streets of London held a better life. He was glad he didn't have a daughter to worry about. It took Eddie all of his time looking after himself.

The bell rang for the end of visiting and he stood up.
"Thanks for visiting Eddie. Maybe I'll see you again."
"Yes maybe. I'm glad you're getting better. Goodbye Patty."
He looked back from the door of the ward and she gave him a little wave and a smile. Yes, he was glad he had come and he was pleased she

was going to be all right. He went home and called Val. She agreed to have a drink with him and quite pleased with his day, he had a bath and got himself ready for his date.

The day following her unexpected phone call, Kerry had made an appointment with her lawyer. With Michael dead, she didn't need her divorce and was now free to do whatever she pleased. She would get the house, the money, the cars and everything else, and without a fight. She hadn't particularly wanted him dead, but it had certainly sorted out her little dilemma. It didn't matter now whether he had been having an affair or not. She was his next of kin and everything would come to her. Fairly confident, she breezed into the office and announced her arrival.
"Hold on Mrs Bradshaw." Her lawyer had stopped her midstream. "It's not quite as simple as that. Let me explain."
"What is there to explain? Michael's dead and I'm his only relative, what could be simpler than that." She smiled her sweetest of smiles, which was easy to do, because she thought she had the upper hand.

"Your husband is missing, presumed dead. That's a completely different story. You see an estate can only be passed on, in the event of a partner's death. Legally, Mr Bradshaw isn't dead, he's missing. And until he is declared legally dead, then the estate remains exactly the way it is at the moment."

Kerry was furious. "What exactly are you saying? I don't inherit anything? I have no money to live on?"

"I'm afraid in cases like this, if your husband is still missing after seven years, and if during that time he has not made his presence or whereabouts known to anyone, then at that point he could legally be declared dead."

Kerry's anger was increasing. "He's hardly likely to re-appear after falling thousands of feet over a cliff in Ethiopia, now is he?" According to the rest of the world, he's dead."

"And according to the law, he's still only missing. And after the seven-year period, you can apply to the courts and have him legally declared dead. His estate would than pass to you unless of course he's left a will to the contrary."

"It gets better all the time, doesn't it."

Kerry had quickly lost her sweetness as the interview had progressed. There was obviously no point in going on with this any further. She would have to reconsider her position.

"I suppose my allowance continues at the moment, just as normal, and I can continue living in the house?"

"Yes Mrs Bradshaw, that's correct. Of course you would not be at liberty to sell the property. Do you understand that?"

"Yes I understand fully. My husband couldn't even have the decency to die outright. He had to make a melodrama out of it. Once a media star, always a star. Thank you. Goodbye."

She breezed out rather less dignified than she had breezed in. Damn him. He couldn't even make a success of dying. Well one thing was for sure. He was out of her hair and she still had the house.

Maybe it wasn't as bad as she thought. Her bills would be paid every month, and she still had enough money coming in each month to allow her to continue to live life as she had always done, and there was no husband to meddle in her affairs. And she still had America to look forward to, without the threat of Michael's private investigator taking any more photographs of her.

The future was looking brighter than she had first thought, and what if she had to wait seven years. In the end, she would be worth more that she would have been if the divorce had gone through.

As the months slowly passed by, Lisa realised that Michael was more and more at the forefront of her thoughts. And when his face was very clear in her mind, she stopped trying to push it away. Some days his face was so vivid, she could almost imagine he was there. Like today, he was here today. She could feel him as she moved around the house. She could feel his touch, so sensitive it would make her jump. They had so few memories, maybe that was why she found it so difficult to let go. It was the week before Christmas and if things had been different, he would have been coming home.

She had to stop this. Tonight was the school nativity play, and she was putting the final touches to Becky's costume. She was to be Mary this year. Jamie was one of three children doing the narration. They were both very excited. Lisa had sent them out to play to get them from under her feet for a few hours. Her thoughts though, still returned to Michael.

When the front door bell rang, she was brought back to reality. She didn't recognise the man on the doorstep.

"Hello Lisa. You don't know me, but my name's Gerard Knight. I worked with Michael."

Courage and Clowns

"Mr Knight, I should have recognised you. Please come in."

She was shaking. She had tried so hard today to get Michael out of her thoughts and now this.

"Can I get you a drink?"

"Some tea would be lovely." He followed her into the kitchen and placed the parcel he had been carrying, on the table. You'll probably be wondering why I'm here. Michael and I became great friends in the short time we were out there. He talked about you all the time. I know what a shock it must have been for you. We were all stunned by what happened."

Lisa poured the tea and sat down beside him.

"Were you the last person to see Michael?"

"One of the last. They should only have been gone a few days."

He could see the tears starting in her eyes.

"I'm sorry, maybe I was wrong to come. But I felt that I knew you because of Michael and I wanted you to know that we all cared for him."

Through the tears she was smiling.

"No I'm glad you came. You see I still feel as if Michael's here with me. Silly isn't it. I miss him so much. If it wasn't for the kids, I don't know what I would have done."

"Where are they today?"

"It's their Christmas play tonight and I was trying to finish the costumes, so I sent them to the park for an hour. They should be back soon. I hope you'll stay and meet them. I'd rather you didn't mention Michael to them, they only met him once." On the spur of the moment she asked him to stay for dinner.

"I'd be delighted. In fact I wouldn't mind seeing the play, if that's possible."

Lisa was very surprised by his suggestion but said that Becky would be over the moon with a larger audience.

"She's making the most of her stage debut. Last year she was only an angel, this year she's the star, or at least that's what she says. She loves the attention."

It was going to be some party afterwards. Meg and Keith would be there, and John Vickers, whom Lisa had seen on a number of occasions, and Jane of course. They were all coming back to the house afterwards for a drink.

Gerard continued. "I should explain the parcel. I hope I've done the right thing. It's one or two of Michael's things. They were recovered from the scene of the accident and I thought you might like to have them. They must have been thrown clear before the truck caught fire."

Lisa touched the wrapping on the parcel.

"Do you mind if I put it upstairs and open it later. You did the right thing, and it was very kind of you."

"Not at all. Whatever you think best."

Lisa put the parcel safely away in her bedroom and then set about preparing dinner, while she chatted to Gerard. She liked him immensely and she could see why he and Michael had been such good friends. She enjoyed hearing about their day to day life at the camp and for the first time she realised why Michael had stayed. She had never understood why before, but she did now and that made it easier.

Jane arrived an hour before dinner. She always seemed to know when her assistance would be needed. They had arranged that she would eat with them before going to the school, but as usual she had turned up early enough to help organise everything.

Dinner was enjoyable and Becky was her normal entertaining little self. Jamie was becoming quite the little man of the house, helping to pour drinks and clear plates. Lisa had to leave at six to drop the kids off at the school. Then she had to get back home and get changed and arrive with all the other mothers, looking as if they did this every day in the week. They met Meg and Keith in the foyer and after all the introductions were completed, they took their seats.

Jamie was very serious and word perfect. He was clear and precise and read the narration as if he was an authority on the nativity. Becky was at her best in front of an audience. She was a born actress. She managed her lines without any prompting and in her costume she looked beautiful. After the performance, Lisa went backstage to collect them both.

"Did you like it?" They both called. Their faces were still pink from the excitement and from being under the stage lights.

"I thought you were both wonderful."

Lisa then had a word with one of the teachers and said how much she had enjoyed the play. She then gathered up their belongings and joined the rest of their guests in the foyer. Gerard was very impressed with Jamie. He thought he was an exceptional lad for his age. Jamie was also very taken with Gerard and asked him a thousand questions about working in a television studio. John had already lifted Becky and was already making his way back to the car park.

Their little party was a lovely ending to the evening. Eventually Gerard decided he would have to leave saying he had an early flight in the morning.

"Thanks for making the effort to come all this way Gerard. I really appreciated it."

"It was the least I could do. I'm glad I've met you at last. Maybe we'll see each other again some day."

"I hope so." Lisa was quite sure they would meet again and she couldn't explain why she thought that.

Lisa returned to her guests. She had a fight on her hands trying to get Becky to go to bed, but at last she had given in. By midnight everyone had gone. John had offered to run Jane home, and Keith and Meg had left a few minutes later.

After Lisa was ready for bed, she lifted the package. Inside the wrapping was a cardboard box, like the kind you used in an office for storage. She lifted out the small backpack. Inside was a hard backed notebook. He had dated each page and kept it as a diary. He had used her name on every page, as if he was talking to her...

Lisa, we've finally arrived. We're only staying here one night before flying out to the coast...

Lisa, it's heartbreaking, you should see the kids. No I take that back. I wouldn't want you to see these kids. God was always blamed for plagues and famines, but he couldn't be responsible for this...

Lisa, I've never worked so hard in my life. We're up before dawn and the best part of the day is having dinner when we stop.

She flicked through the pages. She had been upset that he hadn't written and here it was. He had written to her every day. She turned the pages until she got to the last entry.

Lisa, we should be back at Korem the day after tomorrow. We didn't meet up with the refugees. I hope they've found somewhere safe. I was driving today, the roads are treacherous and it's heavy going. Chris is going to take over tomorrow. He's better on these roads than I am and we'll be a lot safer with him at the wheel. Goodnight my darling, I love you..

She cried softly as she read the words. She closed the book and put it back inside the box. Apart from the backpack, there were odds and ends, pens, knife, and at the bottom, crumpled and torn, was a jacket. It was badly marked by the dust and the soil. She felt inside the pocket and pulled out the postcard. The little girl's face smiled up at her. She was a beautiful child. Her dark skin looked like velvet and she had enormous dark eyes. She turned the card over. Michael had written a short message to say that they had arrived.

Typed at the bottom of the card was the title, 'Smiling Ethiopia'. She put everything back in the box. It was everything she had of Michael, except for an engagement ring and two little rag-doll clowns. That night she cried herself to sleep.

She cried for Michael, who would never be coming home.

In the last few months, Eddie's caseload had increased, partly due to the fact that his own attitude to life had changed. When he thought back to the start of the year, he shuddered and thanked God that he had seen fit to put him back on the right track.

He was actually making enough money now to live on comfortably, and if this kept up, well who knows. His new found vigour for life reminded him of the early days, when as a young policeman his enthusiasm had carried him along at an alarming rate. He still missed the company of the guys he had come through the ranks with, but he was making new friends and accepting less and less cases that involved the low life whose level he had almost stooped to.

And his new assistant was working out just fine. You wouldn't have recognised Patty now. A regular life was suiting her. She had lost that gaunt appearance that Eddie remembered from their first encounter. She was a hard worker and didn't flinch from telling Eddie off when he left files lying around the office. She also had an intelligence he had never imagined. She was quick to pick up on things and her suggestions were always considered. They worked well together.

She had been kept in the hospital for four weeks in total, during which time Eddie had continued to visit her. If she went back to London, all the hospitals good work and rehabilitation would have gone in a matter of weeks. Eddie had tentatively sounded her out and before long she had agreed to come and work for him and stay in Glasgow.

She had gone to London and collected her bits and pieces and Eddie was delighted when she did in fact return, as promised. They had found her a little flat and she had worked wonders with it.

"I think we should shut up shop for an hour today. You could help me pick a Christmas present for Val."

"Only one hour then. We can say we're closed for lunch and we can be back here at two."

She drew him one of her looks.

"Okay Miss Efficiency – exactly one hour." He said laughing. "If I'd known you were going to be such a dragon I'd have put you on the London train myself, with a one-way ticket."

"You know very well if it wasn't for me, you'd still be working in a pig-sty. You couldn't live without me and you know it, so be thankful I decided to stay."

She hit him over the head with the file she was putting back in the cabinet, before picking up her coat and handbag.

"Well, are we going?" She said impatiently.

"God woman, you'll be the death of me."

They locked up and walked the few streets to one of the large department stores. He had no idea what he was looking for. As he looked across the crowded store, he thought for a moment he had seen Kerry Bradshaw. On looking again, it wasn't her. He hadn't heard from her again, thankfully. He laughed to himself when he thought back to the photographs that he had sent her. He would have loved to have seen her face when they arrived. She was a vicious woman and deserved all she got, except for the fact that she would get everything and wouldn't have to fight through the divorce courts. But that wasn't his concern now, he was Christmas shopping and both he and Patty were having Christmas lunch with Val. For the first time in years he felt as if it really was the season of goodwill.

Christmas was one of the best Lisa could remember. They had gone to the midnight service, after which Jane had stayed overnight so that she could be there first thing in the morning to see the children's faces when they discovered what Santa had brought. Meg and Keith, Meg's mother Marjory and John Vickers had joined them for Christmas lunch.

The day had gone off splendidly. John was a regular visitor to the house and the kids adored him, not only because he was exciting, being a detective, he was also good fun. Lisa knew that he wished for more out of their friendship, but she didn't want anything other than that, and she wasn't sure if her feelings would change. She liked him a lot, but she didn't love him.

The snow came and lay like an ivory carpet over the town. It lay undisturbed through January and well into February. With the thaw, came the prospect of the custody hearing. Lisa knew there was really nothing to worry about, but she did anyway. It was finally going to be the end of a long journey.

The shop had been very successful over the winter and her range of evening wear had sold out long before the end of the festive season. People's tastes were changing again and the fancier the outfit, the better they seemed to like it.

It was on a very cold February morning that Lisa heard from Josh, for the first time in months. She was as much to blame, as she had found it easier not to contact him, and in so doing, had saved herself the anguish of having to think about Michael. Even so, it was good to hear his voice.

"Hello there. How are you? It's been such a long time since we've spoken. I'm sorry but I've been so busy. I'm going to be over your way tomorrow and I wondered if I might drop in?"

The following day was Sunday and she had nothing planned, so without hesitating she told him it would be lovely to see him.

She told the kids in the evening that they were having a visitor the following day and Becky insisted on baking. Her efforts were improving and she enjoyed it so much, Lisa didn't have the heart to refuse her.

They were all ready for their visitor on Sunday afternoon. Becky had iced her cakes and placed them very carefully on a plate, and warned Jamie that he wasn't to touch them. Becky still had a tendency to be bossy but Jamie seemed totally oblivious to it. In all the time they had been with Lisa, she had never heard him say a cross word to her. When the doorbell rang, Becky raced to answer it.

"Hello. Are you Josh? I'm Becky and I'm very pleased to meet you. Please come in, Lisa's making tea."

Josh had forgotten about the children being in the house and their presence now made his task all the more awkward.

"Hello there. It's lovely to meet you too. Hello Lisa, it's good to see you." He kissed her on the cheek before noticing Jamie hovering in the background.
"How do you do." The little boy said very politely. "Becky's made some cakes, so she'll be offended if you don't eat at least two of them, and she would be delirious if you managed more than that."
Josh had to laugh at his frankness.
Lisa was all organised and the tea was out on the table in a matter of minutes.

As usual the kids kept the conversation going. Jamie asked Josh what he did and as soon as he mentioned the studio, he told him he had met Gerard Knight at Christmas.
"Are you as famous as him?" He asked, thinking that Josh probably wasn't because he had never seen him on television before.
"No, he's much more famous that I am. I work in the background anyway, so no one gets to see me."
After they had cleared away the tea plates, Josh asked Lisa if he could speak to her in private. She was unprepared for Josh's request, but none the less, she asked the kids to go find something to do for a little while. They both disappeared upstairs with the dog and before long Lisa could hear the television in the bedroom. She made

them both another drink and they went through to the sitting room. Josh's uneasiness prompted her to ask what was wrong.

"Lisa, I don't know how to say this…. they've found Michael."

CHAPTER 15

Lisa tried to let the news sink in. She realised what he had meant to say was that they had found Michael's body. Now there would be a funeral and she would have to live the last seven months all over again.
"When are they flying the body home?"
"No Lisa, they've found Michael. He's alive."
She was laughing and crying and holding on to Josh all at the same time. Michael was alive. But how could he be alive after all this time? What had happened? Where had he been? Did it matter? Did any of it matter? He was alive. She was laughing but the tears were still streaming down her face.
"And they're sure it's Michael? I mean, there couldn't be a mistake?"
"There's no mistake Lisa, he's coming home."
She hugged Josh and cried until she couldn't cry any more.
"When did you find out?" She asked as she wiped the tears away."Only yesterday, before I phoned you. I don't know any more. He'll be in a bad way Lisa. I think you should be prepared."

Courage and Clowns

"I don't care, as long as he's alive. I don't care." Lisa was too thrilled with the news to care about anything else. Nothing mattered, Michael was coming home.

"I have to call today and find out when he's coming. So if you don't mind me using your phone, I'll do it now."

"Of course you can."

While Josh made his call, Lisa tried to get her thoughts straight. It seemed like only minutes before Josh was back.

"He's arriving on Friday. They've arranged an ambulance to meet the flight and he'll go straight to hospital. We can be there for him arriving."

The news was still sinking in.

When Jamie and Becky came back downstairs, they didn't quite know what to make of it. Adults could be very strange people. Lisa looked as if she had been crying, but now she was laughing and saying everything was all right. Josh left soon after, having arranged to meet Lisa on Friday.

That same evening Lisa phoned Meg and Jane and told them the news. Everyone was at first stunned and then thrilled. The rest of the week just didn't pass quickly enough. Josh had been keeping her updated and finally Friday arrived.

She had arranged to meet Josh at the hospital, and together they waited, drank coffee, and waited. When the doctor appeared, Lisa knew by his face that something was wrong.

"Miss Whitford I'm sorry. I'm afraid Mr Bradshaw wasn't well enough to make the flight from London. He's been taken to a hospital in London where they'll monitor his condition and hopefully in a few days, he'll be able to travel. If you'd like to come through to the office, I'll give you the details of the hospital.

Josh and Lisa followed the doctor, and furnished with the information they needed, they telephoned London. The doctor there was very helpful. He said Michael was stable and that he could probably be transferred in three or four days. No, there was nothing to be gained by her coming to London for such a short time. Michael had amnesia; he wouldn't recognise her anyway.

Josh was anxious to hear what had been said. "Lisa what did he say? Are you going to London?"

Lisa repeated the conversation with the doctor. They left the hospital despondent.

Lisa called the hospital every morning and on the third day the news was good. Michael was coming home at last. The flight from Heathrow was at three and at five o'clock Michael was at the hospital in Glasgow. When the doctor called her through, she had no idea what to expect. Josh had come with her and after they were both

Courage and Clowns

gowned and masked, they were taken to Michael. He had a virus that hadn't been identified yet, and the hospital staff were taking no chances.

Lisa approached the bed. She gazed at the man lying there asleep. He had blonde hair, and that was as far as the resemblance went. He looked nothing like Michael. His skin was burnt almost black. His cheekbones stuck out, making the skin hang on either side of his face, as if it belonged to someone else. Was this really the man she loved? As she sat down she reached for his hand. Every bone was prominent. So prominent, you could almost count them one by one. The body stirred and as his head turned, his eyelids opened. Lisa saw that the eyes were the most dazzling shade of blue. It was Michael.

She wiped a stray tear from her eye and smiled at him.
"Michael, it's Lisa. I'm here darling. Everything's going to be all right."

She gently kissed the hand she had been holding. She could feel the heat of his skin through the mask. She wanted to put her arms around him and hold him, but he looked so thin and fragile lying there against the starched sheets. She had the feeling if she touched him he would disintegrate. He was staring at her without a glimmer of recognition. After a few moments he closed his eyes and drifted back to sleep.

A nurse appeared and asked if they could leave for a short time to allow the doctor to attend. They were relieved of their gowns and went in search of the cafeteria. They picked up coffee from the self-service counter and found a table.

"Where did they find him Josh? What's happened to him?"

The tears that she had fought so hard to contain at the bedside now flowed freely.

"He was picked up by some refugees, somewhere near the crash site. But instead of making for Korem, they ended up about three hundred kilometres south. A native guide, who had been at Korem, recognised him. He had apparently been carried all that way. It's any wonder he survived at all."

The nurse they had met earlier came and found them and said that the doctor was ready to see them. They were ushered into an office and a few minutes later the doctor appeared.

"After our preliminary examination and going by the notes we've been sent, there are one of two things that I think you should be aware of. Michael sustained damage to his spine in the crash. We are going to operate to rectify some of the damage that's been caused by the initial fall and the fact that he has been in this condition for a matter of months. The damage could be permanent but we have no way of knowing that at the moment. There are also some injuries to his skull and there could be brain damage. Again we won't know for definite until some further tests are done. I'm sorry, it's not very good news. He's seriously ill at the moment and it's going to take him a long time to recover. He's exceptionally weak and the operations are going to put some strain on his heart, but without them, he wouldn't stand a chance anyway. The injury to his back has left him paralysed from the waist down and really at this stage, the chances of him ever walking again are pretty remote. I'm sorry to give you such bad news, but as I say, we have a long way to go yet." Lisa was speechless. She had been so happy just having Michael home.

The next couple of weeks were exhausting, trying to juggle her shop life, her home life and visits to the hospital. She had tried to explain to the children about Michael, but as they could barely remember him, it was difficult for them to understand why Lisa had to go to the hospital so often. The custody hearing was coming up and everyone, including the unflappable Jane, was beginning to get edgy. Judith had assured her it was now merely a formality, but something in the back of Lisa's mind told her that it wasn't going to be that easy.

And how right she was. It was seven o'clock, and she had only arrived at the hospital. There seemed to be some sort of commotion going on in the corridor outside Michael's room. She hurried the few remaining yards, but was waylaid by one of the nurses.
"Miss Whitford, could I have a moment please."
Before Lisa could answer, a bright light flashed in front of her face and there were voices, all screaming at once. The coldest voice of all, was that of Kerry Bradshaw.
"How dare you try and make a fool of me. Turning up here and telling people you're engaged to Michael. I'm married to him, you little tramp." She turned to the doctor who had been trying to calm her down. "I want her out of here now. Do you understand?"
The doctor was not about to be dictated to by a neurotic visitor.
"Mrs Bradshaw, you're the one who's leaving. Your behaviour is more befitting a street market than a hospital. Now if you don't leave, I'll call the police." He turned to the hospital staff who were hovering around. "Now would someone get these reporters and cameras out of here. Get security up here, I want this place cleared."
He turned to Lisa.

"Miss Whitford, I'm sorry, would you like to come through here?" He beckoned to a door marked private.
They entered what appeared to be a kitchen.
"I have no idea who let that woman up here, but we've had to give Michael a sedative to calm him down. God knows what he thought was happening. She's been screaming like that for at least twenty minutes. Once we get the place cleared, I'll let you in to see him. I know it's none of my business, but where has she been for the last few weeks."
"I've no idea. I've never met her before. Michael was divorcing her before he went out abroad." Lisa was still slightly shaken from the encounter.
"It's going to be difficult to keep her away, if she legally is his next of kin." He continued. "But I could recommend that her visits are upsetting and disruptive."
Lisa had to smile at the doctor's polite description of Kerry's outburst.

It was fifteen minutes before Lisa was allowed through. Michael was sleeping. The operations had been a success as far as the doctors were concerned. But there was little change in Michael. He hadn't spoken one word to her since the day he had been brought in, in fact most days he would only be awake for about an hour of her visit, and during that time he only stared at her and listened to her talking. There was never a hint that he remembered anything. At times it was hard to believe that he even understood the language she was speaking.

She stayed for two hours, arranging his flowers in vases provided by the nurses and talking to him while he slept.

The following morning the papers were full of the story.

Michael Bradshaw's wife and girlfriend have fight in hospital. This was awful. But not quite as awful as when Judith called and told her the hearing would have to be postponed.

Was nothing in her life ever going to work out right?

John had called in the afternoon and said how sorry he was about the newspaper article and suggested that, if she liked, he could come over later. Josh was going to the hospital tonight to give her a break, so it would make a nice change to have some company. She agreed and asked him to come for dinner. Perhaps his presence would settle the kids, as their life seemed to be upside down at the moment.

John arrived earlier than she had expected and she was still finishing of the meal when the doorbell rang. Jamie and Becky were jumping around and talking incessantly to him before he escaped and came through to the kitchen.

"Where has his wife been until now?" He asked as he poured a drink for them both. He handed Lisa the glass of wine.

"I've absolutely no idea, but I knew she had to turn up eventually, but yesterday was definitely the wrong day. Any day would have been the wrong day. I don't seem to be having much luck."

He felt very sorry for her. She looked tired and disinterested, which wasn't like her.

"Lisa, if there's anything I can do. If you want I'll come to the hospital with you when I can. It would at least be company for you."

Lisa appreciated how kind-hearted he always was and wished she could have said yes.

"It wouldn't be very exciting for you. Thanks anyway, but I need to be there on my own."

They passed a fairly pleasant evening, except for three phone calls from reporters asking if she had any comment. Eventually they had put the phone off the hook.

There were more reporters outside the shop the following day and when she went to the hospital in the evening, they were waiting outside. Thankfully Kerry was nowhere in sight. Tonight Michael was sitting up. He smiled as she came into the room, but she knew it was still only out of politeness. Suddenly, because she wasn't expecting it, he spoke.

"Thank you for the flowers. The nurse said you brought them last night. I don't remember,"
"You were asleep that's why. And when did you find your tongue. You haven't spoken a word in weeks."
His speech was slow and slurred but still a welcome change from the silence.
"You've been here every day. The nurse said your name is Lisa. Are you my wife?"
"No, but we were engaged, before the accident."
She had no idea how to explain it all to him in his condition, so she refrained from telling him that he already had a wife.
"Were you there when I had the crash? The doctor's haven't told me very much."
"No, you were in Ethiopia and you've only just come back."
"What was I doing there?"
"You're a television reporter and you were out there working."
Lisa's two hour visit came to an end and Michael had asked questions almost the entire time. Some she couldn't answer but this was wonderful news that he was talking and at least asking who he was. She realised she didn't know enough about Michael's background to fill in many of the gaps and she saw the disadvantage in this. Before she left the hospital, she spoke to the doctor briefly.

"I'm beginning to see that to help Michael fill in the gaps in his life you have to know something about it, and I don't. Maybe his wife should be allowed to visit?"

"No, Mrs Bradshaw's one and only visit probably set Michael back rather than helped him. He was very distressed. What you have to try and remember is that anything could trigger his memory and there's nothing to say that it shouldn't be something that you and he did together. That's as possible as it being something further back in his past."

"I hope you're right. He was talking tonight, so I suppose that's a step forward. Thank you for your time."

She left the hospital that night in higher spirits than she had felt for some time. Michael was on the road to recovery and surely now it was only a matter of time before things got back to normal. Really there had been nothing normal since the night she had met Michael. So what was normal? Lisa's life before all of this had been normal.

As she drove home she thought over everything that had happened since the explosion in Stancroft, and apart from Michael's reported death, she knew she wouldn't change any of it. Her life was going to be exactly what she had always wanted; it was just going to take a little longer.

The following day she had a meeting with Judith. Lisa knew that she wasn't flavour of the month with the care team, but that didn't matter anymore. Everything was out in the open and she'd cope with whatever they threw at her. She had survived the last year and nothing could be as bad as that. When she turned up at Judith's office, she was confident and articulate. She wasn't waiting to be reprimanded for loving someone they might not approve of and she fully intended going ahead with the hearing as soon as possible. And her relationship with Michael would go on along with everything else. Now what did they think of that?

Judith hadn't bargained on Lisa's outspoken and decisive manner. She was not going to back down.

"No Judith, I don't want the hearing postponed again. I'm going ahead with it. I'm not giving these kids up now; not after all I've gone through. Now you can either back me up, or step back and let me do this on my own." Lisa's attitude was slightly short of argumentative.

But she didn't care anymore and from now on she was going to be in charge of what happened in her life. She'd had enough of being calm and trying to please everyone. You couldn't do that anyway, so why try. She knew what was important to her and that was all that mattered.

"Lisa of course I'll back you up. I'm surprised that you even think I wouldn't help you. But you must realise that they have to put the children first and if they feel that your life is turning into some kind of media circus, it will go against you."

But Lisa was adamant the hearing should go ahead. Two days later she received a letter giving her a date in two months time. It was longer than she had anticipated but at least it was settled.

Kerry Bradshaw continued her war through the newspapers, but as Michael and Lisa never provided any counter statements, her arguments were beginning to wear a bit thin. Eventually people lost interest. She had however served divorce papers on Michael, in hospital, and she had named Lisa. It wasn't any surprise when the papers reported that too.

At the end of March, Michael was transferred to a nursing home on the West Coast. Here he would convalesce and start physiotherapy.

Visiting was now more difficult, but Lisa soon settled into a routine of spending one day with Michael during the week and then again on Sunday afternoons. She had waited a few weeks before asking the children if they would like to go with her. To them it was like having a day at the seaside.

When they arrived, Michael was out in the garden. He had been looking forward to meeting the children because he'd heard so much about them.

Lisa had explained to the children on the journey down how ill Michael had been and that he would be in a wheelchair. Of course that didn't stop Becky from mentioning it.

"Why are you in a wheelchair Michael?"

Michael thought there was something very familiar about the little girl, but he had been told that he had only met her once, so it was hardly possible he would remember her. However he did answer her question.

"Because I can't walk and they gave me this so that I could get around."

"You used to walk all right. You took us to the pub and then we went down to the river. Did you just get fed up walking?" She asked with her usual diplomacy.

Michael laughed. She was an adorable child and such a beauty.

"No, I had an accident. But they're trying to teach me to walk again, so maybe one day we'll go back to the river. Would you like that?"

"Yes but we could still go with your wheelchair, and we could take turns pushing you." Becky continued undaunted by the seriousness of Michael's complaint.

Michael for his part found her charming and was enjoying answering her questions.
"That's very kind of you Becky, but I think we should wait until I get out of here. We have a children's play area at the back. Would you like to see it? How about you Jamie?"

Jamie had been very quiet since they had arrived. He remembered Michael and he liked him. He was sorry he was sick but he didn't understand why Lisa had to spend so much time with him. But he livened up at the suggestion and soon he and Becky were running ahead through the gardens to where Michael had indicated.

With the children safely playing Lisa asked how the physiotherapy was coming along.
"I think it's useless. Lisa why do you still come here? You have two beautiful children and you deserve better than having to visit a cripple twice a week. I'm never going to be out of this chair."
Even after everything he had been through Lisa had never heard him talk like this.
"Don't say that. It's going to take time." She tried to sound hopeful but it didn't work.
"I'm so sick of hearing that from everyone. How much time do you all think I want to spend like this? I don't even remember any of you people who constantly visit me. I just can't see the point in all this."

"Michael stop it. Josh and Colin and the others all visit you because we all love you and want to see you well again. Whether you remember us isn't important. I'm trying my hardest so don't you dare push me away."

There was bitterness in her voice that she hadn't intended. "I'm tired Michael. I'm trying to run a business, bring up two kids and I could lose them because of you so don't sit there and give up on me. You don't have the right."

She was near to tears and was beginning to run out of sympathy.

"I'm sorry." He said, looking away from her.

He couldn't bear to see the pain in her eyes.

"I shouldn't have said what I did. I know how much you're doing but I just wish I could remember. Do you have any idea what it's like to not remember your life, or the people that are part of it?"

She wasn't at all sure at that moment she cared, but refrained from saying so.

"Let's get the kids and go get something to eat."

She was still on edge and the rest of the afternoon passed with the cloud still hanging over it. For once, she was glad when the visit was over.

Later in the week he still wasn't any happier, so Lisa asked to speak with someone at the end of visiting. She was introduced to a young doctor that she hadn't met before and he also voiced his concerns.

"He does seem to be going backwards instead of forwards. He's losing interest in the exercise programme because he's got it into his head he won't ever be able to walk again, so why should he waste all this time and effort trying. The operation on his spine was successful and there's now no reason why in time he shouldn't gain the use of his legs. But he has to work on that himself, we can't do it for him."

Lisa wasn't surprised by the doctor's remarks. The change in Michael was all too obvious.

"What else can we do? There must be something."

"His feelings aren't uncommon but they can be difficult to deal with. It all comes down to time. We have to be very patient with him and give him all the support we can."

It was all so easy to say, but Lisa was tired and she really didn't need anything making her life more difficult than it already was.

Michael had just succeeded in wasting another hour of the physiotherapist's time. She wasn't winning here and she knew it. Anne had been working here for four years and no one was more difficult than Michael Bradshaw. He had everything and didn't appreciate any of it. He had more money than he needed and a fiancée with two beautiful kids and still he wasn't satisfied. If anyone in here had something to work towards, it was him and he couldn't care less.

"How about we go for a walk?" She asked tentatively. Anything was worth a try and she had no other sessions that afternoon.

"Is the term 'walk' supposed to be significant?" He bit back at her.

"You really are becoming a real pain Michael. Let's go. I want a walk and you're coming with me."

She pushed the chair along to Michael's room and collected his jacket.

"Now Michael if you don't want to be civil to me, then don't talk to me at all. I really don't mind." She spun the chair around and headed along the corridor and out through the gardens. She couldn't help Michael if he wouldn't help himself.

She continued along the path towards the sea front. There was still a light chill in the spring air, but pushing the chair was a good way of keeping warm.

"Are we going anywhere in particular?" He asked although he didn't really care one way or the other.

Courage and Clowns

"Blowing cobwebs away, that's all."

Anne walked until she came to a bench on the promenade, where they could see over the sea wall and listen to the waves crashing onto the rocks below. She had always liked the sound of the sea.

"Why have you given up Michael? You were doing so well in the beginning and you have so much going for you."

"Well I'm no use to anyone like this. How could I support a wife and two kids from a wheelchair? Now can we go back, I'm getting cold?"

"You're a clown Michael, you're throwing it all away. You're so wrapped up in self pity you can't see what's in front of you. If you carry on like this they'll all leave and then where will you be."

"I'd be better off on my own. I don't need them."

"That's where you're wrong Michael, even clowns need company."

"What did you say?"

Something in her words sounded familiar.

"Nothing Michael. You've depressed me enough for one day. I'm taking you back."

On the walk back he tried to recall her exact words, but nothing now rang any bells. Anyway the cold was getting to him now and he just wanted to get back inside to the warmth, and the peace and quiet of his room.

Once back in his room he tried again to remember exactly what she had said, but again nothing. He looked around the room, his home at the moment. The only home he knew. There was a vase of carnations on the bedside cabinet.

Lisa always brought carnations and when he had asked her if they were significant she had merely said that she particularly liked them, but if he preferred something else, she could bring those instead. It didn't really make any difference to him what kinds of flowers were there, because he didn't remember whether he liked anything else better or not.

Some of his clothes had been brought in and although they were hanging in his wardrobe, they could have belonged to anyone. There were some books, brought in by Josh, but he never seemed to be able to concentrate long enough to want to read them. There were hundreds of cards from well wishers that Lisa had stuck all over the walls, and that was home. He wondered what kind of house Lisa lived in. He had never thought to ask. Was he really the uncaring type of person he had become? He spent a very restless night.

When a nurse rushed in and hurried him into his chair, he realised it was neither morning, nor that the bells ringing were his alarm clock.

"What's happening? Why are the bells ringing?"

"It's nothing to worry about." She said, wrapping blankets around him. "There's been a fire, but there's no need to panic. It's in the east wing. We're not in any danger here but we need to get everyone outside."

Although Michael couldn't see any fire, he could smell the smoke as they made their way out into the car park.

Outside the scene was different. The east wing had flames gushing out of the roof, heading skyward. There was the sound of the fire engines and people screaming. Suddenly, Michael knew he had to be over there near the fire, that he had to help.

Hampered by his chair, it took him some time to get across the garden path. The smoke was stronger here and it burnt his nostrils. He coughed and spluttered but continued until he was as close as he could get before someone shouted at him to get back. A nurse appeared and turned the chair around.

"No you don't understand, Lisa and the kids are in there. You have to get them out. And Chris, you have to save Chris."

The nurse had no idea what he was talking about and returned him to the car park. However much he protested, no one listened. His friendly physiotherapist appeared and tried to calm him down.

"Michael, Lisa's not there. She's at home with the kids. They're safe."

He was confused. He had seen her go into the building. She was going to get the children. Why would no one listen to him? Eventually back in his room, the doctor gave him something to make him sleep.

When Lisa got the phone call in the morning, she altered her plans for the day and drove down. Michael was still asleep when she arrived and she was ushered into the doctor's office.

"I'm sorry but Michael's had a very traumatic night. As you can see we had a fire during the night and Michael seemed to think that you were in the building. We had to give him something to calm him down. He should be awake soon and I thought that if you were here it would reassure him that you were all right."

"Yes of course. I'll go along and wait in the cafeteria. You can call me when he's awake."

Lisa left the office and wandered along the corridor to the café. She stood in the queue and watched some of the nursing staff laughing and joking over breakfast at a table in the corner.

She couldn't remember the last time she had laughed like that. Why did things just seem to get worse? She ordered her coffee and took it over to a table. She had called Josh and he had said he would come down around lunchtime.

She felt as if she would be in dire need of his company by then.

She was on her third cup of coffee before a nurse arrived and told her Michael was coming round. When she reached the room she could hear his raised voice. He was screaming at someone in anger. As she got to the room door, he was struggling to get out of bed and was promptly restrained by the nurses. When he saw Lisa, his face changed.

"Did you find the children? Are they all right? And Chris, did someone get Chris out?"

She walked slowly over to the bed.

"No Michael. Chris didn't make it. He died in the fire. But the kids are out, they're safe."

The nurse looked at her in amazement. No one was dead, what on earth was she saying.

CHAPTER 16

"Can we get a doctor in here?" Lisa's voice was full of excitement, although no one else could understand why. "And can the rest of you leave me with Michael, please."
The nurses left the room.
"Michael, don't you understand. You're starting to remember. Now, just relax, the doctor's on his way."
Michael's head was still fuzzy from the sedative, but Lisa was safe and she was here.

When the doctor arrived, Lisa explained to him the significance of what Michael had been saying.
"He's remembered there was a fire when Chris died. He must have been conscious after the accident. And thinking I was there, was nothing to do with last night's fire. I met Michael after there had been an explosion, when I went to look for the kids. That's the reason I have the kids because their mother died in the explosion. Michael was there with the television cameras and there were lots of buildings on fire and I was running about looking for Jamie and Becky.

Courage and Clowns

Don't you see, he's started to remember." She was so excited she was hugging Michael. He had finally come back to her. Nothing mattered now, nothing at all.

The doctor stayed with them for the next hour trying to help Michael piece together all of the scraps of information that were swirling about in his head. When Josh arrived Lisa told him the good news. For the rest of the afternoon Lisa and Josh talked non-stop until Michael's head was aching. Finally a nurse arrived and suggested they both leave. Michael was having a more traumatic day than the night he just lived through and she told them he needed to rest. Reluctantly they both left the room.

Josh and Lisa drove along to a small café on the sea front. They ordered fish teas and sat down with hot drinks.

"Only time now Lisa and it will all come back to him. It's a dreadful thing to say, but thank God there was a fire."

"Except that now he has to deal with Chris's death along with trying to remember the rest of his life. He's back Josh. I still can't believe it. I was beginning to hate coming here because all he did was tell me not to visit. I know he didn't really mean it but it was soul destroying."

The fish and chips arrived along with more drinks. Lisa realised that she hadn't eaten all day and she was ravenous. She had phoned Jane from the hospital to tell her the news and asked if she would see to dinner for the children.

"Why is it fish and chips always taste better by the sea?" Josh remarked. He hadn't eaten since breakfast and he was enjoying his meal.

They chatted for another hour before deciding that they should be heading home. Josh ran Lisa back to the nursing home to pick up her car. He was desperate to get back to the studio to tell everyone the news.

Over the next few weeks with the help of Josh and some of the technicians, they had set up a miniature studio in Michael's room. He watched reels and reels of news film and bit by bit, it was all coming back. Although he was having a rest from the physiotherapy for the time being, the staff still insisted on visiting him. His love/hate relationship with his physiotherapist, Anne, continued.

"Is there any chance, now that you have your memory back, of bringing your exalted presence down to the exercise room? Providing of course, you don't intend upsetting anyone."

Michael laughed.

"Where did you get your wonderful bedside manner?"

"I think I was just lucky enough to be born with it." She smiled at him sarcastically. "How are you doing anyway? Apart from getting fat, lying in bed all day watching films."

"I am not fat and you'll be pleased to know, I re-start my combat training with you next week. Now there's something to look forward to."

"I can't wait."

Michael continued. "I really should thank you. You are in a way responsible for my recovery."

"And how did you decide on that. If there was anyone here you didn't want help from it was me. It's a bit ironic then. It definitely wasn't intentional, so how did I do it?"

"You said exactly the same thing I wrote on a card, when I bought a porcelain clown for Lisa. That was milling around in my head before the fire, although I hadn't quite made sense out of it."

"I'm very glad that without trying, I managed to help. Now just think what good we can both do for your legs when we're both trying."

She excused herself and made her way back to the unit. Michael Bradshaw wasn't quite the hopeless case she had once thought bit he still ha a long way to go.

Lisa arrived in the afternoon and they went for a walk in the garden. Their conversations were now more normal and everyday topics could be discussed. Lisa told him about the custody hearing coming up.

"I'd like to attend with you. Everyone knows about us now so what difference could it make and I think you've been through enough on your own. I have every intention of marrying you, so they can't ignore me."
"Michael, I'm not sure that's a good idea."
"If it hadn't been for those children, I would never have met you, and that doesn't bear thinking about. For once, we're going to do something together and Jamie and Becky are going to know that from now on, everything's going to be fine, and we'll always be there for them."
"I understand what you're saying." She said hesitantly. "But the last thing Judith wanted was a media circus, and with you there, isn't that just what could happen?"
"There will be no reporters, no cameras, only me. There won't be a circus, as you very kindly put it, although the best part of the circus is usually the clowns.
He smiled and winked at her.
"The only clown here is you, and I warn you Michael, if anything goes wrong, you'll wish you had stayed in Ethiopia."
"What could possibly go wrong?" He kissed her gently. "I thought about you every day while I was out there. But you wouldn't know that. I even bought you a lovely postcard..."

His words drifted off as he remembered the child with the smiling face.

"I know you did Michael but it's all over now. You've finally come home."

Lee Stewart Gilmore